The Vegas Flop

a novel

Kyle K. Wolfson

Also by Kyle K. Wolfson

The Haunting of Abraham Lincoln.
DERT

____

Day 1, 1:54 pm

LUCAS GREEN

I've been on more airplanes than I can count. Different airlines, different countries, different airports. After a while they all start to feel the same. Check-in, security, gate, seat, baggage claim. Doesn't matter where you're traveling to, the journey's the same. However, there's a notable difference when you land in Las Vegas, and that sensation surrounded me as our plane's wheels made contact with the runway, followed by the whooshing of deceleration.

Landing in every other city is an indistinguishable experience from all the others, a release of tension from those who fear flying that we're finally on the ground, but also an anxiety about what comes next. Every person on the plane has a different agenda once they click open their seatbelt. Some are there for work and are jaded; others are on vacation and are excited. Some are there to see family, and that can go either way. Getting their luggage, calling an Uber, tracking down the rental car; the immediate future is going to be chaotic for all of us, and yet all we can do is sit silently in our seats as we slowly approach the gate, waiting for the burst of activity as people with connecting flights try to fight their way forward.

It's different in Las Vegas. The energy is the same throughout the plane; nearly everyone is arriving for a vacation. Some want to experience the natural wonders; the Grand Canyon is nearby, we actually just flew over it, and then there's skiing in Utah or rock climbing at Red Rocks. Of course, most people are there to enjoy the manufactured fun of Las Vegas—drinking, pools, gambling, elaborate live shows, showgirls, and strippers. The expectations are high, as everyone peers through the windows to get a view of the New York-New York rollercoaster or the Luxor pyramid, enticing sights that are clearly visible even from the runway. Even though most of these people will find their sky-high aspirations beaten down over the next few days, they eagerly anticipate the adventure. Pregnant strippers, alcohol poisoning, bad luck at the tables, and terrible sunburn are problems for the flight home, which also has a very unique feel compared to most other flights.

Looking around the rows, a veteran eye can spot those for whom Las Vegas is merely home. Their mind wanders to the practical: where did they park their car, will I-15 be crowded on the way home. I don't know what, if anything, people think when they look at me. I'm here for work. Most people who visit Las Vegas for work are also up for a good time: company dinners, nice accommodations, or planned outings intermixed with meetings or trips to the convention center. My work is in the suburbs, far enough away to be out of the glare of the neon, but still in the shadow of the Strip, as is the entire valley. The Stratosphere tower on the north side of the Strip leers over the breadth of the city. It's visible from every corner of town, constantly reminding the population why this town exists in the middle of the desert. They have been lured in by a siren song to leave their hospitable environment and go live as missionaries amongst the infertile soil of sand and rock. Las Vegas is a religious settlement, like Salt Lake or Mecca, built as a monument to its divine master, money.

The plane lunged to a stop and the frenzy began in earnest the moment the seatbelt sign turned off. It sounded like the end of a rollercoaster while you waited to disembark. It was just me and my backpack, lightly packed. A book, a phone charger, a car key, a laptop, one change of clothes, and a toothbrush. That plus the phone in my hand and the buds in my ears were all I brought with me. People always worry about packing enough things. A tip from a world traveler: they have everything you need wherever you're going.

The terminals in Vegas have a distinct feeling as well, a certain smell to welcome you home, kinda like fresh carpet and cologne. The most obvious are the clusters of slot machines that must be passed multiple times during the walk to baggage claim. I'm surprised they don't have slot machines on the airplane you can play once you enter Nevada airspace, valuable gambling time already wasted. However, we aren't here to complain about gambling; it's a part of life here and must be accepted, like the illegal immigrants on the street who hand out cards for hookers at every corner (though that job seems to be dying off recently, another low-level task displaced by the Internet).

But of all the parts of arriving in Vegas that feel different than other flights, nothing feels more surreal than the first step you take outside the airport doors. After hours of being in climate-controlled environments, the first breath of the hot, dry desert air is a surprise. It's not the gambling or sex that constitutes the backbone of Vegas memories; it's the feeling of walking into an oven as soon as you're outside, even at night. It wasn't to be this time, though; it was October, and even in the desert the heat must fade at some point, sure to return before long.

The journey from the plane to the parking lot is interesting as the crowd grows thinner, people detained by bathrooms, slot machines, snacks, and baggage claim. Getting off the shuttle in the middle of long-term parking is the first time you're truly alone in your journey. The Toyota 4Runner was right where they said it would be, silver with current plates. It looked clean, though being outside for a few days had given it a light coating of sand and dust, nothing that driving wouldn't blow off.

Clicking the key fob, the car beeped in response. It was ready for me. Inside, the car was clean and empty other than the registration and manual. The only other thing in the car was a cellphone in the glovebox. It powered on easily, as phones that have been recently reset are prone to do. The only evidence of it ever having been used is a single call in its history. That's my contact. Only one ring before a woman's voice answered, "Battle Born Renovations, this is Amy, how may I help you?"

"This is Lucas Green calling for Carlos."

"Of course, Mr. Green. Mr. Guerra left a message for you. He'll meet you here at the office at 8 pm. Do you need the address to our location?"

"I do." I double-checked the time on the phone. It read 2:30 pm.

"It's 3636 North Washington Avenue. We're right next to the 7-Eleven."

"Sounds good. I'll meet Mr. Guerra there at 8 pm. Thank you." Five and a half hours to burn before the introductory meeting. It would've been nice to get started immediately, but these Carlos Guerra types always wanted to work in the dark. A meeting about murder couldn't happen during daylight; it would be improper.

Either way, it meant lunch was on the menu first and a trip out west always means a meal at In-N-Out Burger. It's the most popular fast-food restaurant on this side of the country, especially for those of us who are aware of the secret menu items. There are several nearer the airport than the one I choose out in the Centennial area. Of course, the nice thing about Las Vegas is that most everything is nearby, even the other side of town. That's what happens when you build an entire city in a valley surrounded by mountains; the opportunity for outward expansion is rather limited.

A Double Double combo meal with a Coke and a hard plastic seat near the window. It's like I'm back in the 1950s, except for the earbuds and the non-segregated bathrooms. At least out here in Centennial, most everybody is a local, so you escape the overbearing loud tourist types that exist around the Strip. The most defining characteristic of these Vegas suburban residents is avoiding the Strip at all costs. It's like a beach town where none of the locals like swimming.

The comedian Bill Burr finally finished up ranting about the NBA in my ears, ending the latest podcast episode, but he's recently been tacking on episodes from ten years ago to the end if the listener wants to do a bit of time traveling. I don't know what's more out of date nowadays, a burger joint pretending to be in the '50s or the opinions of a comedian from 2009.

Comedy podcasts are what's filling up my Spotify playlist at the moment; not actual performances, just an hour where a comedian will sit around talking with their fellow comedian friends. Fun enough, but still bursting with advertisements and excited updates about new shows added in Spokane or Savannah. I wonder if Lenny Bruce ever ate at In-N-Out Burger when he came out here. Seems like a perfect Norman Rockwell type of painting; troubled and persecuted comic sits quietly eating a burger in pre-Corporate America, scrawling jokes about Eisenhower on napkins and wondering if he'll be arrested tonight for saying things that were against the accepted etiquette. How far we have come as a society. I wonder who would be an advertiser if Lenny had a podcast.

Out the window and across the street is the reason I'm in this particular shopping center, the pet store. I don't like dogs. Don't get all offended, I was bitten once as a child. Animals are unpredictable. It has something to do with their inability to communicate. However, people in general like dogs, people talk to people with dogs; therefore, people talk to me if I have a dog. So, a dog must be had.

If arriving in Vegas has a very distinct feeling, stepping into a pet store has a very distinct odor—fur, animal food, and the unique smell of wood shavings in a hamster cage. "Can I help you today, sir?" A young woman in a red vest caught me quickly; her name tag identified her as Jenny. Only people who actually like animals will work at a pet store; someone like me could never handle the smell or the drool.

"Actually, yes you can. I'm looking to buy a dog today!" I answered her with an enthusiastic smile.

"That's fantastic! They're over this way." She led us toward the barking.

"I just moved into town and need some company. You know how that goes. My dog back in Florida died last year."

"Oh no, that's so sad! What kind of dog was it?" Her concern was not forced.

"He was a black and tan coonhound."

"Aw, I love the floppy ears."

"Yeah, he was pretty cute."

"Okay, so we don't have any coonhounds at this store, but we can see if any here seem like the right fit."

The purpose of the dog is best filled by an aging one, but not one that's ailing. The kind that only bothers you when it needs something, because he hasn't got the energy to keep you entertained. After some searching, I found what I was looking for, a mutt with a gray muzzle and an annoyed expression, like he was sick of listening to all the try-hards in the cages around him. Perfect.

"You made a great choice, Mr. Green. We'll be sorry to see Deputy go. He's so easy-going."

"Deputy?"

"Yes, that was his name when he first arrived. I think it kinda fits him, don't you? A sorta old-timey name for a laid-back pooch."

"Yeah. I could see him driving an old patrol car, chasing the troublesome cats outta town."

Jenny laughed at that. "Oh, I could see that, too! I wonder if we have a little cop hat we could put on him. That would be soooo cute!"

I looked at Deputy. He didn't look like he would think it was cute, though I didn't think he would put up too much of a fight, either. He had the vibe of a grandpa being forced to socialize with his wife's friends at the retirement community.

"Do you already have everything you need to make him comfortable at home, or will you need help finding toys and bedding for him?" Jenny asked once her giggling subsided.

"I don't actually have anything at all, so I guess I'll need a leash, some food, and probably a cage."

"You mean a crate? We don't like to use the word 'cage' here," she answered rather firmly.

"Yes, that's what I meant." I looked back at the glass and metal barriers keeping the un-bought animals in their places. You can call it the Playboy Mansion for all I care; if someone else has to let you out of it, it's a cage.

* * *

It was 7:57 pm when I arrived at Battle Born Renovations, a typical blocky building with a chain-link fence surrounding the perimeter. The gate was locked, and the business was obviously closed for the night. Only the pickup truck parked in front gave any sign that people were there. Pulling in next to it, I saw a man sitting behind the wheel. "You Lucas?" His voice carried through my newly lowered window.

"Yes."

"Hop in," he ordered. It was a gentle command, yet a command, nevertheless. The foolishness was annoying. It wasn't enough to put this meeting off until it was dark, but now they were also demanding a surprise location change.

"Looks like you'll be hanging out here for a while alone," I said, looking into the rearview mirror to where Deputy was sitting in his crate. He didn't seem to care; he'd probably enjoy the peace and quiet. I cracked the windows. It was popular convention, even though the temperature was low enough that there wasn't any chance of overheating.

"Is that a dog?" the man asked as I climbed into his truck. I recognized him as Javy Santana from my research on my new employer.

"Yes, it is." I pulled the door shut.

"Why is there a dog in your car?"

"He was hitchhiking and said he needed a ride to the land of stupid fucking questions, so I brought him here." Javy didn't respond, he still seemed to be processing what I said to him. "Where are we going?"

"Mr. Guerra doesn't like to conduct your kind of business here. BBR is a clean operation." He had the vibe of a person who had just gotten done waiting out in the parking lot for someone who didn't show him the level of respect he believed he deserved.

"Where are the supplies I asked for? I didn't see them in my car."

"Mr. Guerra thought it'd be better to deliver them in person, just in case anyone poked around the car while it was waiting for you."

"That's highly unlikely, unless you have an undue amount of attention on you already," I answered steadily, my tone suggesting I was dealing with amateurs.

"Nothing like that's happening, and your job is to keep it that way," he answered back with a hint of edge in his voice. He wasn't just an errand boy for the Guerra organization, he was a ranking member, unused to anyone disagreeing with him, and he wanted me to know that.

After another twenty minutes of driving, we finally came to a stop in the driveway of a house on the northwest side of Las Vegas, not that far from where my work would take place. The outside of the house was in good shape from what I could tell in the darkness, the new coat of paint glowing under the street-lamps. Through the windows, I could see that the interior was bathed in the bright electric glow of work lights, bouncing around the bare walls and concrete floor. Things were starting to make sense now; this house was being renovated, which made it an easy place to meet up. Not many cops would waste time with a stakeout; their microphones would be flooded with the sound of tile saws and hammering. Plus, there was the ready-made excuse for why so many people were coming and going at this location.

Carlos Guerra was waiting for us in the kitchen. Several chairs had been arranged in between the cabinets that had been disassembled and laid out around us, waiting to be sanded and painted. I hadn't met Carlos previously, though we'd had several brief phone calls over the past few weeks while we negotiated the engagement of my services to him. The pictures I had tracked down on Facebook did justice; he was short, stocky, with a nervous energy about him. Short men tended to be a bit on the high-energy side, obviously overcompensating for something. Carlos Guerra tried to play the part of the regular joe, a guy who was simply in the home renovation business, but his style and energy reeked of drug dealer. Which, of course, was also true.

He was standing in the kitchen, engrossed in his phone as we entered, probably part of his tough-guy show he'd be putting on over the next few minutes, acting like my arrival wasn't worth looking up from whatever he was tweeting about. Taking the chair facing Carlos, I sat down patiently. Javy remained standing near the part of the kitchen counter that still remained in place, just covered with a drop cloth.

Finally, he ended his texting, sliding his phone back into his pocket and bringing his eyes to mine. "How long will it take?" he asked abruptly.

"How long will what take?" I replied calmly and evasively. He was looking for a reaction to his purposeful rudeness.

"Your work?" He finally took the seat opposite me.

"My work is an art, not a science. If you want to

work with me, it'll take as long as it takes."

"Two weeks is the limit."

"As I said, if you want to work with me, it'll take as long as it takes."

"You can't kill someone in two weeks?" Javy interjected from the side of the room with a sneer.

"You'd be surprised how quickly I can kill someone." I turned my gaze to Javy. The veins in his neck pulsed under the tattooed skin. "But that isn't why I'm here, is it?" I turned back to Carlos.

"This is a situation that needs to be handled delicately," he admitted with a nod of his head toward calming Javy. Clearly, Javy was offended that he wasn't being given the opportunity to handle this situation himself.

"Delicate means art," I said, directly looking at Javy, "and I imagine the closest you've ever been to artistry is when you're huffing spray paint next to some graffiti."

"You gringos always got such a mouth on you, until I show you what I'm good at," Javy growled, taking a step forward.

I responded, "What *I'm* good at is knowing everything about the target. I know why Grant's girlfriend left him, I know what medical procedures he's had, and I know what he thinks about before he falls asleep."

"Yeah, I can use the Internet, too, but we're trying to kill him, not suck his dick."

"Anyone can do what I do, just as anyone can do what you do. But no one else does, which is what makes my work special. With everything I know about

Grant Anderson, I'll be able to resolve this issue quickly."

"Either way, the two-week timeframe remains." Carlos took over the conversation again. "Your work may be delicate, but so is mine, and I'm footing the bills. It needs to be ended in the next two weeks, no exceptions."

"Expediency is always at the top of my priorities," I answered back sweetly. It was standard practice to have this type of conversation with clients. Hiring me is a form of surrendering control, being done by people who survive by always remaining in control. It's only natural for them to try and exert as much influence over the proceedings as possible, even if it's just for show.

"Judging from what you've said, I guess you don't need what we've put together on Grant," Carlos said.

"Actually, I welcome every offer of assistance that can be rendered. Anything you've compiled on him would be most helpful to paint a complete portrait."

Carlos motioned over to Javy, who pulled a manila folder out of one of the tool bags on the counter. "This is what we've put together on him since he arrived in town," Carlos said as Javy delivered the folder.

"How about the uncle?" I asked, accepting the folder from Javy. "Isn't he the nexus of this whole endeavor?"

"He's dead, so he doesn't matter anymore. Now, it's the nephew who's the problem."

"I think the uncle matters greatly. If not for him, his nephew wouldn't be in this position, and I wouldn't be here now." I had my theories on what had happened with Paul Sherman, but hearing it from the horse's mouth would be better.

"He worked with us, he stole from us, and he had a heart attack before we could deliver our message."

"My work doesn't lend itself very well to delivering messages."

"The message will be received by those who need to hear it," Carlos answered coldly. He would clearly prefer a more noticeable message than I specialized in delivering. However, events had boxed him in on responses. "Once the work is complete, there are also items that need to be removed, unnoticed, from his home and office."

"I trust you've already made arrangements to deal with that yourself?" A statement phrased as a question. Recovery was a premium feature in my portfolio of services, and Carlos was still on the basic subscription.

"Of course. Once we confirm the death, Javy and boys will go to work."

"Very good." The silence hung in the room after that, Carlos and Javy continuing their obvious show of strength by playing tough and trying to subject me to some sort of job interview evaluation. Clearly an intimidation technique, though lessened by the fact that they had to resort to such methods. If you're the type of person who has to go to great lengths to intimidate people, it's because you're not very frightening to begin with. The most intimidating people I've ever met are the ones who don't have an act that goes along with it, but rather it's just who they are to their core.

"What kind of setup were you able to arrange for me?" I had sent very specific requests to expedite my work.

"We were able to get you in the house across the street from Anderson. The furnishings are already in there."

"Across the street. That's excellent."

"Paul taught us a trick or two when it comes to homes," he said, smirking a bit.

"How about the required equipment? Javy said I could collect them here."

"Yes, they're in the garage, everything you need to make the house look like yours. Some of the stuff you requested is very expensive."

"If killing people was cheap, anyone would do it."

"You have all your fancy tools. Why do you need a gun, then?" Javy asked. Carlos might have been playing difficult as part of his tough-guy act, but Javy was less act and more just a disagreeable personality.

"Why do *you* carry a gun?" I pointed toward the slight bulge in his waistband.

"Because no one'll buy me a bunch of fancy toys," he answered surprisingly well.

"I guess it's just a security blanket for me. I usually never have to use it, but having it around makes me feel a bit safer."

"Maybe you just like having us buy expensive things for you."

"Oh, is the Sig P239 too costly?" Sig Sauer handguns were what I always used. The lack of safety scares off some people, but the extra-long trigger pull to cock the hammer for the first shot made the weapon safe to carry. It's the gun I'm most comfortable using, which is why I always ask for it on a job.

"A gun is a tool," Javy grumbled. "Buy the one that works, not the one with the biggest price tag." He fumbled with the tool bag before producing the black plastic case Sigs came in, tossing it over to me.

"Sometimes price does matter. I notice you don't have many cut-rate tools laying around here. You spend the money and buy the good stuff." I motioned to the pile of newer-looking Dewalt power tools in the corner. Javy remained silent. Despite his position in the company, I doubted he spent much time touching power tools. "So, what do you use?" I continued. "I'm always open to hearing opinions." He pulled up his shirt to reveal the grip of a Glock holstered inside his waistband. "Ah, a Glock. Looks like a classic 19. I've —"

"It's a Glock 17," Javy interrupted. "Two extra rounds in the mag and a longer barrel."

"Interesting. Well, maybe I should give it a try at one of the gun ranges down the road if you recommend it so strongly."

"It's what all of our people use. It's the most practical gun on the market." He sounded annoyed. "You said you just need fifty rounds?" He held up a generic box of 9mm ammo.

"I need some to get a feel for the gun down at the range, but something more dynamic would be nice to actually carry. Do you have any hollow points?"

"Yeah." Javy pulled out a smaller box. Hollow points are often sold in twenty-count boxes since they're shot far less often than regular bullets. "These are what we carry. It'll get the job done."

"I appreciate it. Hopefully I'll be returning all of this to you very soon, gently used." I thanked them with a smile.

"Is there anything else you want?" Carlos asked.

"I think we're good at the moment, if you have the rest of the things I asked for."

"It's all in the truck, ready to go," Javy answered.

"Very good. Well, all that's left to do now is convince someone to kill Grant Anderson in the next two weeks."

Day 2, 7:58 am

GRANT ANDERSON

Grant Anderson woke up at 7:58 am. Is there any worse feeling than waking up right before your alarm goes off? Two minutes of sleeping lost. Getting out of bed has always been Grant's least favorite part of the day, and this bed makes it even worse. The guest bed in his uncle's house hadn't been bought with comfort as a priority; in fact, he wasn't sure why his uncle even had a furnished guest bedroom. Uncle Paul wasn't the type to have guests visit. During Grant's childhood, the only two times Grant's family visited Las Vegas to see Uncle Paul, they had stayed at a hotel. They hadn't even stopped by Paul's house during the visit. Instead, Paul would just meet them for dinner or for a drive out to the Hoover Dam.

Maybe the bed had been left here when Paul bought the house. It did seem to be in better shape than the mattress in the master bedroom. Grant could feel the coils poking through the thin fabric the one time he tested it. After a few minutes weighing his options, he had settled on the slightly less gross guest room as his residence. Still, it wasn't much better than sleeping on the floor at this rate. Since the guest bedroom was on the first floor and the rest were upstairs, it meant that the bathroom was out in the hall. Technically, it was a common bathroom, but since there wasn't anyone to share it with, it served as an open-concept-style master suite.

Bathroom routine out of the way, it was time for breakfast. The kitchen in his uncle's house was decently sized and attached to the living room. Most houses in Las Vegas had a fairly simple layout. The Vegas population boom began in the early '90s and had been growing steadily ever since. The big rush of people to the desert meant that homes needed to go up fast and easy. Basic '90s-style layout and decor defined this new belt of suburban homes. Like rings on a tree, the city showed how it expanded from an intersection in the desert to a valley-wide metropolis. At least, that's what the books Grant had been reading seemed to show. He was actually a newcomer to the Silver State. The two prior visits had really just been excuses for his father to gamble and enjoy the nightlife, while their mother split her time between the designer stores and hotel spas. Grant and his sister spent their time at the pool or the arcades created to occupy children while their parents were busy with their own version of an arcade.

Uncle Paul had passed suddenly from a heart attack in August. Grant, the only member of the family who wasn't busy, had been assigned to travel out to deal with the wrapping up of his life. He had planned his uncle's sparsely attended funeral and the cremation. The urn remained in the house, still in the funeral home's original packaging. Paul's end-of-life wishes were chaotic and vague; however, the will was clear that, having no children of his own, he considered Grant, his nephew who had been given the middle name "Paul," his sole heir. That had brought Grant the sudden windfall of a three-bedroom house in a quiet neighborhood, as well as a 2011 red BMW Z4 convertible (both paid off), and finally, ownership of Paul's company, Port Harvest Real Estate.

Whatever little amount of cash there had been was mostly depleted by funeral expenses, taxes, and paying off some credit card debt. Uncle Paul had passed away inside the BMW on the top level of the parking garage at one of the off-Strip casinos scattered around the town. The summer sun of August had been in full effect, and it'd been two days before Paul's corpse had been noticed by some passing guests. Needless to say, the BMW was sold far below market value to a car restoration company. The lingering scent would be passed on to some unsuspecting buyer, who would spend the life of the car covering up the unidentifiable smell with assorted air fresheners.

After having to sell the car for pennies on the dollar, the thought of selling Paul's worn-down and cluttered house under market was too bitter a pill for Grant to swallow. Piling what possessions he needed into his 2009 Yaris, he drove across the country from Georgia and took up residence in his new house, diving into reviving his uncle's business. Port Harvest was a small real estate company, but it had made a decent living for Paul, despite his poor stewardship of its revenues. Perhaps with a steadier hand, Grant could build it into a successful enterprise. He had passed the Georgia licensing exam years ago, but his credentials weren't transferable to Nevada. So he had devoted a considerable amount of time the past two months to speeding through the Nevada licensing process, so he could get the business up and running.

His freshly attained license was a bright spot among the landslide of rubble his uncle had left him. However big the task of building a successful business was, the more daunting the challenge turned out to be cleaning up the house and office. When he had first entered the house back in August, he understood why they had never visited. Every available inch was covered with stuff. Some of it was garbage—empty Diet Coke cans, wine bottles stacked to the ceiling in the dining room, and junk mail stacked like cordwood by the front door. However, most of the mess was made up of just random stuff. Outdated electronics and folded piles of clothes were just the start of it. It looked like the entire contents of several Goodwills had been dumped into the house, and that Paul had existed solely on the thin trail that wound through the mountains of his belongings.

Grant had started with the essential living spaces like the kitchen and bathroom. Once they were cleared out, the tide could be turned against the upstairs and garage, which were jammed with every imaginable piece of junk that could be bought and stored. The Port Harvest office was another island to conquer, too. It seemed like Paul had spent nearly the same amount of time in its cramped spaces as he did at home.

Grant's entire existence these days was confined to the small spaces between the debris that his uncle had left behind.

He decided it was a breakfast biscuit kind of morning. The microwave had been the first item to get cleaned. If Grant had been able to figure out how to detach it from the cabinetry, he would've replaced it outright. The tray had been nearly glued into immobility from the splattering of gunk throughout it. Left to its own devices much longer, Grant feared the radiation of the microwave might have actually given birth to some sort of science-fiction organism. It was sparkling clean now as it heated up the frosted breakfast meat and cheese.

Grant flipped through the book that laid on the counter. There were plenty of books in the house—the shelves in the front living room sagged under the weight of the dusty hardcover clutter—but this book was an exception. Clean and prominently displayed, it was the first thing besides the mess Grant had noticed when he first arrived. It was hard not to, with its bright white cover, the picture of his father smiling broadly, and the familiar phrase at the bottom, "By Ted Anderson, owner of Teddy's Homes."

His father was the original source of real estate interest in the family. Ted had grown a thriving business in the ever-growing Atlanta suburbs since he had moved there at twenty-two. He'd been successful enough to feel entitled to write a book with his insights into the business. Grant had already read it a few times. It's really hard to read a book written by someone you know so well; their voice practically screams the words off the page at you. Part of being a force in the real estate agent business is marketing yourself, and writing a book about yourself is a great way to do that. Each chapter was headlined by a quote from Ted himself that he thought was especially insightful. They rang a bit hollow with Grant. He had spent his entire adult life working for his father, "climbing the ladder from the bottom", as Ted insisted with much theatrics. If his son was going to be in the business, he'd often declare, he'd be treated no better than anyone else. Of course, this didn't take into consideration the fact that with Grant's education and practical on-the-job training he'd gained from years of assisting his dad, he could've easily secured a job of higher stature than receptionist at the company if his dad hadn't been the owner.

Uncle Paul had left behind a series of erratic and misguided business ventures in the '90s, inspired by or jealous of his brother-in-law's growing revenue. He decided Vegas offered the best opportunities to grow, so that's where he settled. He wasn't wrong—with the building boom, there were new houses to sell every day —however, while he was every bit a self-promoter as Ted, he was missing the fact that Ted actually enjoyed his work. Paul enjoyed not working…or more accurately, he enjoyed scheming about ways to make money that didn't involve working.

The microwave announced that breakfast was thoroughly warmed. Grant flipped the book closed before going for the plate. Did Paul buy this book and set it somewhere to be seen as a tribute to his successful in-law, or was it spite? Grant didn't consider a breakfast that had been frozen solid two minutes before to be worth sitting down at the table to consume, which was a good thing, since the table hadn't been cleared yet. It housed a multitude of finished puzzles on it, each one stacked on top of the previous one. Despite his uncle's obvious distaste for throwing things away, somehow the boxes for the puzzles were missing, which left Grant in a conundrum on what to do with them—toss them in the trash can, or salvage them? Maybe the original boxes were just hiding somewhere.

The uncertainty meant that the puzzles remained, so Grant ate his breakfast from the kitchen counter. After the food was swallowed, he wiped the dish down and rinsed it off quickly. Doing the dishes in a timely manner had never been something Grant worried about; but here in this house, he had made a vow to stay ahead of the mess, so dishes got washed right away. The line had to be held against disorder.

The Yaris was parked in the driveway. Most cars lived in garages here in Vegas. Avoiding the sun was always job number one in this town. You would start sweating on the walk from your parking space to the store; no reason you should sweat in your driveway. However, Paul had either decided that the BMW should be shown off, or he had filled the garage with so much stuff, he had given up trying to fit the car inside. Regardless of Paul's motivations, the Yaris waited outside until space could be cleared.

Day 2, 8:15 am

TRACY COOK

"You shouldn't be eating that." Bill Strider's voice broke through the confused hum of the police station.

"Really? I shouldn't be eating a frozen Ding Dong and a Coke for breakfast?" Tracy Cook responded without looking away from her computer. This month's crime statistics had just been released, and Tracy always enjoyed studying them.

"You don't want to end up like Bert over there." Bill kept his lecture going while nodding his head to a large detective spilling out of his chair a few desks over. "Cops are some of the most unhealthy people in the world." He slid into his seat across from his partner. The health of the people in his immediate view was his favorite topic of conversation.

"And what's that you're having for breakfast? Mulched grass?" Tracy countered, allowing herself to look away from the percentage of car break-ins that happened in parking garages and glare at the senior detective around the screen.

"There are things other than grass that are green," he replied calmly, holding up his smoothie bottle. It was bright green this time, which was better than the mud-colored stuff he normally drank. "I'll make one for you tomorrow. It tastes better than it looks."

"No. That last one was disgusting."

"It was ginger," he answered, shaking his head. They had already had this argument a few times. "Ginger is good for you. It helps the heart."

"It tastes terrible," Tracy argued back, pushing away from her computer. "Besides, my heart is fine. I work out all the time."

"I keep telling you, the meals are the most important part. It doesn't matter how much you work out if you're eating *that* every morning." He gestured to the Ding Dong as Tracy finished off the last bite.

It was hard to argue with Bill; he actually practiced what he preached and appeared to be the healthiest person in the entire Las Vegas Metro Police Department. He was correct that the majority of the officers were either overweight or denying they had a drinking problem. Tracy Cook, the only woman in the detective division of the 10th precinct of the Northwest Area Command Section, was the smallest person in the office by at least a hundred pounds, with Bill probably being the next lightest despite being well-built. The cops who did pay attention to their fitness and didn't overeat or drink tended to be muscleheads who were also trying to go up another uniform size.

Bill seemed to dislike the Hans and Franz types as

much as he disliked Ding Dongs. He focused on bodyweight exercises, endurance, and eating healthy. He had gone on several long pronouncements in the car and once at a department-wide barbeque that if a police officer would ever be called upon to put their muscles to the test against a suspect, it was most likely going to be their legs, not their chest or arms. Criminals were prone to flight over fight, so they were going to opt for a footrace instead of a boxing match. He insisted that the meathead officers would be huffing and puffing into the radio for backup just trying to chase down a wheelchair. Needless to say, that didn't go over well at the picnic. But it didn't stop Bill Strider. His trim frame was built to chase down suspects and hassle Tracy about her eating habits.

Tracy dropped the still chilly wrapper into the waste bin. "Where did you put my hair ties?" she demanded, pushing her hair back. She always left the house with the goal of leaving it down through the day, but it never lasted long.

"I don't know," Bill shot back.

"You were playing with them yesterday when I was on the phone." She shuffled things around on the desk, looking for them.

"I don't think so."

Spotting a single one looped multiple times around a pen, Tracy reclaimed it. "Did you hear back from North PD about those cookie jars?" she asked, slipping back to her work.

"Not yet. They said they'd call me before lunch. But I'm thinking they're the ones we're looking for. There can't be that many hot cookie jars in southern

Nevada."

"My grandmother collected cookie jars. She'd take me to antique stores and yard sales every weekend, looking for certain collector editions."

"It's like baseball cards for old ladies," Bill mused. "Did she actually keep cookies in the jars?"

Tracy paused, looking away from her computer and down at her vibrating phone. "She did, but in a plain one. The fancy ones were all on display out of reach." Her voice drifted into the absentminded tone one has when they're distracted. The caller ID on her phone read "Mom" as she reached for it.

"Makes sense," Bill said. "You don't want the kids trying to open up some collector's item just to get another Oreo."

Tracy pressed the ignore button. It was too early in the morning to deal with her mother, plus she was at work. Whatever her mom wanted could definitely wait until after work, and probably even longer. Bill was looking at her as she set the phone down. "Sorry, what did you say?" she asked.

"We were talking about cookie jars."

"Oh yeah, I hated eating Oreos out of the jar. They were always too hot, so the frosting was kinda melted."

"That's just 'cause you like everything cold."

"Probably where it started." She admitted that she had a bit of a neurosis about eating only freezer-cold desserts.

The sound of a phone vibrating cut through the desk again. If it was her mom again, she better be dying, Tracy thought as she looked down. Her phone screen was still blank, however. It was Bill's phone this time.

"Strider," he answered with the slickness of a TV detective, few words and serious looks.

Day 2, 8:45 am

GRANT ANDERSON

Grant turned the volume on his phone a few clicks higher. Podcasts had the tendency to get quiet at important moments. The more important the thing someone is saying, the quieter they get. Drinking was a common part of comics' podcasts, so the tempo often veered between loud drunken revelry and quietly intense conversations.

Flipping the blinker on, he drifted out of the center lane and into the far right lane. The car in the center lane had tape holding the rear window together, never a sign of someone you should be driving behind. He had timed out the commute to the office during his first weeks and was confident that the center lane was the quickest route. Less cars turning from the center lane, and no chance of the turtle-like city buses getting in the way. The biggest variable on his drive were the traffic lights. The number of cars on the way never made much of a difference, which was about as different as it could be from the metro Atlanta commute. If you were making a list of pros and cons of Vegas compared to Atlanta, the traffic would be the number-one pro, far more important to everyday life than gambling at gas stations.

One downside of the short drive, though, was that it made it hard to finish his podcasts. Listening to a two-hour podcast took a while when you tried to do it in ten-minute segments. He had tried playing them in the office, but he couldn't handle working and listening at the same time. It was easier while he was cleaning at home, but that was mostly reserved for the weekends.

Checking the time, Grant realized he should probably factor in being cut off several times into the math of his daily commute. The drivers in Vegas were empowered by the straight flat roads to take more risks than you would expect to see on the twisty, unpredictable roads in Georgia. Everyone ran red lights out here, and pulling out in front of traffic was routine.

Grant pumped the brakes hard and sent his phone flying to the floor as the moped traveling next to him veered too far into his lane. Mopeds were the preferred mode of transport for people who had lost their license, and it showed in their driving. Fishing his phone off the floor, he checked the time. Looked like he'd be two minutes late today. It really didn't matter; he knew there wouldn't be anyone coming by for a drop-in. Still, Grant couldn't shake the mantras his father had preached to him his entire life. In Teddy's view, showing up late would lead to slacking in other areas, eventually leading to a complete failure of ambition, resulting in destitution.

The opened door revealed the smell of liberally applied air freshener. It wasn't that the office space had stunk when he had taken it over, just that it had a musty smell that clung to his clothes all day. So, he had doused the space in scented air, and once he cleared enough space to access more of the electrical outlets, he had decided to get some of those plug-in scent diffusers. The office in general wasn't much at all; located in an aging strip mall on Sahara Avenue, it was just on the wrong side of the invisible border between social classes. In Vegas, there were clear distinctions on what part of town you were in. Where Grant lived was an area inhabited by comfortably middle-class types. Then there were the gated communities where the high-rollers lived. Besides the gates and guards, their neighborhoods were recognizable by the amount of greenery spilling over the walls.

And then there were the slot machine areas. The issue with Vegas was that it attracted people from all over the country who were down on their luck. They imagined that could all be changed in Sin City. For some of them, like Paul, they found enough success to stay afloat, but that was partly because he hadn't looked for his good fortune to come out of a slot machine or roll of the literal dice. Those who did envision the casino as the path to the easy life were chewed up and spit out into certain areas of town. Those areas were clearly obvious when passing through, but also rather randomly situated through the city. In Atlanta, the poor areas were avoidable; in Las Vegas, it might just be that one street or a particular intersection where the down-on-their-luck types congregated. They were randomly interspersed throughout the entire town.

The space Paul had picked out for Port Harvest Real Estate's corporate office was inside one of the poor perimeters, though being on the edge meant it had a very reasonable price tag while only being slightly farther down the street than you would want. It wasn't as much of a detriment to business as it might be for some other venture. Meetings at the actual office were rare for anyone who wasn't a super-agent like his dad. For someone like him, bringing clients in to wow them with the professional feeling was part of the strategy. For the agents down in the trenches, most worked from their home anyway. Paul's office clearly didn't have many visitors, since the lobby was nearly as cluttered as the rest of the office was. It looked like he had tried to keep the mess from spilling over into the lobby but had finally lost that battle.

That was where Grant had set up his space, pushing the boxes and papers deeper into the building. He dragged Paul's grimy computer out of his office and set it up in the lobby, along with a small folding table to serve as a desk, and went to work on his laptop and newly purchased printer. Paul's ancient desktop was used for reference as he tried to demystify the nearly two decades of Port Harvest's history, bills, income, and filings, all of which needed to be sorted out and recorded. New digital folders were created, and paper originals scanned and dropped in their respective folders. The paper copies were also deposited into a new filing cabinet that sat across from Grant's table. It was nearly full by now, so another one would be needed soon. What was taking so long was that none of the files had ever been organized; they were pretty much just piled around the office randomly, so no one folder could really be said to be complete. It was an ongoing process—pick up a piece of paper, try and figure out where it belonged, then move on to the next one in the pile, most likely from a completely different year and concerning a completely different client. The biggest folder was the unassigned pile growing alarmingly large next to Grant's table, paper that couldn't be identified as belonging to a specific person or transaction at this point. Maybe once the whole office was cleared, they could find their home, retroactively.

Today the agenda was a bit shifted. The office opened at 9 am, which was just a formality, but a routine to be honored. That left only about an hour before it was time to meet the Duvalls to show them a couple houses. So instead of file organizing today, which could consume hours, it was general clean-up. Separating the actual paperwork from the assorted junk mail, scribbles on various pieces of paper, and printed-out MapQuest directions from the mid-1990s was enough to keep Grant busy for the next fifty-eight minutes.

Day 2, 10:36 am

TIM "TIMBO" CYRUS

"You sure that's the house?" Tim "Timbo" Cyrus demanded.

"Yeah, man, you saw the boxes," Ray Williams answered back.

"I saw *boxes*. They didn't say what they were. They could've been moving boxes for all we know," Timbo shot back.

"Nothing else comes in boxes like that. It had to be a TV," Ray argued.

"When is she leaving? We're just sitting out in the open here." Timbo changed the topic but continued with the complaining. Tim had grown up in Las Vegas, his parents bringing him here when his dad got transferred to Nellis Air Force Base. His parents' relationship had already been struggling, and it didn't hold up well under the Las Vegas heat; or maybe it was the strippers that finally did it in. When his dad,

Marcus, was transferred to Texas, Tim remained in Vegas with his mother and two sisters. That was the last he saw of his dad. After his mother ran out of luck and boyfriends in the valley, she decided to move back to South Carolina with her family. Nicki and Taylor went with her, but Timbo, recently a legal adult, decided to stay behind. First, he worked as a security guard, but he quickly realized that he couldn't even pretend to care about protecting someone else's property, something his bosses picked up on after repeated break-ins at the upscale condos where he worked. Once he got the taste of living on other people's work, he was hooked for life. He tried out several different schemes for robbery before finally meeting Ray by chance. It was a match made in heaven.

"How would I know when she's leaving, man? You're in charge of that shit!" Ray shouted back at him.

Timbo checked the mirrors again. There had been an elderly couple walking a dog a little earlier, but they didn't last long. Even with the heat fading away this month, it was still against people's nature to go for walks in Las Vegas, as if the summer's heat might return suddenly like a flash flood.

Their white panel van was sitting on the opposite side of the street and several doors down from the house they were watching. Mrs. Smith was still home, but she was supposed to be going to pick up the kids from school soon.

Ray Williams was a young guy from New Mexico. He was an Amazon delivery driver during regular business hours, but today was his day off. His job put him in the perfect position to get a feel for what was being delivered in the nondescript boxes he handled every day. Computers had a certain weight to them, and TVs were marked "fragile," though like he said, not much else shipped in the tall skinny boxes. He kept his eye out for expensive items being delivered, and then Timbo would scope the place out. Mrs. Smith had received several shipments lately that looked pricey, so Timbo double-checked Ray's hunch by checking out her recycling bin that week. Several Amazon boxes had been folded up inside the garbage can. If they were buying new TVs, there were probably a few more high-end electronics sitting around inside there.

"I can't believe this is the house we're hitting. Maybe a new TV. That's what we're going for," Timbo berated Ray. "That's the best you could find?"

"Well, fuck you, then. You haven't found anything else to hit. You're too lazy to go box sniffing, so this is what I've found."

The uncomfortable silence returned to the cab of the van. Ray just shook his head. Timbo always got this way during the waiting. He didn't like just sitting there in the open. Ray understood the fear, but it was part of the job. They hadn't done anything yet, so no reason they couldn't be sitting here on the street.

"I'm giving this bitch like ten minutes, and then I'm just going in. I don't care if she's there or not," Timbo declared, slamming his fist on the steering wheel.

"If she doesn't leave, we can just come back some other day," Ray reasoned.

"Bullshit. We aren't coming back and leaving our asses hanging in the wind a second time. People will notice us being here again."

"That's less risky than going in while someone's still there. That's crazy dangerous."

Timbo shook his head. "Don't be such a little bitch. You're strapped. What are you scared of?"

"I'm scared of getting shot! My cuz got shot when I was a kid, and he was messed up, man. Never walked right again."

"You don't sound scared when you're singing about that shit," Timbo countered.

"That's different, man." Ray brushed him off. Sure, his lyrics were a bit on the violent side, but he was a rapper. What was he gonna sing about, slingin' boxes for Bezos?

"I don't know why you even bring that with you." Timbo motioned to the tattered notebook sitting on the dashboard, the telltale sign of every aspiring song writer.

"In case I have an idea. You never know when it's gonna hit you."

"I got one," Timbo sneered. "Bitch better get yo blouse and get outta the damn house. I'm 'bout to roll up and grab dem fucking toys."

"I like it." Ray nodded along.

"Now you go."

"What do you mean?"

"I mean I made a verse, now you sing one."

"Oh, it don't work like that."

"You're just too fucked up to sing shit right now. What did I tell you about getting glassy when we're working?"

"I have to, or I'd be all edgy like you, man. This lets me focus."

"That's fuckin'…" Timbo's voice trailed off as the red Honda they had been waiting for backed out of the driveway.

"That's her," Ray commented.

"No shit," muttered Timbo. "Hit the clock."

Ray leaned over and turned the old eggtimer knob to five minutes. The *rat-tat-tat* of the timer started immediately. Five minutes was how far away they believed a person needed to be to not return home if they forgot something.

The timer continued to count.

Day 2, 1:03 pm

LISA SMITH

"Max! Give that back to your brother!" Lisa Smith shouted while watching through the rearview mirror.

Max tossed Charlie's iPad back to his brother in disgust. He had forgotten his at home that morning and made sure everyone knew how angry he was that his mother hadn't turned back around, even though they had only been six minutes away. Seven thirty am was when he had to be in his seat and ready to leave. Normally, he played fast and loose with that mandate, but not this morning. Today, they only had a half-day of school, and their mom would be picking up him and his brother to go to lunch at noon. That exciting change to the monotonous routine hurried him along as he got ready.

It was 7:36 when Max realized he had forgotten his tablet in the bathroom where he had been watching videos while he brushed his teeth. But his mom steadfastly refused to turn the car around, so he had to go the whole day without it. It was supposed to only be used for schoolwork while at class, but that was more of a suggestion in Max's eyes. He had tried to weasel Charlie's away from him several times, but his brother had refused to even let him look at his tablet the entire morning. Only once they got in the car after lunch at Cafe Rio did Charlie put it down long enough for Max to snag it. He was too busy cramming his leftover chips into his mouth to even notice until they were halfway home; then suddenly it was something to cry over.

"He isn't even using it," Max protested to his mother, as Charlie tucked the iPad out of sight in his backpack.

"It doesn't matter. That's his and you can't just take it because you don't have yours."

"I need to go to the bathroom," Max shot back.

"You can wait until we get home."

"I need to go real bad."

"Well, you're still going to wait until we get home."

Mr. Smith, Jerry, was away for work in Texas for a few weeks, and it was starting to wear on her. It was supposed to get easier as the kids got older; that's what all the parents said. It was all a lie. *I wonder if the second husband is easier than the first*, she thought.

Finally, they were turning onto their street, and she hit the garage door remote. It still hadn't moved by the time she glided into the driveway. Jerry had said a dozen times now that he'd look at the door, but he still hadn't even changed the batteries. Jamming down on the button again, the door finally started to roll up. She closed her eyes as she waited for the door to fully open. Only eight hours to go until it was time for them to get in bed. Fucking half-days.

The van wasn't even turned off when Max was fighting to open the door. "Max, wait until we're stopped," she warned, but he kept fighting with the child lock until it gave in and he was finally free, running for the house and presumably the bathroom he'd needed to visit so urgently just a few minutes before. Though Lisa would have bet good money that he didn't need to go anymore.

"Charlie, come on," she said. He was still in his seat, munching on chips. "You can eat those inside."

"I wanna stay here," he mumbled through a mouthful of food.

"Fine. Whatever." She got out of the car and walked into the house herself.

In the kitchen, her eyes strayed to Jerry's liquor cabinet. *What's the point of living in Vegas if you can't occasionally get day drunk?* she thought.

She loved being a parent; it would just be easier if the kids were a little quieter. She always side-eyed the boring women who were self-medicating during naptime. But the desire to experience a little less motherhood had been lurking in the back of her mind. All she had in reach was Advil and liquor, but Jenny had a prescription for Xanax that she bragged about every playdate. All the moms agreed, she did seem a lot happier, even though her kids were notoriously the worst behaved on the block. Just a taste, Lisa thought. Plus, pills were a lot more discreet than drinking. And they were actual medicine; the doctor wouldn't prescribe them if they didn't help.

"MOOOOOOMMMMM!" Max's wailing came bouncing down the hall.

"What is it?"

"MOOOMMM!" he screamed again.

"If you need something, come out here."

Max's footsteps came rushing down the hallway. "Mom, my iPad is gone! It's gone!"

"No, it's not. You probably just left it somewhere and forgot."

"THE TEEEEVEEEEEE!" Max screamed. She walked into the living room where he was, to see that the TV was missing. The cables were still hanging there on the outstretched arms of the wall mount that had held the TV that morning. It was like the TV had been ripped right off the support. Her eyes moved lower. The Xbox was gone, too, just cables remaining.

BANG! The sound made both of them jump in the quiet living room. The front door had swung open and slammed against the wall. "RUN!" Lisa screamed, grabbing her son's arm and sprinting back the way they had come toward the garage.

The pair knocked Charlie over in the doorway of the garage, sending his remaining chips flying. "GET IN THE CAR!" she screamed, pulling the keys from the hook beside the garage door opener and mashing the button. Her voice was one that the boys had only heard on rare occasions, the voice every child knew meant that there wasn't any room for disagreement or time-wasting, only silent obedience.

Max jumped into the front passenger seat and Charlie followed him. Lisa dropped into the driver's seat and hit the ignition on the keyless engine, slamming the shifter into reverse and hitting the gas.

CRASH! The car lunged into reverse through the garage door that had failed to open once again. Lisa slammed the brakes, but the car was already halfway through the thin aluminum paneling of the rollup door. It was at this point that all three of the Smiths in the car started to cry.

Day 2, 1:40 pm

TRACY COOK

It had been a busy day for the two detectives. They had been dispatched to an overnight break-in at a warehouse near the North Las Vegas local airport. Housed in nondescript warehouses was a company called EventRig, specializing in concert production. Tracy wasn't much of a music buff, live or recorded. Bill had taken a great interest in the work they did, indulging himself in a guided tour of the facility by the building manager, Mark. The equipment they rented to the touring industry was spread across several of the warehouses, so the tour took longer than usual, as they gathered evidence about the robbery of five laptops and two bins full of cabling that occurred during the night. The pair of detectives had been dutifully checking the local scrapyards when they stumbled onto the thief. They had barely gotten him in cuffs before they were redirected to the optimistically named

Tropical Parkway, though other than the heat, there wasn't much tropical about the street. Once they were in the neighborhood, the house was an easy find, with the two patrol cars that had arrived on the scene first still sitting in front of the house with their lights flashing, and crime scene tape blowing in the wind around the boundaries of the property. Several other police cars were parked in the open spaces down the street.

"You don't see that every day." Bill broke the silence from the driver's seat as he eased the car to a stop at the end of the driveway, motioning to the car sticking out halfway through the garage door.

"Surprised it doesn't happen more," Tracy answered.

A very tall, uniformed officer named Holmes met them in the driveway. "Detectives, we've searched the property and it's all safe," he said. "The owner and her kids are waiting in the back-yard."

"Very good," Bill said. "Take your men and start working the street. Look for the usual stuff—suspicious activity, doorbell cameras pointing in this direction."

"Yes, sir," Officer Holmes answered, before leaning in a little closer to the detectives. "Mrs. Smith isn't handling this very well." He nodded his head toward the rear of the house before he walked off to gather the rest of the uniforms who were milling around on the property.

"Do you want to go back and talk with her?" Bill asked Tracy.

"Because I'm a woman?"

"Yes." He peered over his sunglasses at her. Tracy didn't answer. "You have a nice face. It'll calm her down more than my angry Irish one will."

"Fine. But only because you admitted your face is ugly."

"Whatever you want to tell yourself."

Bill led them down the walkway to the front door, which was swinging gently in the breeze. The chuck with the locks in it laid just inside the doorway, with sawdust and splinters covering the whole area. "Looks like they drilled a hole and then stuck a saw through," Bill explained, inspecting the evidence of the cuts on the door. "Probably used a Sawzall. It'd be a little noisy, but it'd get the job done quickly. It's these damn recessed doorways. Park the car in the driveway, someone would have to be standing directly in front of the house to see anyone messing with the door. The neighbor across the street wouldn't even hear it. You want to warn the public about something, warn them about not trusting anyone they see walking around with a cordless saw."

"You really hate power tools," Tracy commented, stepping through the doorway and heading for the rear of the house.

* * *

Two hours later, Tracy and Bill were sitting at a small Mexican food joint down the street. "So, the TV was brand new?" Bill asked, mostly rhetorically as he flipped through his notes. "Did she say what they did with the box?"

"Da vox?" she mumbled through a mouthful of taco.

"Yes. A seventy-inch TV requires a big box."

"She didn't mention it."

"Probably put it out for recycling. These smash-and-grab types scope out the recycling piles on trash day, looking for houses that are throwing away boxes for expensive things."

"I can call her and ask if you want me to."

"No, it's okay. Let's wait and see if CSI discovers anything useful. What else are we missing?" He jabbed the open notebook with his finger.

"I think it's all in there. I'll start cross-referencing it against any similar crimes in the area," Tracy said, taking a break from the tacos. "But first, I need to get more queso."

Day 2, 9:03 pm

GRANT ANDERSON

"I hate the colors in here." The Duvalls, Cindy and Jack, were doing their latest house tour with Grant. So far they hadn't liked any of the homes seen in the Fountain View area, yet they insisted that they wanted a house in this neighborhood and no other. "It's all so bland," Cindy continued. "How many shades of yellowy white can they put in one house?" She finished her criticism off with an insincere chuckle, designed to get Jack and Grant to agree with her.

"Paint's the easiest thing to change about a house," Grant responded.

"You do a lot of painting?" Jack asked, not even bothering to hide his sarcasm as he headed back for the front door. He had seen the foyer and hated it, and that was enough for him.

"I'm sorry this isn't what you were hoping for. I can keep digging in deeper to find that diamond in the rough."

"Look, Grant," Jack said self-importantly. "No offense, but this isn't working out with you. We've decided to go with a different agent."

"Oh, I'm sorry," Grant answered, stuttering out an apology. "Is there anything I can do to change your mind? I've been trying really hard to find something up to your standards."

"We keep telling you what we don't want, but you aren't listening. You just keep showing us the same crappy houses over and over." He gestured at the structure behind them. "I don't like hearing excuses, and that's all I get from you. It's that simple."

"Well, I'm sorry things didn't work out," Grant responded meekly. One door slam later and their Charger was roaring down the street toward some other agent. Probably some guy they'd seen on a bus stop bench, the Vegas version of Teddy Anderson. Marketing yourself is the path to success in real estate; his dad had said that over and over. In fact, it was the title of one of the chapters in his book.

* * *

The days blurred together. At home it was cleaning the house, at the office it was all about paperwork. Taking over Uncle Paul's business would've been easier if there'd been some sort of client list or advertising budget, but there wasn't. The best Grant could surmise was that Paul worked exclusively by word of mouth and referrals, which would probably dry up now that the word of mouth was that he was dead. The Duvalls were one of the few leads Grant had created on his own, a bit of Internet stalking, but that wasn't a long-term strategy. Cold-calling was the lowest of the low, but it could at least be done on the cheap. None of it had been successful in creating any serious interest, only a couple of callbacks and all of them dead ends.

It was after 9 pm when Grant finally flipped the "Open" sign over and slipped out to his car. He didn't turn toward home, but instead set course for downtown; not to the Strip proper, but old Vegas, centered around Fremont Street, the original site of the gambling town. The nightlife in Vegas was obviously legendary, with nearly every casino boasting some kind of nightclub or flashy bar. However, as a local resident, there's also a need for low-key bars that service the desires of the regulars who aren't looking for an epic night of partying. Oddly enough, that's also hard to find in Las Vegas. The bars around town that don't cater to tourists instead serve the career alcoholics, looking for a quiet place to drink their life away while playing video poker on the machines embedded in the bartop. Those bars all served the same unappetizing food and smelled of smoke. The only women to be found were the waitresses who had aged out of the big Strip places, now banished to a life of pouring drinks for blue-collar-and-below workers who weren't ready yet to do all their drinking on the sidewalk outside a convenience store.

On Fremont, there was one bar he had found that had a ring of reality to it, The Phoenix. Even though it was on a famous street, it was far enough out of the range of the neon lights that the masses of tourists didn't stumble upon it. It was mostly for locals and the occasional visitors who were looking for a relaxed vibe. Grant had never been much of a drinker; neither of his parents drank either, and his teenage years had been mostly spent on the computer playing video games, or helping his dad get another house ready to show, so now as an adult it was more of a forced habit. Holding a beer at a bar was a better look than just a Coke. The straw made it surprisingly juvenile, like going to a bike park with training wheels. Still, a straight Coke would have been his preferred drink if he didn't feel so foolish holding it.

Trying to pick up girls at a bar felt like the romantic version of making cold calls, although even worse because you had to do it in person. Grant had an entire bag of tricks for dealing with potential clients to distract them from the fact he was only interested in the commission he would make for selling them something. In a bar, there was no denying that the only reason he was there was to try and hook up. All of his skills at chit-chat failed him at a bar, though, because he really didn't care what a woman's cat was named or what she did for a living. (Spoiler alert: it's always a teacher or a nurse.)

It was a weekday night and even in Vegas, people have jobs, so the dance floor was shut down. The lounge part of the bar was sparsely populated as well. A couple of groups were spread out on the sofas, and a large group of couples were piled into the booth in the far corner, being extra loud. Grant ended up finding a seat at the bar. He didn't have to wait long before a group of four girls came in and occupied the space next to him. They were dressed for going out, but not excessively like tourists would have been. The girl closest to him was petite, maybe a hundred pounds at most, medium length brown hair and a perfect smile. "Hey," he said to her.

"Hi," she answered with a smile.

"I'm Grant."

"Hi, Grant. I'm Vanessa. Nice to meet you." She accepted Grant's handshake.

"Are you from around here?"

"Sorta. I'm living here while I go to UNLV."

"That's cool. What are you studying?"

"Early education. I'm going to be a teacher."

"That's awesome," he replied, trying to hide his surprise. "You like teaching?"

"Well, I'm not really doing it yet. I'm still studying."

"Oh, right."

"And what do you do?"

"I'm a real estate agent."

"That sounds fun."

"Sometimes, I guess."

"Every job is probably like that," Vanessa answered genuinely.

"I wouldn't know. This is all I've ever done, and honestly, I hate it. The people are the worst, and the houses smell terrible. I've been asking myself what I'm even doing out here, living in my uncle's disgusting house, showing mid-life-crisis rich assholes houses for their swinger parties. This place sucks." Vanessa just nodded politely, so Grant filled the pause with a sip of his drink. "It's just hard, I guess."

"Yeah," Vanessa answered. "That sounds rough."

"Yep, and my only clients fired me today."

Before she could answer, her friends on the other side grabbed her attention and quickly the whole group was climbing out of the chairs. "Are you leaving?" he asked Vanessa's back.

She turned around. "Oh, yeah. We're supposed to meet some people and they ended up back that way a bit." She jerked her head in the direction of the casinos. "It was nice talking to you, though. Hope things get better."

"Yeah, uh, you, too." Gripping his glass tighter, like a driver speeding into a corner faster than he should, he added, "Could I maybe get your number?"

She smiled politely, saying, "That's so sweet of you," before turning and following her friends out the door.

* * *

If there was one good thing about being a single guy in Las Vegas, other than strip clubs and weed stores on every corner, it was Roberto's Tacos. All over town and open 24 hours a day. In Atlanta, restaurants went dark early unless it was a Waffle House. Out here, instead of waffles, they had tacos. He needed something to help him stop replaying his embarrassing encounter at the bar over and over in his head. Even as he had been talking to her, he was regretting the sound of his own voice, but hadn't been able to stop. Hoping the next thought might be the one to right the ship and charm Vanessa. "Idiot," he mumbled at himself. So far his ventures out to the social scene had ended in fiasco.

Instead of finding a girl he could talk to, yet again he would be burying his feelings under a pile of food. Tacos could take the edge off, even though he had been counter-productively listening to some of Bill Burr's podcast on the drive. It's not great background noise; the Boston comic's voice sounded like a perpetually angry garbageman. Grant already had tickets for the next time he came to Vegas. Guess that's a second positive for this town; comics always have scheduled dates in Vegas. Not that they avoided Atlanta, but they were drawn to Las Vegas.

Turning right down Anadarko Valley brought him back to his uncle's house. Of course, there wasn't much point in meeting girls at bars; there was no way he could bring them back to a house that looked like this. They would probably assume there were bodies beneath the piles.

The house across the street had been dark ever since he arrived in town. He knew it hadn't been publicly listed for sale or rent, because Grant kept close tabs on the houses in his neighborhood. Tonight, however, the lights were on. For the first time since Grant had moved to Vegas, he had a new neighbor.

Day 3, 8:36 am

LUCAS GREEN

The amount of traveling I'd done in my life meant I was used to sleeping on foreign mattresses. The bed that had been provided for me here was clearly the cheapest version of a bed that Carlos and his crew could find, but it worked well enough. As for my roommate, Deputy the dog didn't mind his crate at all. After having spent some time behind bars at the pet store, he seemed more comfortable sleeping in there than in the open.

I woke before dawn and roused Deputy as well. He wasn't eager about the early morning, but he accepted it without complaint, not that Deputy had much getting ready to do. Some food, then slipping on the collar and leash, and he was prepared for the day. The rest of the house had also been furnished by Carlos's lackeys up to a livable standard. Besides the bed, there was a couch, TV, WiFi, and enough kitchen supplies to fill out a bachelor's kitchen. Other than the bed, the rest of it wasn't strictly necessary, but it would look better if anyone ended up visiting the house during my stay. Yesterday, I got the lay of the land and watched Grant leave for work in the morning. I had decided against venturing after him; I needed to be familiar with the neighborhood first. I was watching through the window when Grant returned home last night at 11:24 pm. Obviously, he hadn't been at work the entire time, but his demeanor during the walk to the front door didn't give any clues to where he'd been. He was dressed in the same clothes he'd had on when he'd left for work, and he was carrying a bag of takeout food. Carlos had aggressively pitched the idea of using his men to tail Grant in the preceding weeks to build a reliable history of his movements, but I didn't think it was wise. If Javy was any indication of how his men worked, they couldn't be trusted to handle the subtle work of observation. So I was starting at square one with tracking his movements.

All homeowners in Las Vegas had heavily invested in blackout curtains. The unbearable sun was a relentless alarm clock and liable to cook things through the windows if the interior wasn't blocked off from its gaze. So watching Grant's house during daylight wasn't going to reveal much. Only at night was the soft glow of light visible around the edges of the windows. Today, there was no sign of life until 8:36 am, when he exited the house for the first time.

"Action," I ordered Deputy as my hand fell on the door-knob. Deputy refused to budge. "Let's go," I said, yanking the leash again. The dog laid his head down on his paws, averting his eyes. Grant was on his way to his car as I knelt down. "Listen to me," I said, grabbing ahold of his snout and forcing him to look at me. "You have one job left in life, and that's to go out for a walk." Deputy snorted, finally unwinding his body as slowly as possible as he climbed upon his many feet.

Even though I had been peeking through the curtains for a while, the brightness of the Las Vegas sun was shocking the first time I stepped into it. The sound of the door opening immediately drew Grant's attention to me. Pausing for a moment in front of his car, he gave a wave. "Hey, neighbor." His voice drifted across the narrow street.

"Hello," I replied, giving a half wave back.

"I love your dog. What's his name?" Grant had abandoned his route to the driver's seat and instead started down his driveway, toward us. A real estate agent could always be trusted to start conversations with strangers.

"Oh yeah, he's great. His name's Deputy, but he isn't a morning pooch."

"I don't blame him. Mornings are the worst." Grant kept speaking as he crossed the street, now on our side. "I'm Grant Anderson. I live right there." He pointed back at the house he had obviously just exited.

"Nice to meet you. I'm Lucas Green." I accepted his hand.

"Did you buy this place? It's been empty for a while."

"No, no, I'm just here for business. My company got it for me."

"What kind of work do you do?" Grant inquired, bending down to pet Deputy.

"I'm a real estate investor. Or a real estate scout, I guess. I work for an investment group."

"Oh, really? What a coincidence. I'm actually a real estate agent."

"How funny." It wasn't that far-fetched. It seemed like nearly everyone was involved in real estate in some capacity. "We're looking for a couple of apartment buildings or commercial structures to buy out here."

"If you need any help, I'd love to be of service," Grant responded, pulling a business card from his pocket with the skill of a blackjack dealer. He had his business cards locked and loaded before he even left the house. "I'm new in town myself, but if you need anything, let me know."

"Thank you. I'm new to this area, so let me ask what you think of it. I haven't spent much time in Vegas outside of the casinos downtown." In my experience, most people like to talk if you simply give them the opportunity to. Let's see if Grant is like most people.

"It's alright. This was my uncle's house. He passed away, so I moved in a couple of months ago. The area isn't too bad. Everything's close by, and the 95 is just that way, and the 215 is behind us. You can get anywhere pretty quickly."

"You know what they say about location!" I gave him a bit of a laugh.

"Yeah, this is my favorite part of the town I've seen."

"How about crime?" I pressed him. "It seems pretty safe around here."

"For the most part. If you go down Cheyenne or Craig, it starts to get rougher on the other side of Rancho as you get closer to the Air Force base. But stuff still happens. There's been a couple of break-ins in these neighborhoods since I've been here." He gestured around our neighborhood. There were several developments around us that each contained a subdivision surrounded by decorative block walls, but the entryways were completely open, so it wasn't like it was secure.

"Interesting. I'm from Miami, so it feels kinda similar, just with a desert vibe instead of an ocean one." It felt like places built in the heat had a common design to each other, a lot of stucco in all of them. Of course, in Florida, nature was trying to claw back every square inch of space at all times. Turn your back and the grass was creeping, or there was an alligator under your car.

"Well, then, you must be used to the heat," Grant said.

"And the crime. When I first lived down there, the cocaine wars were just ending, but it hasn't completely left yet."

"That sounds scary. I'm sure there are drug problems here, but I don't know about it. Most of the crime just seems to be break-ins or drunk kids causing trouble. Though I keep a gun nearby anyways."

"Oh, really? Did you need one back in Georgia?" I asked.

"I didn't. I never owned a gun back there." He paused. "Wait, how did you know I was from Georgia?" he asked.

"The bumper sticker," I said, pointing to the Tomahawk decal on his car. "I used to watch them on TBS all the time."

"Oh yeah, those were the days."

"So you didn't bring a gun, but you have one now? Was your uncle one of those guys with a gun under every ledge?"

"Ha, more like he just lost them in there. I found a shotgun in with the brooms, and a .38 Special sitting on top of a pile of toilet rolls. Who knows how many more are in there."

"Sometimes when nature calls, you have to be prepared."

"Yeah, I don't know what he was planning on shooting in there. Hopefully it was just part of his general messiness," Grant answered with a laugh. "I haven't even been able to clean out the house fully yet. I'm still sleeping in the guest bedroom. There was less stuff to move in there."

"Yikes. Well, if you see any mice, maybe Deputy can handle them for ya."

"If you hear any gunshots, it'll be me shooting at them."

"Copy on the gunshots. It's only the mice."

"Well, I better be getting off to the office. I hope you enjoy your walk. There's actually a dog park like two blocks past the neighborhood that way." Grant motioned over his shoulder to the northwest.

"I guess that's where we're heading, then. He could use some time to stretch his legs out."

"Have a good day. Give me a call if you need any help. I'm always available!" Grant offered his hand again.

"Of course. I'll probably be bugging you all the time." I accepted his hand for the second time.

Grant turned and started walking back across the street when I stopped him. "Hey, Grant, I actually do have a question." I followed after him into the road. "My company got the utilities set up here, but I think they forgot to get the trash service started. Do you know what day the recycling pick-up is?"

"Oh yeah, it's on Wednesdays, about 10 am."

"Okay. I have a bunch of boxes for the TV and stuff. Do you think I could toss them on your pile? I hate not recycling."

"Yeah, man, no problem. I just park the cans right here on the sidewalk. Help yourself."

"Awesome. Well, have a good day. I really appreciate it." I finished before turning away down the street in the general direction of the dog park he had mentioned.

Even though the weather was perfect for a walk, it seemed like a chore after a few minutes. Despite Grant's suggestion, the dog park was never on the agenda, though it was visible from the far end of the neighborhood. Deputy seemed to shy away from heading in that direction. The faint sounds of yelping from the park didn't entice him at all. The whole goal of the morning had actually been achieved as soon as Grant came across the street. The rest of the walking was just for appearance's sake and general surveillance. The subdivision was practically indistinguishable from the others around it. Cookie-cutter neighborhoods took up every block on this side of town. The one I now lived in had three entry points through the seven-foot-high block walls, one on every side except for the north. The perimeter looked about the same as it had from the vantage point of Google Maps, no surprises anywhere to be found. Deputy wasn't very interested in anything we passed, either. It seemed like he felt duty-bound to participate in the walk, even though he wasn't very keen on the idea.

Walking is helpful for thinking, a monotonous activity that lets the brain cycle through ideas more effectively. By the time my house was back in sight, I had settled on the details of the plan I had been grasping for this morning with Grant. I even ran over the risk ratios before I got back.

My profession was very unique in that there was no official research to lean on, so being an assassin like me who eliminated targets by getting third parties to kill them was intellectually draining work. If the goal was simply just to eliminate the person, I could've been done already. I had a gun, I could get a knife if needed, or fashion some kind of bomb. Those were all tried and true methods. However, I needed to engineer this death through circumstances that couldn't be traced back to either me or my client in any way. In fact, it couldn't even look like the death occurred in any other way than happenstance; being in the wrong place at the wrong time, with an easily identified stranger holding the smoking gun.

In theory, it's easy; however, manipulating someone else into committing the deed is another matter. But the walk had given me time to lock in the thought. General Patton claimed that creativity is everything a person knows, experience and ideas all jumbling together in the subconscious until a unique thought pops out. Not everyone I've mentioned that philosophy to has agreed with it, but I think it makes sense. Obviously, it takes a certain personality to create the winning thought. No matter how much I study, I'm not going to create like John Lennon or Walt Disney. But even artists of that level weren't just pulling concepts out of thin air; there was some underlying thought or experience that brought that new idea to the forefront. It would be interesting to hear a creative mind go back and explain each step of how they formed their thought. "Oh, that reminded me of this one time in school, and I connected it to this thing I saw my friend's dad do when the lawnmower wouldn't start."

Fishing out the cellphone I'd been given, I hit redial. The phone's one and only purpose was for calling a single number. "Battle Born Renovations, this is Amy, how may I help you?" the familiar voice chimed through the phone.

"Hi, Amy, this is Lucas Green, calling for Carlos."

"Of course, Mr. Green. Mr. Santana has actually said he's able to assist you on anything you might need. Would you like me to direct your call to him?"

"Sure." Typical; Carlos Guerra wasn't going to let himself be on speed dial anytime I needed something, so instead I got to deal with Javy and his attitude.

There were a couple of clicks and a pause before Javy's voice came through. "Mr. Green," he spoke pointedly.

"Yeah. I need some boxes."

"Boxes?"

"Yes, empty boxes for electronics. A big TV box, a new Xbox, and a Playstation. Maybe a soundbar or stereo system, and an iMac box."

"You just want the empty boxes?" he asked, sounding puzzled.

"Yep. I don't care if you buy the items, steal them, or dig them out of the recycling. I just need the boxes before Wednesday."

"Okay. I'll call you when we're ready to deliver." He hung up.

Not the most elegant of plans, but it would work well enough, I hoped.

Day 3, 9:13 am

TRACY COOK

"What did you do last night?" Bill asked, taking his seat across the desk.

"Nothing much, just watched TV and ate dinner," Tracy answered. "How about you?"

"Hunter had a tee-ball game last night, so it was family night at the park and then dinner at Chili's."

"Chili's. That seems so 'fat cop' of you," Tracy answered with a smirk.

"They have salads there. You just have to skip the 900-calorie dressing."

"How's Becky doing?"

"She's good. She keeps bugging me about wanting to go over to see your new house and bring you a housewarming gift."

"Oh, that's really sweet of her."

"I told her I can bring it here and give it to you, but she insists on delivering it to your house. I think she just wants an excuse to see the place. I can never understand people like that."

"Women?" Tracy said with a smile.

He rolled his eyes. "No, extroverts. Why go see someone when you can just drop a gift off or have it delivered?"

"I think some people enjoy making personal connections with others."

"I guess so. Seems like a lot of effort, though." Bill sighed. In addition to rubbing a lot of his colleagues the wrong way over his stance on their eating habits, he also offended them with his lack of interest in social activities. Cops were always finding reasons to hang out off-duty, but Bill almost always refused to participate. When Tracy first met him, the word around the office was that he was just a miserable person; but the more time Tracy spent around him, the more she saw that he was actually always happy. It seemed to Tracy that he would genuinely just rather be at home with his wife and kids instead of hanging out at bars with people he only knew from work. The desire to be home with his family was probably the most confusing part for the other cops. They could make sense of an introvert, but not a man who would rather be at a tee-ball game.

"You, Becky, and Hunter are invited over any time for a visit, though there isn't much to see at this point. Mostly empty rooms and boxes."

"You've seen one house, you've seen them all," he grumbled.

"Ready to get started on these files?"

"Yeah," he answered glumly. Tracy pulled out her

notepad as Bill flipped open the manila folder. "First up, we have the Dupree case."

"Bill. New girl." The voice sounded over Tracy's shoulder, cutting Bill off before he got started. Both detectives looked up. It was their captain, Walt Snitker. He had been running the robbery division for a couple of decades now. He had found a position he liked in the department hierarchy and had nestled in tightly. Bill had told Tracy that Walt had already looked ancient even when Bill had first started, and that he would likely look exactly the same when Bill retired.

"Yes, Captain?" Tracy answered as he reached their desk.

"You're being assigned to the task force up on the third floor," he said, pointing at Tracy.

She blinked for a moment before Bill cut in. "What? When did that start again?"

"Today. Detective Dean is back," he grumbled, turning away from them. "Report to him up there as our representative."

"Dumbass state trooper," Bill grumbled as well. He seemed to know more than her already, so she just looked at him, waiting for an explanation. "He's some hard-on with connections and a state badge. He was running an investigation up there for months, wasting everyone's time, until he got pulled off for some stupid leadership training thing with the FBI. But I guess he's back now." The local police and state police were natural enemies, like lions and other lions who wore stupid park ranger-looking hats.

"What's he investigating that he needs one of us up there?"

"No idea, but the captain's sending you because you're low man on the totem pole. The good trooper just needs bodies to make it seem like he's important, so now you get to play along with him."

Tracy gathered up her notebooks and bag. She hadn't spent much time on the third floor; it was mostly conference rooms. Getting attached to a task force seemed like a good thing, but neither Bill nor the captain seemed to think so. "Have fun," Bill called out as she trooped off. "I'll text if something comes up."

The printed-out piece of paper taped to the door of the largest conference room read "TASK FORCE X." Tracy partly expected to be welcomed by a bald man in a wheelchair, but no one at all greeted her as she entered. Against the back wall was the most impressive suspect board she had ever seen. It spanned the entire wall, over fifty printed-out headshots with different colored strings stretching between them, all leading to the face in the center, Edgar Mencia. "Hey," Tracy addressed the room. "I'm Tracy from Robbery. My captain sent me up here."

There were three other people in the room. Two of them didn't even turn their heads. The women on the left side of the room responded by looking back. "Grab a seat," she suggested. All of them were already sitting at the line of folding tables set up in front of the suspect board. Tracy followed the suggestion and sat at the table with the other woman. "I'm Tina," the woman said. "Homicide."

"Nice to meet you. This is a pretty friendly room, huh?"

"Think of this as detention. No one wants to be here. We—"

She was cut off as the door opened again and a smartly uniformed state trooper entered. The man marched to the front of the room where he turned around to glower at the assembled people. "Welcome to Task Force X," he barked out. He paused for a moment, as if expecting them to react to the name. "We'll be picking up where we left off when we last met. What progress has been made on the assignments I left each of you?" He looked first to the man at the opposite side of the room from Tracy. "Special Agent Chavez?"

"Nothing to report. The agency hasn't gotten any new tips."

He turned to the next man, who responded, "Haven't seen anything new, either."

Tina shook her head when he looked at her. Finally, his eyes fell on Tracy. "Well?"

"I'm sorry?"

"Have you made any progress on the bribery angle?" he demanded.

"Um, I was just assigned to this a few minutes ago," Tracy answered.

"Who are you?" he snapped, going for the folder on his podium.

"I'm Tracy Cook. I'm with Robbery."

"She took Will's spot as the local precinct presence," Tina cut in.

"Okay, so did Will make any progress while I was gone? Where did he go? I expected all the same people back."

"I think he got promoted," Tracy said. Bill had mentioned a Will who'd been promoted and moved out to Henderson.

"You people all know the governor's personally invested in this investigation, and nobody made any progress while I was gone?" he said, glaring at everyone in the room. The rest of the people shifted in their seats, avoiding looking at the trooper. The name plate on the podium identified him as Dean Wilson. Now she wished Bill had given her more of a heads-up about what to expect from him.

"I'm not even sure what we're investigating," Tracy offered.

Dean stood aside and thumped his hand against the picture of Edgar Mencia. Even though Tracy had never personally worked on a case involving him, his face was fairly well-known in police circles. He was the local representative of the Cortez cartel, the organization that controlled the import of nearly every illegal narcotic in the valley. "This man is our target!" he declared. "And more importantly, who he's funding in the political arena." He gestured up to the pictures that had been placed above Mencia's photo. Now that she focused on them, Tracy recognized most of them from their campaign videos.

"Now you know why the governor's so interested," Tina whispered as Dean continued his tirade.

"Mencia is funneling money to all of these politicians, and I want to nail him on it."

This announcement made the whole arrangement much clearer to Tracy. Dean Wilson had wrangled a mandate for a political witch hunt, pressuring various departments into playing along. However, none of them were interested in actually being useful to his delusions of grandeur, so they contributed as little as possible, which was why the "new girl" had been sent up by Captain Snitker. The other three people at the table with her looked completely disinterested as Dean continued explaining how they were going to crack the code on the political money laundering he was sure was happening.

If the cartel was adept enough to sell a product that produced millions of dollars in the United States and escape detection, she was sure they'd be able to funnel thousands of dollars to local politicians without raising any flags. Starting an investigation with the goal of finding an infraction was a violation of many moral and practical rules when it came to being a law enforcement officer. She let her gaze work over the rest of the suspect wall as Dean talked about how obvious it was that these officials were on the take, despite not having any actual evidence of that fact.

"Wait!" she said suddenly, sitting upright in her chair. Her eyes had fallen on the very last picture tacked to the wall at the far left side. "I know that guy!"

"Who?" Dean leaned over his podium to get a look down the wall at where she was pointing. The rest of the room had actually looked up as well. Anything that interrupted Dean's lecturing seemed to be of interest.

"That's Paul Sherman," she said. "He was my real estate agent when I bought my house."

"So? Should we put your picture on the wall now?" Dean snapped.

"What?" Tracy said. "Why?"

"You seem so proud of knowing a criminal. Maybe

your face should be up here."

"Dean!" Tina interjected.

"I just thought it would help to know I know him," Tracy sputtered back. "He's in my phone. I can easily talk to him."

"He's nobody," one of the men on the other side of the room offered. "He was just the real estate agent on record for some of Mencia's home purchases."

"If he isn't important, then why is his picture up there?" Tracy shot back.

Dean stomped over to the end of the wall and snatched Paul's picture off. "Here, look at it all you want!" He flung the image toward Tracy. The air caught the picture and sent it fluttering off in the other direction.

Tracy got ready to argue back, until she felt Tina's hand grab her hard on the thigh. Glancing over, she saw Tina shaking her head. Letting her breath out, Tracy fell back in her seat, her jaw still set firm.

"Now that that's over, let's get to the actual work." Dean pointed to a cart in the other corner of the room, sagging under the weight of paper stacked upon it. "Those are the donor and expense reports for all these people's campaigns. Mencia is in there somewhere. I want to find him."

Day 3, 2:30 pm

LUCAS GREEN

It has always struck me as funny, the kinds of establishments that are located right next to the Strip. Just outside of the neon glow is a railroad which leads to warehouses predating the growth of the casinos. It's also where the shady strip clubs are located and multiple gun shops. And those are the shops that are reputable enough to advertise. The rest kept their business to themselves, their parking lots lined with hand-drawn signs and chain-link fences suggesting that unless you had received an invitation, you were in the wrong place. The Gun Depot was on the list of visits today. Javy had talked so glowingly about the Glock 17, maybe it was time to give it a try and see how it felt in my hand. Glocks are the most common handgun in America; it couldn't hurt to be more familiar with it.

But before that was one more stop. The flickering sign only read "Harold's," but that was enough if you knew what you were looking for. Pulling through the unlocked gate, I parked next to a beat-up old pickup truck. It was the only vehicle around, so it was probably a safe bet that it was Harold's. The Vietnam veteran sticker on the window suggested that as well.

The door didn't chime as I walked through it, but the sudden appearance of the deeply elderly man out of the corner told me that somehow he knew it whenever his door was opened. He didn't say anything, just glared at me like an intruder, as opposed to a customer.

"Hello," I started. He was definitely going to be able to help me; the room was filled from floor to ceiling with assorted gadgets and electronics piled up on tables and wall shelves. "I'm Lucas. Montgomery gave me this address. Said you could help me out with some equipment I need."

The man's face relaxed when he heard the name. "Montgomery, you say?"

"That's right."

"He sure is a good guy. Sent me plenty of business over the years. How do you know him?"

"She and I are in the same business." I slightly emphasized the "she." I could tell he'd deliberately used the wrong gender as a test.

A smile broke across the old man's face. "That's all I needed to hear. Welcome to Harold's House of Spycraft and Extraction. What can I do for you?"

Fishing a paper out of my pocket, I held it out. "I've got a few basic items on there, and maybe a few unique ones."

He took it and studied it. "I got most of this ready

to go, but this last one might take a bit. How long-range does it need to be?"

"Across a street and through a wall."

Harold thought for a few moments. "I can do it, but we'll need the make and model."

"I don't have that yet, but I will."

"That's alright. You'll be able to program it yourself simply enough, once you know. It'll cost extra, though."

"That's not an issue."

"Good man. I'll get started right now."

"Okay. I've got a few other places to visit. I'll be back in a couple of hours?"

"Sounds good, Mr. Lucas."

Day 3, 5:05 pm

TRACY COOK

"How'd it go?" Bill asked, taking his seat at the desk. She'd been sitting there staring at the ceiling for nearly twenty minutes since the task force meeting wrapped up for the day. They'd spent the last few hours shifting through generic paperwork, cataloging every penny that passed through the campaigns as Dean preached about corruption he was sure was hiding just under the surface.

"It was the worst experience I've ever had," she answered, immediately launching into a full recounting of her morning.

"He really threw the photo at you?"

"*Yes!*"

"That guy's a piece of work. The captain fought hard to keep him out of this building, but we're the precinct nearest to his house, so he refused to go anywhere else."

"Everyone else seems to hate it, too. Only Tina was the least bit friendly."

"Tina Flores?" Bill asked.

"Yeah, you know her?"

"We used to have a thing."

"Bill!"

"It was before I met Becky!" he shot back. "But it's still awkward. Did she mention me?"

"No, we didn't get around to discussing prior lovers."

"Stuck to just real estate agents, then?"

Tracy glared at her partner. It was easy to be cavalier about the experience when he got to sit down here goofing around all morning, instead of being assaulted with glossy headshots. "If he knows Mencia, we need to talk to him!" she hissed, lowering her voice.

Bill nodded his head up and down a few times. It was his thinking pose. "If he's been in Mencia's homes at any point, he's more in the know than any of us. We're lucky just to see Mencia's front gate before his lawn decorations come to life as angry defense attorneys."

"So I'm not crazy."

"I didn't say that," Bill answered, eying his partner. "You want to call Paul and set up a meeting, don't you?"

"Would it be so crazy if I happened to see a house I wanted to look at all of a sudden?"

"Hey, look at this crown molding in the foyer! By the way, do you remember any incriminating details about that drug kingpin you sold a house to years ago?" Bill mimicked her voice.

"Give me a little credit. I'll at least wait until we make it to the kitchen."

"It'd be borderline interfering with an investigation at best."

"That's not an investigation up there," Tracy said. "It's a glorified fishing expedition. Dean's just hoping he finds a golden nugget in a shit river of paper that he can take to the press. 'Hero Trooper Proves School Commissioner In Bed With The Cartel!'" She held her hands up like she was reading a newspaper headline.

Bill leaned back in his chair, drifting back into his thinking form. "Getting anything on Mencia is practically impossible. The cartel's become so hands-off that they can't be tied to much at all anymore. Mencia is directing a multi-million-dollar enterprise without doing anything more than fielding a few phone calls. He makes sure the product is delivered to the north and the money is delivered to the south, and that's it."

"And if he's funding politicians, it'll be even vaguer," Tracy interjected.

"But Sherman might actually provide some insight," Bill mused, as if he hadn't heard her. "Property is perfect for laundering money. It could lead to a real case being built through the back door."

"So I should call him?"

Bill shrugged. "You're always talking about remodeling that new house of yours. Maybe you could look around and get some ideas."

Tracy smiled. Dean was clearly obsessed with breaking a big case, but he was going at it the wrong way. He already knew the crime he wanted to prove and was only accepting evidence that supported that. It meant he was missing the actual insight his investigation had uncovered, someone unconnected to the cartel who might actually know more than they should.

Reaching for her phone, Tracy started to stand up, when Bill said, "Wait, we have actual work to finish. I made some calls while you were sorting paper up there." He held up the Lisa Smith case file. "I talked to a Detective Gillis down in Henderson. He's had two similar cases over the past year, but nothing to go on. No suspects or leads, and he seemed pretty uninterested in discussing it." Bill flipped the page over. "However, Detective Levy in Spring Valley was more helpful. He has a blurry photo from a doorbell camera of what they believe the perp's vehicle looks like."

"Oh, really?" Tracy's interest was piqued instantly.

"Yep, and he emailed it to me."

"And?"

"Where does one find emails?" he answered pointedly.

Clicking away from the open windows, she headed to her inbox and the only unread email in it. The attached photo was as blurry as described and looked to be a standard white panel van with no markings. "A white work van," she muttered.

"Yep, the most generic-looking vehicle on the road. No shot of the plates or any markings on the exterior."

"Well, now that we at least have an idea what

we're looking for, we can re-canvass the area tomorrow."

"Isn't tomorrow your day off?"

"Oh, yeah." Tracy stopped for a moment. "But I don't really have anything going on." Spending a couple of hours knocking on doors wasn't a great off-day activity, but there wasn't much else she had planned on doing. Binging episodes of *New Girl* could be rescheduled.

"Yes, you do."

"What?"

"I also got a phone call from my wife. She wants to come over for dinner tomorrow night. She'll provide the dinner if you can provide a table."

"Oh, of course. I have a table," she answered quickly. She did have a table, didn't she? Yeah, it was there, but still out in the garage, buried under a mountain of unopened boxes and junk mail.

"How mature of you. Six pm work?"

"Yeah, that'd be great." Tracy's mind ran through all the things she'd need to do to get the house ready for guests. Getting the dining room table inside was probably the most important step. The Striders were laid-back people, but having dinner in the garage might be a little too informal. Also, the guest bathroom didn't have any toilet paper, even though it had caused an issue once or twice already. She had been dragging her feet on finishing the move-in process, but now there was a reason to get it all done.

"There's still some phone calls for me to make," Bill said, shaking Tracy out of her momentary daze of planning. "You going to make yours?"

Day 3, 5:10 pm

GRANT ANDERSON

Whack. The Phillips-head screwdriver in Grant's hand had just gone flying, after the third attempt at forcing together two pieces of the drawers that looked practically the same as three other pieces. Why aren't the pieces clearly marked? You're supposed to be able to tell them apart, according to the poorly drawn instructions, emphasis on *poorly drawn*.

He had gone shopping at IKEA that morning, his office was finally cleared out enough he could start making the space his own. It took nearly an hour to get the desk put together, the backboard with the cubbies and the dry erase board still looming in its packaging. But that had to be simpler, right? That's when Grant's phone rang. The screwdriver went sailing again, this time going through the doorway and into the back office. Closing his eyes and taking a deep breath, Grant cursed himself. It was just a desk, and it shouldn't be getting to him like this. Even worse, throwing the screwdriver into the back office meant it was now part of the endless mess and would probably take more effort than it should to retrieve it.

The phone continued ringing. It was an unfamiliar number but carried the 702 local area code, perhaps a good sign that the caller wasn't just a spambot. Answering with his happiest voice, it was good fortune he did once he heard a real human on the other end, a woman named Tracy Cook, who apparently had been one of his uncle's old clients. His conversation with Miss Cook was quick and to the point. She had a house she wanted to look at, tonight if possible. He had evaded the questions of where his uncle was in every professional conversation he had been a part of since taking over the business. He still hadn't figured out how to handle explaining his uncle's death to people in a business-like manner. Potential clients normally didn't want to hear about anything dramatic happening in their agent's life. It was a reminder that the agent had priorities other than their own wants and wishes. So Paul's passing would only be mentioned if absolutely necessary, preferably after the closing.

Balancing his laptop on his lap, he made the appointment and promised Miss Cook that he would see her soon. With that finished, he transferred the laptop to its resting place on his new desk. It might have been a disaster to build, but it felt good to be working on a surface designed for computers and not roadside lemonade sales.

Some of his favorite work was digging into comps for a home. Uncovering what was happening in the neighborhood and where it was going was research and art at the same time. Much less stressful than dealing with picky clients who didn't like a property because of the paint color. Everything in a house could be changed, there was just a level of difficulty to each. Want to add an office or move walls? That was going to be difficult and involve contractors. However, most of the upgrades people wanted to make to their homes were a lot simpler than it seemed at first. People were just so used to customizing everything in their lives *before* they bought it. One that hasn't yet been customized scares people into thinking it's not their dream home.

He wasn't sure what Miss Cook was looking for; she had been kinda vague on the phone, and he hadn't seen anything in the mess of paperwork that had her name on it. Finding the property in question she'd asked about, Grant moved his mouse cursor to the print button, when he realized the printer was still on the folding table, unconnected and out of his reach. He thought about how he might need another desk for the printer, then immediately said out loud in response, "No way I'm going back there."

Day 3, 6:28 pm

TRACY COOK

It was 6:28 pm when Tracy rolled to a stop in front of 2021 Champion Street. A red Yaris was already parked in the driveway and the door to the house was open. Paul had always been late to their viewings; apparently, the nephew was a bit more prompt.

Before she could open her door, a man exited the house. He was average height, though with a slim build, with carefully combed and gelled brown hair. Button-down light gray shirt and blue jeans. The business-casual look was marred a bit by him wearing sneakers instead of dressier shoes. He was coming straight down the walkway to greet her, his laptop bag swinging at his side. "Miss Cook, I presume?" he spoke lightly.

"That's me. And please, just call me Tracy." She shut the door behind her and accepted his hand.

"Awesome. I'm Grant Anderson. It's great to meet

you." He gave her hand a firm shake. "I've already done a quick walk around the outside and everything looks good. No signs of settling in the walls or foundation. You're really going to love the backyard. It's perfect for entertaining."

"Oh, okay."

"Are you ready to go inside?"

"Yeah. Let's start there," she said, as if she was in charge of this viewing. It felt more like Grant was the host of a game show and she was the unwitting audience member dragged up on stage.

Inside, the home immediately lived up to expectations. Modern tile in the entryway and around the fireplace in the living room. You wouldn't think of needing a fireplace in Las Vegas, but most of the houses came with them, though it was rare to ever see them used. Maybe it was a desire to fit in with the rest of the country. New England had fireplaces, so why shouldn't the citizens of Las Vegas? Probably because it routinely got over 110 degrees and snowed once a decade. Yet you could still see chimneys sticking out of nearly every house you passed.

"This is all the listing information," Grant announced, handing the single page over with the specs of the home. "Would you like a water?" He produced a SmartWater bottle from his laptop bag.

"Oh, no, thank you," Tracy answered. The occasional Uber driver tried to spice up the drive with amenities, but it was new for a buyer's agent to try the same tactic.

"I've also done some quick comps on the area, and this home is near the top of the range in price, but it's also near the top in contemporary style and features. Notice the pot filler over the stove." He pointed to an odd-looking spout protruding from the wall above the range surface as they walked into the kitchen.

"What is it?" Tracy asked, reaching out for it. It was double-hinged and stretched out over the stove.

"It's for filling up pots with water, if you need to boil something."

"That's interesting." She hadn't ever considered needing something like that in her life, but she pulled her phone out for a photo anyway. This was supposed to be a fact-finding trip about upgrades to her own house. "How long have you been working with your uncle?" she probed, while Grant examined the refrigerator.

"I've only been out here for a couple of months," he answered, unlocking the sliding glass door to the pool deck. "Do you know my uncle very well?"

"Yes, he was my agent when I bought my house a few months ago. Did he not mention that?" She followed Grant onto the bright white concrete that surrounded the pool. He hadn't been lying when he said she'd be impressed with the back-yard.

"Oh, so you're a recent home-owner! Congratulations. Are you already looking to add to your portfolio?" Grant continued.

"Well, actually, this viewing was mostly to get an idea of what the nicer homes are looking like in the area. I live just over that way." Tracy pointed east, toward her house, where you had to carry the pot over to the sink if you wanted water in it.

"You picked a very nice one to survey, then. The

renovations here are expertly done. I noticed the cabinets are solid wood, not the composite stuff you normally find in quick reno jobs. The composite paneling is prone to warping and bulging if it gets wet." He patted the exposed side of the cabinet before turning toward the open dining room space. "The floors also look to be engineered hardwood, not the vinyl stuff you find in most flips."

"Is that what you would recommend?" She bent down to touch the floor.

"That's a hard question for me to answer. I grew up in Georgia, and carpet was what we lived on. That's what makes me feel at home. However, it would seem like I'm in the minority nowadays. So if you don't want carpet, engineered is the way to go. True hardwoods are very expensive out here, and vinyl's always going to be looked at as a bit cheap." He led her into the garage. It was larger than Tracy's. Hers could fit two cars in tightly, while this one could've easily fit a third, if needed. "Oh, I love the floors," she said, taking a look around. Most garages looked like garages, but this one was gleaming floor to ceiling.

"Yes, so do I. It's just concrete paint with the flakes tossed in while you paint it. Very cheap to do. They sell the kit at Home Depot. It just looks so much better than bare concrete."

The rest of the house was as beautiful as the beginning was. The master bathroom was stunning, a walk-in shower with two rain heads and a freestanding tub in front of the window. Even the master closet was impressively outfitted with a professional organization system. This house was obviously much bigger than her house, so she could never fit all of this into her existing space. However, the walk-in shower was feasible. It would be much nicer than the oversized bathtub-shower combo that was in her master now.

They had wandered through the whole house, commenting on the features and Grant offering his opinion on their feasibility. Again, a much-noticed contrast between him and his uncle; Paul would wait near the front door and offer the blandest opinions on the house. The more she thought about it, the more it seemed like Paul wasn't as great of an agent as she had initially thought. It'd been her first home buying experience, so she didn't really have anything to compare it to. However, he'd been adept at the negotiations. He had gotten over eleven thousand knocked off the purchase price, and another five thousand after the inspection showed some water damage. They both had agreed it wasn't much of an issue, but Paul beat the sellers over the head with it and forced the price down. Maybe negotiating was Grant's weakness; if so, he and his uncle would make a great team, Grant handling the customer side and Paul the arguing side.

Back at the front door, Grant got the lockbox closed up and suddenly had a business card in his hand in the blink of an eye. "This is my card. It's got my email on it. If there are any other houses you want to look at, just send the addresses over and I'll get them set up."

"Alright, thanks. But I'm not really looking to buy any time soon," Tracy answered as they strolled back to their cars. He seemed so excited at the chance to make a client of her, but she was only looking at houses out of curiosity about Paul's old clients.

"No worries, I'm new to town, so I need to see as many houses as possible to get a feeling for the market. I'll look at any house that piques your interest."

"That's nice. I felt like your uncle got bored looking at so many with me."

"That's not surprising. I got the same feeling whenever he had to hang out with me," Grant answered with a laugh.

"Had? Past tense?" Tracy said, turning fully to face Grant.

Grant paused and licked his lips. "Uh, my uncle actually passed away a few months ago. He had a heart attack," he answered softly, avoiding her eyes.

"I'm so sorry. I had no idea." Her assertive body posture quickly melted away. That'd been the last thing she'd expected to hear. She was assuming rehab or something of that sort.

"Yeah, it's been hard, but I think I can keep Port Harvest going. He would've liked that."

Tracy simply nodded. She hadn't prepped for any follow-up questions for something like this.

"Anyways, it was great meeting you, Tracy," Grant said just a moment before Tracy could get her next question out. "Shoot me a call, text, email, anything, whenever another house catches your eye. And I'll be on the watch for homes that might be worth looking at in this neighborhood." He had stepped far enough away from her now that the conversation had died a natural death.

"It was great meeting you, too. See you later." She gave him a smile and a small wave as she dipped into the driver seat.

* * *

Tracy had finished off a few more errands and picked up what she would need for dinner. She had pushed the Paul issue out of her mind for the time being. All that new information needed time to settle in her mind before she could really make any progress.

She was almost home when her phone rang again, the screen flashing "Mom" once again. With a sigh she swiped the answer button. She didn't have a good excuse to ignore it this time, so she might as well get it over with. "Hey, Mom," she said.

"Tracy, are you there?"

"Yes, Mom, I'm here." Even though phones had been around well before Shelly had been born, she always treated them like they were some newfangled technology. And that was even before she got a smartphone, with which she struggled mightily to achieve even the simplest tasks.

"I've been trying to call you!" she yelled into the phone.

"Yeah, I've been busy, Mom."

"I need to see you. Something's going on at work and I might be in trouble."

Tracy scoffed. There it was, the predictable drama. "What's going on at work?"

"I found out my boss is stealing from the casino, and he's trying to set me up for the fall."

If an eye roll could be audible, it would've sounded like a cannon shot in Tracy's car at the moment. "Mom, no one's stealing from the casino."

"How do you know that!"

"Because we aren't in a movie! People who stole from the casinos got buried in the desert and voila, no more stealing."

"He is, though. I can prove it. I just need you to get involved before it's too late."

"If you have proof, just turn him in to his boss." Tracy tried to reason her out of a face-to-face meeting.

"Tracy, it's not that simple. I need to see you. Can you meet tonight?"

"No, I can't."

"Why not?"

"Because I already have plans, Mom," Tracy shot back.

"How about tomorrow?"

"Fine, I can meet for lunch." When her mom got like this, there was no stopping her until she got someone to listen to her latest conspiracy theory.

"Where at?"

"I don't know. I'll have to text you when I know what I'm doing tomorrow and where I'm at."

"A text? What if I don't get it in time?"

"I don't know what that means, Mom."

"Texts don't work on my phone. I never get them."

"Okay, then I'll call you, because apparently you have the one iPhone in existence that can't receive texts."

"I'm dyslexic!" Shelly shouted.

"Right."

"Alright. Don't tell anyone what I told you. I don't want anyone to hear about it."

"Yep, gotta go. Talk to you tomorrow."

Day 4, 11:55 am

LUCAS GREEN

Deputy didn't get a walk this morning. He didn't mind. He didn't even move when I left, just his eyes following me through the house. I had been up early and took my car one street over and waited there. From this position I wouldn't be able to see Grant leaving his house, but I'd be able to see him when he drove by on his way to work. There was no reason to assume that Grant would be watching for someone tailing him, but this was how the business worked, caution at all times and in all things. Deputy would have to spend the day alone at the house so I could be waiting for Grant before Grant was even awake.

Sure enough, the red Yaris eventually slipped across my bow as Grant left the neighborhood. Shifting the car into gear, I drifted along behind him. I had mapped the route a few times yesterday at different times of day, and every time it came back with the same path as the fastest. The Vegas grid system of roads made plotting courses pretty simple; just get on a road in the right direction and it'll get you there eventually.

Grant made a right into the strip mall that houses his office as I cruised past to the light and made a U-turn. That's how I ended up in the parking lot across the street, watching the front door of his office. This business had gotten more bearable since podcasting became widespread. Listening to morning radio DJs was the absolute worst thing I'd ever experienced in my life, and I once had to go to a Justin Bieber concert. Next time you're driving to work, put on one of the inane morning shows and keep track of how many minutes are spent on music, how many on advertising, and how many listening to the host and his cast of annoying characters trying to be funny.

But like I said, now we have podcasts, which my study of Grant had shown he liked, so I was listening to every comedian-hosted podcast I could find so we would have something to talk about when the time came. He probably didn't have anyone in his life who liked discussing comedy. It'd be a powerful tool against him.

Three hours dwindled away on this stakeout with no visible sign of life at Port Harvest. Grant went inside at 9:00, turned the "Closed" sign to "Open," and had been in there ever since. Pulling the notebook out of my pocket, I made a note: check the security on the *office door*. Getting inside and looking through his computer's calendar might make this easier. At the very least, I'd have an idea of where he was going at all times.

My new phone started vibrating on top of my dashboard. An unfamiliar number flashed on the screen, but it was local. "Hello," I answered with a flat voice.

"I got your boxes." Javy's snide voice was on the other side. "Meet me at the Home Depot, on Charleston, in 30 minutes."

"Fine." I ended the call. It was more satisfying when you could snap a flip phone closed; mashing the "End" button on a touchscreen was less dramatic. I hated having to bend to Carlos's and Javy's demands. It was like letting children run the show, if those children also carried guns and bad attitudes. But dealing with them was part of the project, so I had to go along with it the best I could.

Charleston Boulevard was only one major street over, I knew that easily enough, but I wasn't sure where the Home Depot was, so I had to google that. It was only twelve minutes from my current location. At least Javy was considerate enough to set the meeting nearby.

One more look at Grant's office. It'd be hard to get any kind of robbery to happen at work; it was obvious that the strip mall was not raking in the cash, and tricking anyone into believing there was some secret stash in his office would probably attract too much attention to me. Pluss it'd be far easier for them to break in at night and clean the office out. The home invasion was still the best bet. Watching Grant like this was just busywork, but it was either sit here and watch or sit at home with Deputy and wait for him to come home.

The five hours I had spent in the car was wearing

on me, specifically my bladder, so if I was going to leave my post, I might as well leave now and make use of the extra time to avoid using the bottle I had brought. People always make the mistake of bringing a water bottle or something like that. A Gatorade bottle is the way to go, extra-large opening. I slipped the 4Runner into reverse and eased out of the parking lot. Hopefully Grant wouldn't leave before I got back; it would suck to have spent all this time watching nothing happening, only for him to disappear while I was having to deal with Javy, who could've just as easily left the boxes at the house or had me come pick them up when it was convenient for me. Unpleasant assholes and petty power displays; it was enough to make a person want to change professions.

Day 4, 12:05 pm

TRACY COOK

Her mother had already texted that she'd be late, or at least that was what Tracy gathered from the garbled message. Shelly Louis only seemed to distrust text messages when she needed the information; for sending info to other people, it was good enough.

Tacos El Gordos was a staple of Las Vegas cuisine. In a city brimming with five-star restaurants and designer foods, El Gordos was as simple as it got, and still rivaled the best food in town. Tacos were pretty much the only thing on the menu; you walked in, picked a line which was dedicated to a certain type of meat, and shouted your order across the grill top to the tacoist back there. Beef and pork was all that Tracy was going to eat, although you could get plenty of meats that were less commonly eaten in the United States if you so desired, which Tracy did not.

Four pork and four beef soft tacos later, Tracy had

a table and plenty of food for the both of them when Shelly entered. "There's no parking here!" she scolded at no one in particular as she stomped over to the table. Shelly looked just like what you would expect a sixty-something Las Vegas cocktail waitress to look like—hair that was a little too blond, skin that was a little too tan, and teeth that were a little too white.

"Hi, Mom," Tracy greeted her as she slid into the opposite side of the booth.

"Hi. Where's your partner?"

"This is my day off."

"But don't you think he should hear this, too? This is a serious case, and it shouldn't be just you working on it."

"Mom, have a taco," Tracy said, pushing the plate forward. Tracy knew Bill would be polite if he had to listen to Shelly rant; he was a professional and wouldn't hold a crazy parent against her. But even still, the less people who had to deal with her, the better.

Shelly calmed down a bit as she worked on her taco. Her energy was always up. Tracy hadn't figured out if it was completely natural or chemically enhanced at this point. "You said you were having trouble at work?" she asked her.

"Yes. My boss is stealing." Shelly took a dramatic look around the room, as if her shift manager was stalking her to a taco shop.

"You've seen him stealing?"

"No, I just know he is."

"But the cameras don't see it?" Tracy countered. It was well-known to anyone who had ever seen *Ocean's Eleven* that every inch of a casino is covered by cameras to keep every chip accounted for on the floor.

"No, there aren't cameras like that in the theater. I've been taking extra shifts in the theater shows. For a while it was that country guy with the butt, but now it's a comedian." She sighed. "No butt." Tracy nodded along. "The theater has less cameras because there aren't any chips in there. The cameras are all pointed at the money. There are big gaps backstage where nothing's being recorded."

"Okay, so what's he stealing, then?"

"Anything he can get his hands on. Boxes of alcohol are missing."

Tracy cut in. "If he's walking out with cases of liquor, someone would notice that."

"But he isn't walking out with them," Shelly said, tapping her finger against her temple like she had just solved the case.

"So he's drinking them in the bathroom?"

"No, he's collecting the stuff he steals in moving cases like the productions use, and then getting the case shipped out of the building when the shows change over. No one bothers looking, because they think it's just extra cables or whatever, and then he must go fetch it somewhere else later."

"Okay, so you've seen this happening?"

"Sorta." Tracy gave her mom the universal look for *go on*. "Whenever we find something that got left after the show, cellphones or wallets, whatever, he has us put them in these funny bags and bring them to him in the back hallway."

"That makes sense. He's keeping them organized."

"That's what he says, but where do the bags go?

They should go to security, but I've never seen security use bags like that. And there's a road case in that hallway that always sits there locked. Why would it be locked? Everything else back there is open or empty."

"Even if he is doing that, why are you in trouble?" Tracy asked, grabbing another taco. So far Shelly's theory had been heavy on speculation and light on actionable intelligence.

"Because last week, he had me collect the lost-and-found bags from everyone and take them to the back hallway and leave them on the road case. He said he'd go back there and get them later, and then they were gone."

"Yeah?"

"So all the other ushers and waitresses saw me collecting them. If it gets reported, they'll say they saw me with them last."

"Alright, that makes sense." Shelly's word against the whole staff and her boss wouldn't carry much weight.

"But that's not the worst part. He's using fake credit card readers."

Tracy perked up at that statement. Stealing an occasional lost phone or a bottle of tequila wasn't going to garner much attention from anyone, but skimming off customers' credit cards sure would. "What do you mean?"

"He's been giving me a different credit card reader than everyone else. The other girls say it's the same, but I can tell something's off with it."

"Interesting."

"That's why I need your help. If anyone finds out,

it'll look like I was doing it on my own."

"What do you want me to do?" Tracy asked. Internal casino problems were normally handled by their security staffs, with the culprit getting handed over to the police after they caught them red-handed. A detective showing up and sniffing around was going to raise a few eyebrows, especially if the guilty party tried to blame the detective's mother. "Just go to his boss and explain what's happening. Their security lives for stuff like that."

"So you won't help me!"

"I'm just saying—"

Shelly cut her off. "I've had some trouble with management. They won't listen to me."

Tracy looked at her. Her mother was prone to believing everyone was out to get her.

"Fine. Garrett's boss is Sarah Brantley. She runs the theater. I met her husband at the bar one night and we were having fun, but nothing had happened, and then Sarah came up and freaked out on both of us."

"You were hitting on your boss's husband?"

"We were just having fun at the bar. Is that so illegal?" Shelly shot back. "So I can't go to Sarah because she already wants to fire me, and Garrett knows that."

"Okay, I still don't know what you want me to do."

"I don't know, tap his phone or arrest him and make him tell you what he's up to."

"Arresting him without evidence of a real crime isn't going to work. Right now, it's just your word against his."

"I'm reporting the crime right now."

"You're reporting a suspicion of a crime. You haven't seen anything leave the property. You're just guessing that's what's happening."

"I'm not guessing, I *know* it's happening. I talked with Ethan, and he told me that case isn't part of the production, and he doesn't know why it's there, either."

"Who's Ethan?"

"He's one of the roadies. He's working with the funny guy with no ass."

Tracy paused with her next bite and set down the taco. "And how do you know *him?*"

Shelly shrugged and avoided eye contact. "Oh, you know, we met at one of the shows, and we've been hanging out since then."

"You're sleeping with a roadie?" Tracy shot back. Her mom didn't just "hang out" with male friends.

"It doesn't matter what we're doing off the clock. Ethan told me that case isn't part of the production's equipment!"

"Alright." Tracy checked her watch. "I have some stuff I have to do."

"Tracy, I need help! If he pins this on me, I'll lose my job and go to jail."

"I understand." Tracy stood up from the table. "I'll think about it, and get back to you with a plan or something."

"Okay, but call me soon with this. It's really stressing me out."

"I will," Tracy answered, walking away from the table.

"Thanks for lunch!" Shelly called after her.

Day 4, 12:25 pm

JAVY SANTANA

Javy spun the wheel of his company truck and turned onto Charleston Boulevard. This wasn't the closest Home Depot to the place they'd set up for Lucas, but Javy figured that prick could use a little hassle. Anything that messed with him was worth doing in Javy's mind.

"Fucking empty boxes," he muttered to himself while changing lanes. They should've dealt with Paul Sherman the moment Miguel realized he was skimming money. Miguel had dragged his feet because he'd been the one who hadn't realized that Paul was scamming them. That was how the Guerras operated; Miguel made dumb decisions and the rest of them had to obey. Even though Miguel was probably the weakest out of all of them, he had the inside track with Edgar Mencia, so he stayed on top, forcing his brother Carlos to do all the real work.

Javy hated being under the thumb of someone like Miguel. Carlos was the true boss; he couldn't be replaced. Miguel was pretty much just an accountant at this point. He'd stopped doing real work years ago and was now easily replaceable; everyone knew it, but it was never said out loud. When Miguel finally acknowledged that Sherman had been cheating them, Carlos was ready to go skin him alive that minute; but Miguel made them wait, and then Paul died on his own, which caused Miguel to call the whole thing off and refuse to let them move against the nephew. Miguel had always been naive about how things worked. You didn't steal from the cartels because if you escaped judgment, your family would pay the price. That kept people in line.

So to keep his brother in the dark, Carlos had to go to all the trouble of getting this dumbass assassin to come out and deal with Grant in a way that wouldn't fall back on them. Carlos had always followed Miguel's orders; he'd complained about them, but in the end he did as his brother said. This was the first time he was taking an action his brother had expressly forbidden. Javy hoped it was a sign of things to come. But that'd have to wait, because right now he had to deliver a bunch of empty fucking boxes to this fake-ass white boy. With what they were paying Lucas, he could've just gone and bought the stuff new. Instead, now it was Javy's job to chase down his bullshit.

Not like he didn't have enough going on. He'd done everything the Guerras had asked for years now. He started out on the street, hanging with Carlos and backing him up in his hustles. Then when they got a real business going, Javy had spent the time to get his legitimate general contractor license. Battle Born Renovations was a real company doing real work; not something Javy would've expected for his life, but at this point, he was as qualified to handle the delivery and distribution of the cocaine, heroin, and meth shipped north by the cartel as he was to install a new kitchen with granite countertops and a farmhouse sink. Whatever the gringa ladies wanted, he could get it built. He'd begged for the chance to eliminate Grant, but Miguel had forbidden him from acting, and Carlos had restrained him privately. Carlos had a plan, and Lucas was the plan, and Lucas had a plan that involved empty boxes.

Of course, he wasn't going to get the actual boxes himself; he was the right-hand man to the number-two man in the organization. He had delegated that work instead to Juan Heredia. Juan had been around the business a long time, even before the Guerras were up and running, and he'd been an electrician before that, like his father had been. Juan was a little passive for the business, even though he'd been around it for most of his adult life. He'd accepted the bitch work without complaint, unlike the new kid William Rosario, who had a mouth on him. But he was eager and aggressive, which was what Javy wanted.

Pulling into Home Depot, Javy spotted Lucas's car immediately, parked off by itself near a cart corral. Gliding into the space across next to him, he turned his truck off and jumped out. "Am I driving this time?" Lucas asked, his brown hair flapping gently in the wind and a stupid smirk behind his sunglasses.

"I have to get some caulk for a job," Javy sniped back. "Why did you think we were meeting here?"

"Just figured your kind was used to getting picked up in this parking lot."

"What the fuck did you say to me!" Javy yelled, pushing forward like he was going to shove Lucas, who remained motionless.

"Go get your shit, I haven't got all day," Lucas said slowly, like he was daring him to do something.

"You work for us, don't forget that!" Javy spat back, jabbing his finger as he stepped toward the store.

"We work for the same person, Javy." Lucas climbed back into the driver's seat of his 4Runner. "Go do your shopping, I'll wait here."

Javy spit on the ground in the direction of Lucas, though he didn't respond to the insult, just calmly turned the car back on so he could sit in the air conditioning.

Day 4, 12:40 pm

LUCAS GREEN

Javy had refused to speak when he came out of Home Depot; he just tossed the bag of caulk into the bed of his trunk. I climbed into the passenger side, he remained silent the entire drive to the house they were working on, though he did crank some angry Hispanic rap music on the radio. I couldn't tell what the DJ was saying. Maybe radio stations are better in Spanish.

The no-talking act was fine with me. I didn't want to talk to him, either. This whole nonsense about getting picked up and going to meet at a third location was overly dramatic and pointless. Especially if we met at the same place every time. Not just that, it wasn't even a secret location; it was a house being renovated by Battle Born. If anyone was watching our movements, they weren't going to be fooled by such lazy spycraft.

The house looked the same as it had the other

night, just now with more trucks and people. The exterior paint was being touched up, the window trim in particular. Javy led me through the construction and entered the garage, where Carlos was waiting. The garage was serving as a break room for the crews at this point, with folding chairs and a couple of tables set up. I took my seat next to Carlos. Javy remained standing. "So what's this about?" I demanded once neither of them offered to speak.

"I just wanted to know how it's going," Carlos said casually.

"It's going. As I've explained, this isn't a Jiffy Pop. It takes time."

"What do you need the boxes for?" Javy interjected.

"I want to build a fort for my dog to play in," I shot back.

"He's fucking with us!" Javy hissed, turning to Carlos.

Carlos ignored Javy and kept looking at me. He was working on playing the calm and cerebral crime boss, but his impatient temperament still showed through his eyes. "How many of these jobs have you done before?"

"I've done enough to know what I'm doing, you know that. That's how you heard about me."

"What types of marks do you normally deal with?"

"All kinds—lawyers, a couple of accountants, even a cop."

"How about people in the business? You ever go after them?" Carlos asked as he subtly fidgeted with his watch. This was starting to sound like a job interview.

"People in the business are hard to deal with, since everyone is suspicious no matter how they die. Heart attack, must have been poison. Car crash, someone must've cut the brake lines."

"But you *have* done it?"

"I've made clients with all types of motivations happy, if that's what you're asking." I leaned forward like I was going to whisper to him. "Why, do you want me to deal with Javy?" I said, louder than I had said anything else.

Javy just glared at me, but the rest of his demeanor told a different story. He wasn't sure where his boss was going with this train of thought, either.

Carlos smirked, leaning back and looking at Javy. "Remember when we first started?" he said to him. "You were just a kid. You were on the street, taking orders, and I was handing them out. Just like Miguel told us to do."

Javy nodded. "That was a long time ago."

"It was, but we moved up in the world. And we can go higher." He turned his eyes back to me.

"Except there's someone already in the corner office," I guessed.

"Our organization has outgrown my brother," Carlos said evenly. Javy stiffened noticeably at the statement. It seemed like we were both hearing Carlos utter those words out loud for the very first time.

"So this Grant Anderson thing's just an audition?" I asked.

"The nephew needs to die on principle, but Miguel won't hear of it. He says the money Paul stole is already gone and we'd just be wasting time. Miguel doesn't like taking chances. Murder is a risk and he refuses to believe it's worth it."

"But you?"

"Our business is all risk, and showing weakness is the riskiest move there is," Carlos said strongly.

"I come out and handle Grant and you think since I'm here, maybe I'll kill your brother for you, too?"

Carlos laughed. "I'm not asking for a favor. I know Miguel will be more difficult than Grant, but I'll make it worth your while. Save you another trip out here."

"I told you, killing someone in the business is very hard. You said Miguel's well-connected with Mencia. You think he'll just accept the death and you as his replacement, but I wouldn't be too sure about that. My experience is that the cartel is more of a 'cut your face off while you're still alive and then ask questions' type of organization."

Javy had remained silent during most of the discussion, focused on listening once Carlos got going. It was apparent that even he hadn't been brought into Carlos's thinking until just now. That would probably have a warming effect on our relationship, now that he knew my arrival wasn't just denying him a chance to kill Grant. Regardless of his self-confidence, he knew better than to want to kill Miguel himself. He'd be putting a huge target on his head. That's what they wanted me for.

"I'll worry about the cartel," Carlos insisted. "We know how to handle them." He could be right; the money was the most important thing to the cartel. If Carlos could ensure the flow of money wouldn't be interrupted, they might be soothed. Or they could light the whole region on fire trying to smoke out anyone involved in the killing. Carlos was concerned about looking weak by not killing Grant, but the cartel would view the death of one of their franchise operators the same way, and they had far less qualms about killing anyone possibly involved.

Carlos could see I was about to speak, but he cut me off. "I'm not asking for you to decide anything now, and in fact I haven't even made a real offer of anything. Just think about it while you work on Grant. Maybe some inspiration will strike you, like the idea of having enough money to disappear permanently." He stood up, signaling the end of the meeting. "The boxes are in the back of Juan's truck. He'll drive you back to your car." He nodded to the older Hispanic man who was standing out by one of the trucks. "Let us know if you need anything else."

"Okay." I stood up from the improvised office and walked out to the sidewalk. "You got the boxes?" I said to Juan.

"Yes, sir," the man answered, leading me around the back of the truck. They were all there, lying flat in the bed under a couple spools of electrical wire to hold them in place.

"All the tape on these boxes has been cut," I said. "I need them still in their box shape."

"Oh," Juan answered, just staring at them.

"Do you have tape here?" I saw his hand drop toward his pocket where the round shape of a roll of electrical tape was showing through his pants. "Not electrical tape. Clear tape, like packing tape."

"Yeah, we got some inside. I'll get it." He walked off. I didn't mean to belittle him—he seemed genuine enough—but if his boss was Javy, he was probably used to being berated. Maybe I should tip him when he got back, I thought. That would be funny.

Day 4, 2:03 pm

GRANT ANDERSON

Grant had been in the office all day. It was the day he dreaded the most. Cold-call day. All week he compiled a list of properties the owners might be open to selling. Back taxes was a big one. Homes reported for unkempt yards or other maintenance issues, which indicated the owner was losing interest in the upkeep of their home. Deaths were also a good target, family members looking to unload a house quickly and without a fuss. Grant could help with that. It sounded unpleasant when you described it that way, like an ambulance chaser, and it was even worse actually doing it. Mostly because the people you talked to, when they were willing to talk at all, had other things on their mind than picking a real estate agent.

He had made it a quarter of the way through his list by lunch time. Starting too early was a no-no; waking someone up with a cold call was a surefire way to get blocked. His lunch today was warmed-up chili, just like his mom made. She had emailed him the recipe a few weeks ago and he was getting the hang of making it himself. It was nice to mix it up from his standard BLT lunch he'd gotten pretty adept at making. It was hard to make much more; the office's mini-fridge didn't have much room in it, so there were only so many ingredients he could store.

He had avoided making cold calls by pulling up similar listings in the area to the one he'd shown Tracy last night. She said she wasn't really looking to buy, but maybe she just needed to see the right home. Even if she wasn't going to buy, it was a lot more fun looking at houses with her than it'd been looking at ones with people like the Duvalls. Tracy had seemed to actually enjoy poking around the house the other day. Still, no amount of procrastinating could change the fact that he still had calls to make. So far, the fifty or so calls he'd made had resulted in two possible leads. One young-sounding woman who was dealing with the estate of her grandfather had said she hadn't decided what to do with the house, but that she'd call back tomorrow; and one man who'd been repeatedly cited for trash in his yard seemed eager to get out of the city and land somewhere that would look the other way at his hoarding. Even though that man had sounded pretty drunk on the phone, Grant had been able to make an appointment to meet the next morning.

Now Grant was working on a grocery list for stuff to stock the office with, plus general supplies. He was running low on trash bags, and the bathroom needed more toilet paper. The office could also use some speakers. Background music would help with the endless filing; it would feel like a movie montage. The space also needed a rug or something. The more carpet that started getting exposed as the papers receded, the worse the floor appeared. It looked like it'd been salvaged from a '60s-era casino; the patterns were ugly and it was worn down to the threads by this point. Maybe a trip to Lowes was in order, to see if there was anything he could buy for cheap just to cover it up until the room was clear enough to get a steam cleaner in there. After that, maybe money for new carpet could be found.

It was right then when the front door jingled. Grant jumped from his desk. The only person who entered the office other than him was the UPS delivery man, and Grant wasn't expecting any packages. Turning to the door, he saw Tracy Cook standing there, her eyes adjusting to the dim lighting inside. Her hair was pulled back into a ponytail, and she was wearing a loose-fitting LVMPD t-shirt and capri-length leggings over Under Armor trainers.

"Miss Cook," Grant said, standing up from his desk, still holding the pen he had been using to write out his shopping list.

"Hey, Grant. How's it going?" Tracy smiled, her eyes finally adjusting well enough to see him in the corner. She stepped into the office and surveyed what should've been the lobby, but instead was Grant's temporary working space. On the opposite wall was a folding table with a printer and stacks of papers next to a large shiny filing cabinet. A walkway had been cleared down the center of the space, leading into the back rooms, but even in the lobby there were still mounds of assorted papers laying around.

"Uh, it's going very well. Did I miss a call from you? I wasn't expecting to see you today." Grant moved away from his desk and pulled a folding chair out for Tracy. "Would you like to sit down?"

"I see why he never invited me over to his office," Tracy said, taking the seat Grant provided.

"Yeah, it's designed more as a workspace than an entertaining spot," Grant answered, putting the best possible spin on the disaster around them.

Tracy's face screwed up as she thought for a moment. "How much do you know about your uncle's business?" She reached for her pocket where her wallet was.

"I mean, I'm living in it right here. He was dyslexic, so instead of organizing his paperwork, he just stacked papers randomly on the ground, and now I'm here reliving his life one contract at a time."

"Found anything interesting yet? Maybe regular clients of his?" She fished her business card out.

"No, not really. I was in contact with a few when I first started, but they moved on while I was still getting started out here. You're really the first one to reach out."

Leaning forward, Tracy handed the card over. Grant accepted it and looked surprised when he recognized the police logo. "So you're a detective?"

"I am."

"And you want to talk to my uncle?"

"Sorta." Tracy shrugged. "I found out he was loosely connected to a prominent drug trafficker." It was Grant's turn to be startled by a statement. "It was years ago, but I thought it was worth looking into."

Grant didn't answer, but just kept looking at the card. Uncle Paul wasn't one to shy away from getting his hands dirty, but high-level drug trafficking was a bit much from him.

"Is there something that information makes you think of?" Tracy inquired.

The first thing he thought of were the guns he'd found in his uncle's home. The shotgun in the closet, leaning against the wall along with a mop, broom, and broken shower curtain rod didn't seem to indicate anything other than insanity. The .38 Special had been lodged between some rolls of toilet paper in the upstairs linen closet. It might have been suspicious if there hadn't also been a collection of change, a receipt for a haircut, and an unopened DVD of *The Prestige* nestled in with it.

"There's a file cabinet at his house," Grant said slowly. "It's very well kept. The rest of his house looks like this, but with more diversity to the junk. But upstairs there's this file cabinet filled with paperwork that looks perfectly organized, like he was being very careful with all of it."

Tracy sat up straight. She wasn't sure she knew what she was looking for, but she knew she'd know when she saw it, and this was it. "Did you look through it?"

"Just a bit out of curiosity. It's all pretty standard stuff: purchase contracts, closing paperwork, receipts. It's what the files here are supposed to look like."

"Hang on just a minute." Tracy jumped up and hurried out the door. She always had her work bag with her in case she got called out to something randomly. She needed her notebook.

Grant looked around the room quickly. He'd never even considered the idea of a client dropping by, much less a cute police detective. It looked like he was sorting recycling instead of selling properties in this space. It meant he had nothing to offer his guest; the only source of water he had was his steel water bottle. He kept the water bottles he gave to clients in the trunk of his car, even though he'd told himself a dozen times to bring them inside.

"That was fast," Grant said as she came rushing back to her chair. He had risen to a half-standing position, looking for something that could pass for a refreshment he could offer. "Would you like a, um, some water? Or chili. I have some in the fridge."

"What?" Tracy asked, looking up from her notebook. "Chili?"

"Yeah, I had some for lunch."

"I already had lunch," she answered, looking back to her notes. "Okay, I need you to give me all the dates —when Paul died, how you found out, when you moved out here, and so on." Her pen hovered ready over the blank page.

Grant walked her through the past few months the best he could remember, checking his phone several times for emails or messages to confirm the dates of things. After about twenty minutes they had caught up to the present moment, sitting in the office talking to Tracy.

"Alright, now tell me about the file cabinet."

"Okay, it's three drawers. Each one is mostly full. Dates start at the back of the bottom one and work forward to the top drawer. Each folder is a different property, all of them sold, and all the paperwork for it. I only flipped through a few of them, but they all looked about the same."

"What makes those properties so important?"

"Well, they're all for the same company. It looks like an investment company of some sort."

"So it's probably Paul's biggest client?"

"Yeah, I suppose so. Getting an investment company working through you is a big deal. I guess that's why he kept the paperwork so organized." Grant realized there was a big question to be asked that he hadn't thought of yet. Tracy beat him to it.

"Have you heard from this client since Paul passed?"

"No. I called the only phone number listed several times, but never got through, not even a voicemail. I was hoping they might need a new agent."

"Does that seem strange to you?"

"A bit." Grant spoke softly, realizing how strange it actually was that he hadn't seen anything from this mysterious client in the emails or in Paul's contact list. If they had such a long and lucrative history together, you'd think they would've reached out at some point by now. He'd just focused on the novelty that his uncle was capable of organizing detailed files if he put his mind to it.

"Now for the biggest question. What was the name of this company?"

"It was..." Grant searched his memory, focusing in hard at the client's name on the sales agreements he'd read. "...G-Inc."

"Gee Inc?" Tracy asked back. "That's it?"

"Yeah, that was it. Just the letter G, Incorporated."

"Is there anything else you can remember about it?"

"No, it was basic stuff, but I can look through it when I get home. See if there's anything weird about the transactions in the files or something." Grant was now eager to get back and sort through the papers, but he was also going to need space to do that, and currently there wasn't enough space in that house to empty a whole file cabinet out and sort through every file. That meant a lot of cleaning needed to be done.

"And you'll tell me if you find anything?" Tracy pressed.

"Oh, of course. If there's anything strange, I'll let you know. I don't want to be caught up in anything. I just wanted to be an agent on my own, and this was a chance to get started."

The tension broken, Tracy relaxed a bit as she set the pen down. It was still just a filing cabinet and could simply be that Paul really valued them as a client and made sure to handle their work with extra care. "It's probably nothing serious. Cartel members need homes as well."

Grant nodded. It still seemed like a stretch that Paul was working with drug dealers, though his uncle *was* the kind of agent they'd look for. Someone like his dad wouldn't go anywhere near a property that might tarnish his reputation. Paul would just need the proper compensation. "I don't know if you're interested at all," he said, "but I do have some properties similar to what we looked at last night." Grant held up a few printed-off sheets he'd put together earlier in the day.

"Oh, really?" Tracy remarked, slipping her notebook back into her bag.

"But I guess you weren't really looking at the house, after all," Grant said, putting Tracy's motives together in his head. "You just wanted to see Paul."

"That was why I originally called, yes," she admitted. "But I really am looking to remodel my home, so it does help to look around."

"Yeah, that makes sense."

They both stood up, and Tracy said, "Please let me know what you find in those files. If you need any help, I can come by and look through them, too. But you'd probably know better if something looks out of place."

She held her hand out for Grant, and he took it. "Yeah, I'll see if anything looks odd. And I'll check for secret compartments, too."

Tracy laughed. "I hope that's not what we're dealing with. Stuff could be hidden anywhere in this chaos." She nodded back at the mess.

"You should've seen the house when I first arrived. It was even worse."

"Oh my. Well, have a good rest of your day, Grant. Thanks for all the help."

"No problem, detective. I'll let you know if I find anything."

Grant waved her off as she walked back to her car. At his desk, he sat back down and grabbed the phone. The prospect of the file cabinet holding some actual interesting information gave him the buzz he needed to push forward with the cold calls.

Day 4, 6:35 pm

BILL STRIDER

"Hunter, stop messing with the doors," Bill ordered from the front seat. The two Strider men were waiting in the minivan for Becky to bring the last load of covered dishes out. The passenger side door slid closed, and the metallic click of the lock engaged. Bill drove a Ford Bronco; not the new dumb-looking ones, but an original, like O.J. had made popular. His wife, on the other hand, drove a two-year-old minivan equipped with all the latest features—assisted steering controls, automated braking, and sliding side doors you didn't need your hands to open. All of it was very frustrating to Bill, who enjoyed the basic dial radio and a cigarette lighter in his truck that could actually light cigarettes. Those were all the features a vehicle needed, in Bill's opinion. Some things just didn't need technology added to them, especially when a six-year-old was around who enjoyed just messing with it for fun.

"Hunter, go in and see if your mom needs help carrying anything else." They had each already carried an armful out, but something was keeping Becky in there now. "Wait, here she comes." But it was too late; Hunter had already opened the door and he instinctively tried to stop it, which sent the smart door into a frenzy of indecision in several directions before it finally opened all the way.

"Stop messing with the doors!" Becky shouted from the back of the van, where she was carefully arranging the dishes.

"Dad told me to open it," Hunter protested.

Becky shot him a glance he caught through the rearview mirror. She was very fond of all the features of her van.

"Are we ready?" he asked as she climbed into the passenger seat.

"Yes, I think we got everything. Just drive slow so the gravy doesn't slosh around."

"Okay," Bill answered as he let the car roll backwards. The whole car bounced as the wheels left the driveway for the road.

"Bill!"

The drive to Tracy's was about twenty minutes. Bill did it in twenty-five on account of the gravy. The door to Tracy's house was already open when Bill glided into the driveway.

"I love her yard," Becky said, unbuckling her seat belt. Bill grunted. It looked like most other desert-scaped yards to him.

"Hey, guys!" Tracy was already strolling out the

front door to greet them.

"Tracy, I love your house! It looks so nice," Becky exclaimed, giving her a hug.

"Oh, that's really nice of you to say, but all I've done is put out the welcome mat," Tracy answered back, grabbing a dish from the back of the van.

The last dish had barely hit the counter when Becky insisted on the tour. Tracy had been ready for it and had the place cleaned up, all the underwear in the hamper and no dirty plates sitting in random corners of the house. Becky was interested in every aspect of the rooms, Bill pretended to be interested, and Hunter looked positively bored with discovering just how big Tracy's shower/tub combo was.

Back in the kitchen, Becky was back in charge. "Hunter, help Tracy set the table," she directed as she started popping the lids on her dishes.

"The plates are in that cabinet."

A few minutes later, the four of them were seated around the table, digging into Becky's pot roast. "Did you look at that house last night?" Bill asked once everything had fallen silent.

"I did. The nephew showed it to me. And there's a twist."

"Tracy, are you buying another house?" Becky exclaimed.

"Oh, well, no. I was looking at a house so I could talk to my agent about some clients he used to have."

"Oh, so this is about work, then." Becky's voice went flat with a hint of malice in it.

"Sorta."

"Dad isn't supposed to talk about work at the

dinner table," Hunter interjected.

"Is that right?" Tracy asked, looking at Bill.

"That's the rule."

The silence returned to the table. Tracy had been waiting all afternoon to fill Bill in on what she had discovered, but it was going to have to wait.

"So, Tracy, have you been dating at all?" Becky restarted the conversation in a more appropriate avenue, the ins and outs of Tracy's personal life.

Day 5, 8:45 am

LUCAS GREEN

Deputy was looking a bit more perky this morning. He was going to need it; today wasn't going to be the short walk he was used to.

Last night I had prepped the boxes in the garage, some of them folded up, some still in their box shape, whatever seemed like the best way to display what they were to a passing eye. This morning, we waited inside until Grant drove off to work. His trash cans had been at the edge of the street since last night. He had already agreed to me putting my boxes in his bins, but there was no reason to remind him of that fact. I had already decided I would need to speak to him tonight, when he got back from work. He's a real estate agent and I'm looking at properties. No agent worth their salt would turn away someone knocking on their door asking for help with comps. Once inside, I'd have a better idea of how things would play out in there, and maybe get the answer to my most pressing question, why I'd witnessed a police detective visiting his office the day before. Having a cop sniffing around already was just asking for trouble once the events started playing out. The best way to deal with cops was to give them a nice and tidy solution after the fact. They show up, the bodies are cold, and the case is practically solved for them. They love those kind.

Deputy waited inside while I moved the boxes. The oversized TV box I jammed into the can so it stuck up over the side. The rest of them I stacked haphazardly around the cans. It'd be impossible to miss them for anyone paying attention to what kind of boxes were being thrown away. "I hope you're well-rested," I said to Deputy as I attached the leash. "We might be out there for a while." He just looked up with his usual face. He was pretty stoic for a dog.

Outside it was warmer than it had been, the sun coming back to remind the valley of what it could do. I was uncomfortable in the khakis and collared shirt, not the best clothing for a forced march, but it was manageable if I kept a slow pace. We didn't want to overdo it. The walk needed to look casual if anyone noticed us out here. Slipping an earbud into my right ear, I set us on the path I plotted for us, a tight route that allowed for the best visual on cars entering this side of the neighborhood, and any that had come in through the east entrance. The comedy podcasts were wearing thin, so I selected a murder episode. That was more my speed. Maybe I'd learn a thing or two from the babbling female hosts. It never hurt to hear more about murder when your job is murder, just as long as none of my victims were featured in an episode.

Day 5, 8:50 am

TRACY COOK

Tracy had beaten Bill in this morning. Nothing new had come across their desk, so she was free to do her own investigating. She had the notebook opened up in front of her, with everything Grant had told her about Paul and his favorite client, G Inc. It was time to see what the Internet could tell her about those two. Or more specifically, the online police databases.

First was Paul's death. Grant had been a little vague about the circumstances, and once Tracy found the report, she understood why. There were only a few photos, but you could tell it hadn't been a pretty scene when it'd been discovered. The coroner's report matched up: a massive heart attack, Paul dead in moments. No signs of foul play anywhere; his system was clear of everything except alcohol and his prescribed blood thinners, which fit with a cause of heart attack. Tracy made a note that no surveillance footage had been pulled from the scene. She marked that down as something to follow up on. Even if her mother insisted that cameras didn't cover the backstage area of the Metro, it was Tracy's experience that casinos had cameras on everything. She was sure there had to be some footage of Paul before he died, what he'd been doing at the casino, or if anyone had been around him in the parking garage.

Next was whatever information she could find about him professionally and his estate. His name brought up hundreds of documents; being a real estate agent resulted in a lot of official paperwork in one's life. His nephew was named his sole heir and everything had passed to him without issue, just as Grant had said. Scrolling back through the documents, she saw nothing that stood out as unusual. Business license, taxes, and closing documents as expected. She would have to narrow down the scope of her interest if she was going to start searching those files, and a certain timeframe would be needed. She kept that page open as she typed in the next search, this one for G Inc. records. In Nevada, it just brought up the deeds and closing paperwork for their properties.

Bringing up the expanded search window, she saw that G Inc. was a corporation based in the Cayman Islands. Other than owning properties in Nevada and paying its required US taxes, there wasn't any more information. The only additional information was its legal representative, which was a Cayman Island-based firm. That was about as much of a dead end as one could ever find. The Cayman Islands were famous for their lax laws and resistance to law enforcement inquiries. G Inc. being based there could be a sign that the company was some sort of a front for money laundering, or it could just be legitimate real estate investing being conducted through a shell company. Shady, though not really illegal, and definitely beyond Tracy's ability to investigate. She picked up her Ding Dong and took a bite. It'd been out of the fridge for a while, so the cold chocolate had warmed up considerably.

There wasn't much more information to find from her searches. G Inc. was as buttoned-down as one would suspect from a faceless corporation, and Paul's documented life was uninteresting. It'd been two days and her investigation was already on life support. Grant finding something in his file cabinet was the only hope at this point.

She checked her watch. She was due upstairs for the daily convening of Task Force X in twenty minutes, and she still hadn't finished the homework Dean had sent her home with, watching hours of footage from the various campaigns, looking to see if Mencia showed up in any of them. As if that would prove a single thing.

"Now that Becky isn't here to stop us, tell me what happened yesterday." Bill dropped into his seat across from Tracy.

"Well, Paul Sherman died of a heart attack a few months ago."

Bill nodded, wide-eyed. "That is unexpected."

"I met his nephew who's taken over the business." Tracy proceeded to give Bill the rundown on what she'd uncovered, which at this point still wasn't much; Paul was gone, and G Inc.'s properties' transactions weren't much to go on.

"There's plenty of ways to launder money through real estate," Bill mused at the end of the story. "That'd be the most obvious motive for G Inc."

"Yes, or it could be some hedge fund types trying to pay less taxes."

"Equally likely. What's your next move?"

"I'm going to wait and see if Grant calls me back about looking through that file cabinet at his house. If he doesn't, I'll call and press him on it. Maybe he'll let me look at it myself."

"Sounds like a fun date, poking through the records of his dead uncle."

Tracy rolled her eyes. "What have you been working on?"

"I've got a list of ten possible candidates for the break-in on Tropical. Nothing special, just people with records who are linked to white vans like our description."

"So just shots in the dark?"

"Pretty much. Unless they have the TV sitting in the front yard, we don't have anything on them. But, I like dropping in on these types as a reminder that we're watching them. Maybe it keeps them on the straight and narrow if they think we're keeping tabs on them."

"That also could be construed as harassment," Tracy said, looking over the sheet he had passed her. It had ten names with mug shots next to them, all of them picked up for some kind of robbery in the past two years and with possible access to a white van.

"I'm very polite!" Bill answered with some mock outrage.

"You think any of these guys are actually our perp?"

"There's a chance. You can tell when a cop shows up at their door if they have something to hide, because they get all sweaty. Or maybe they want to tell me they loaned their van to their questionable brother-in-law who spends a lot of time down at the pawn shop."

"Alright, if you think it'll work, I guess that's the best option we have at the moment."

"It's a start. This isn't our perp's first crime spree. No one starts off with breaking into houses to steal iPads unless they're twelve-year-olds. This is the robbery version of a dive bar. These guys are like a thirty-five-year-old second baseman in triple-A."

"I don't know what that means."

"Women and sports." Bill shook his head.

"Guys and sports," Tracy sniped back.

"What do you think it means?"

"I don't know. Touchdown?"

"Now you're just embarrassing yourself."

"Sure I am."

"Thirty-five is old for a baseball player. Second base is the easiest position. And if he's still in triple-A, he's desperate to get back to the big leagues. Our perps are guys who've been around the block and have found a low-risk, low-reward ploy of box sniffing and middle of the day break-ins. They're in the system for sure."

"Well, I hope you enjoy that. I have to go listen to Dean and his conspiracy theories about how every elected official except the governor is working for the cartels."

Day 5, 9:15 am

TIM "TIMBO" CYRUS

Timbo took another hit from his vape pen. This one was cotton candy-flavored and his favorite; however, the local stores had stopped stocking them and refused to respond to his shows of displeasure.

Ray was doing his Amazon delivery work, which was starting to seem pointless since he never could recognize anything in the generic boxes. It could be a new tablet or it could be a book, which was practically worthless. Timbo had been getting suspicious for a while that Ray was purposefully not looking for boxes to steal and was instead just doing the work as a regular employee. A few months ago, Ray was spotting something every day they could jack; they had to plan out their recovery trips to avoid suspicion and to fit them all into the available time they had. Now, it was maybe once a week at best. That left the heavy lifting to Timbo, doing the daily rounds looking at people's trash, which was utterly humiliating. TV boxes were the only ones easy to spot, because of their unique size, and yet TVs were becoming worth less and less. You could roll up to Best Buy and get a brand-new flatscreen for a couple hundred bucks; stealing them was barely worth the time at this point. They needed bigger prizes, but those didn't come in easy-to-spot boxes, or they were too big to carry out. Grills and fridges were expensive, but not easy to toss in the back of a car.

Timbo continued grumbling to himself as he slowly drifted through neighborhood after neighborhood, the highlighted map fluttering next to him with the recycling schedules outlined in different colors for each day. A lot of big boxes you saw stuffed into the blue bins ended up being for furniture or something else that was equally hard to steal and transport. It wasn't an effective way to run a business, but Ray was fucking around and not holding up his end of the bargain, so it was all on him now to keep the venture functioning. Recycling days were the worst, because those trashmen started early; they didn't want to still be slingin' bins in the middle of the day, so they got going with the sun. Which meant Timbo had to be ahead of them, but waking up at 5 am wasn't something he enjoyed doing. It was starting to feel too much like an actual job instead of the easy life he expected. Maybe that was what Ray was learning, that he'd rather be working a nine-to-five than be breaking windows to earn about the same amount.

Timbo punched the brakes as a car pulled out of its driveway without looking, directly into his path. He laid on the horn, shattering the mid-morning calm of this neighborhood. The driver of the vehicle jumped in their seat, apparently oblivious to how close they had come to a collision. "Fucking hell!" He slammed his open hand against the steering wheel. The only hard and fast rule of his industry was don't draw attention to yourself. And now he was noticed; the driver wouldn't forget the white van, and there were probably several neighbors peeking through their blinds right now to see what all the commotion was about. Now the entire neighborhood was off-limits this week, and probably even next week, too.

The poorly driven car finally finished pulling out, and Timbo followed them very closely as they drove together toward the exit onto Alexander. They turned north and Timbo turned south. There were only two more subdivisions to prowl through, and he still had found nothing worth their time yet. These next two weren't any more promising. Pulling through the main entrance, he turned left and started his usual route—all the way down, right turn, and then right again down the next street. It did make it easier that all the streets were laid out in a similar pattern. There was no getting turned around in here or backtracking.

As soon as he turned onto the second street, he noticed the overflowing can at the far end of the street. The boxes were even spilling out into the road itself. "Hello there," he said with a smile. It was the first good sign he'd seen all day, as long as they weren't furniture boxes.

Slowing down, he crept forward to the prize. It was part of his act that he was looking for a specific address, so he kept looking in both directions as if he was searching for the right house number until he was right in front of the trash cans in question. The large multicolored TV box stuck out of the top of the can, holding the lid up. Next to it on the ground were several more boxes, each more interesting than the previous: Xbox, Playstation, a MacBook.

"Hey! What are you looking at, you piece of shit!" The voice startled Timbo; he'd been so focused on the loot that he missed the man who was now standing in front of the house, holding the leash of his dog. The dog didn't look very threatening and neither did the man, even if he was acting like he was.

"Fuck off!" Timbo shot back instinctively.

"I'll wring your scrawny little neck, asshole!" the man shouted back. "Stop looking at my shit and get the fuck out of here before I make you."

Timbo's hand slid down to the door handle. Who did this guy think he was? If he wanted to fight, he was about to get his skull cracked right here in front of his own house, with his dog watching.

"I'd knock your teeth out if you had any," the man continued shouting, backing up toward his garage, "but I just got the Porsche detailed, and I don't want to be scrubbing your blood off my steering wheel. So get the fuck away from my house!"

It took everything Timbo had to put his hand back on his own steering wheel. If this yuppie motherfucker thought he could talk to him like that, he was going to regret it. He had no idea who he was messing with.

"Have a nice day, sir," Timbo gritted out through a clenched jaw.

The man just spat in his direction. The wind almost blew it back onto his collared shirt and nice khakis, which would have been funny, but Timbo was crafting his own plan for splattering something all over him tonight. He had mouthed off to the wrong person and was going to regret it. Easing his foot off the brake, the van rolled forward toward the exit. The man was still in the driveway, waving him off like he had won some kind of competition.

Day 5, 2:00 pm

GRANT ANDERSON

Grant was finally back in his office. He'd had the appointment this morning with the drunken hoarder he'd spoken to the day before, which had gone as badly as possible, since Mr. Morill had forgotten about the appointment and was very agitated when Grant knocked on his door at 9:30 in the morning. Turned out he'd changed his mind on selling the place and was going to court to fight over the fines he'd been assessed. So selling his house was a no-go, but Grant left his card. Maybe when Mr. Morill got the right amount of drunk, he'd reconsider.

There wasn't anything new to do in the office, so Grant lugged in the three drawers of files he had brought with him today. The G Inc. file cabinet was too heavy to move on its own, but the drawers came out easily enough, so they rode to work in the back seat this morning. That was his objective for this morning, figure out what was in them.

Clearing as much space as possible, he started on the drawer that had been in the bottom of the cabinet, since its dates were the oldest. The file farthest back in the drawer was dated about ten years ago, so that's where Grant started, a three-bed two-bath in the Enterprise area on the southwest side of town. The market had still been struggling through the effects of the 2008 housing crash and ensuing recession, so houses could be had at a steal back then. This one was no exception. Bought for 112K by G Inc., with Paul Sherman signing on the faceless corporation's behalf. After the executed contract came the assorted bills: HOA fees, gas, electric, water, all paid with G Inc. checks, filled out and signed by Paul Sherman. After that was a four-page bill from a renovation company for work done on the house—new tile, paint, landscaping, carpet, and so on. That bill was around $55,000, also paid for with a G Inc. check, filled out by Paul. The final document was the executed contract for the sale of the house at 144K to a married couple, last name Tomlinson.

Grant checked the math again and confirmed that this deal had lost money; G Inc. was into the house for around 170K total, but they sold it for 26K less. Not a great investment, but these types of investment groups weren't always as concerned about making money in a conventional way. Losing money on a project would result in a write-off somewhere on the corporate ledger.

The next file was pretty much the same, except there was about 15K in profit made. Looked like the renovation budget was smaller and had been spent more precisely, which ended up making the house profitable. Grant kept working through the files, making notes on his legal pad as he went. They bought from different buyers and sold to different sellers each time. The houses were spread around the valley at random, no pattern appearing through the first drawer's worth of transactions. G Inc. got better at managing their flips as time passed; the ones that lost money got fewer and less costly. By the second drawer, the market had started an upwards trend and selling at a profit got easier, even with less renovation being done. G Inc.'s investments had gotten much more aggressive in the past couple of years, which made sense considering how the real estate market had boomed. Houses they'd bought ten years ago in the low 100Ks were over 300K by now and still climbing. That meant, of course, that G Inc.'s flipping had been profitable, though not as much as one would expect. They were spending lavishly on renovations, which chewed into the total profit margins; but with the rate they were flipping, it'd become a very lucrative business. Still, there was nothing out of the ordinary that Grant could find. Recently, they'd started selling to large groups like Zillow or OpenDoor, but that was pretty normal, too; those companies had been gobbling up homes across the whole country. And they were a little less touchy about things, which would make it easier to cut corners on the renovations if they wanted. But that wasn't a crime; in fact, it was almost expected in this industry.

Pulling his phone out, Grant dialed the number for Detective Cook on her business card. She answered on the second ring. "Hey, this is Grant Anderson," he said.

"Oh, hey, Grant. How's it going?" Her voice softened when she recognized him. "I'd meant to call you earlier to check in."

"It's been good today. I've been going through all the files in the cabinet. There isn't anything that stands out as fishy, pretty much just contracts and receipts for flips done by G Inc. It looks like my uncle managed the accounting for them. He signed most of the checks."

"That seems odd. Why would he be signing them?"

"It's not entirely unusual if the investors are hands-off. They tell him what kind of house they want, and he finds it, buys it, and gets the work done and back on the market. Otherwise, they'd have to have someone employed full-time out here managing everything."

"Okay, so there's nothing else interesting in there?" She sounded rather defeated.

"I don't know. Nothing specific stands out, but all together it does seem a little odd. I was wondering if you want to come over and we could look through it tonight? Maybe two sets of eyes will see something new."

"Sure, I can come over tonight. You said the files are at your house?"

"Yeah, we can meet there."

Grant gave her the address and set the time for this evening. The files were technically not at the house currently, but they would be by then. Checking the time, he realized he'd need a couple of hours to get the house in order before Tracy showed up. He flipped the

"Open" sign on the door over and started loading the files back into their drawers. There wasn't any use in wasting time here.

Day 5, 5:05 pm

LUCAS GREEN

Deputy and I had been resting comfortably in the living room ever since our encounter across the street with the local criminal element. Grant had returned home unexpectedly in the afternoon; he was normally a stickler about keeping his place open until 5 pm. Changing back into my own clothes, I watched him through the upstairs window, moving some stuff from the back seat into the house. I wondered if it could have anything to do with the visit from the police detective yesterday, the wild card in our deck at the moment. Deputy just kept watching me from his bed. He seemed apprehensive that I might try and force him on another walk; the longer than usual one this morning had put him in a disagreeable mood so far today. "It's okay, you don't have to go outside," I told him. He reacted as if he understood my words, dropping his head back down to his paws. What a world-weary dog I'd ended up with.

I decided to give Grant some time to get settled into the house before I visited. The floorplans I'd tracked down online gave me an idea of what was in there, but it always helped to actually put eyes on it. "Go to sleep if you're so tired," I said to the dog who was still eying me. "You're done for the day."

An hour later, I decided it was finally time for a visit. Grabbing my folder, I marched across the street. I knocked on the door and Grant answered very quickly. He was still wearing his collared shirt and khakis, though he looked a little harried. "Hey, neighbor, how's it going?" I greeted him warmly once the door was open.

"Hi. It's going good. How are you, Lucas?"

"Very good, very good. Been driving around town all day today. The traffic's worse than I thought it'd be out here."

"It's all the tourists, people driving in from LA," he answered distractedly. "Come on in. Is there something I can help you with?"

The place was decently lit, although a couple of bulbs were burned out in the ceiling fan lights. The front room had the vibe of a place being hastily cleaned; several garbage bags were full on the ground and the vacuum was sitting against the wall.

"Actually, there is," I replied, holding up the folder I'd brought with me. "I have a few properties I've looked at in here. Thought I might get a local opinion on them."

"Oh, sure. I'm just in the middle of trying to get this room cleaned up. I have someone else coming over soon to look through these files." Grant motioned toward the stack of drawers sitting on the fireplace mantle.

"I can help if you need to get done in a hurry. I'm pretty good with a vacuum." I grabbed the handle from where it was leaning against the wall.

"You don't have to do that. Just give me a few minutes and I can look at them."

"Nonsense. I'll help you out, then you can help me." I tossed the folder onto the top of the drawers.

"Sure." Grant shrugged and picked up the nearest two trash bags as I flipped on the vacuum and started working the carpet. Grant hadn't been lying about his uncle leaving the house messy; there was plenty on the floor to keep the vacuum busy. The depressed lines of carpet still showed that the space had only recently been cleared. Grant was definitely trying his best to make a good impression on the soon-to-be-arriving guest. All that remained in the room once the trash bags were cleared out was a wall of bookshelves, which like everything else in the house was sagging under the combined weight of all the random books and papers that'd been stacked on it. Farther into the house was still pretty messy. Grant had his work cut out for him just finishing this room. Getting the whole house in order wasn't going to be an easy task.

"That looks pretty good," I said, turning off the vacuum. "What do you think?"

"It looks great," Grant said as he sprayed half a can of air freshener around the carpet. "Would you like something to drink?"

"No, I'm fine, thanks." I wrapped up the vacuum

cord and stowed the whole thing away in a broom closet.

Grant picked up the items I'd seen him carrying in earlier. They were file cabinet drawers missing their cabinet, stuffed with documents. I grabbed the one closest to me from the kitchen counter. "What are all these?" I asked.

"Records from my uncle's business. There's a detective coming over to look at them." Grant started pulling the folders out in order and laying them on the freshly cleaned carpet.

"A detective?" I asked, handing him the next file.

"Yeah. I don't know what she's looking for, but I told her about these folders and she wants to see them."

"Do you mind?" I asked, squatting down and picking up the first folder.

"No. In fact, you might know better than I do if there's anything odd here. You're on this end of the business, after all."

I opened the folder and started laying its contents out in neat piles. "That's the one that had the phone number on it," Grant said, crawling over to the pages I had out. The top of the page had the G Inc. letterhead with a phone number underneath it. "I didn't see any calls to that number in my uncle's phone, though."

The doorbell chimed before he could say anything else, and Grant went to answer it. Sure enough, it was the detective I'd seen the other day, and he greeted her with, "Come on in, Detective."

"Just call me Tracy. I'm off the clock here." She stepped inside, her eyes adjusting to the change in brightness, then noticed me sitting cross-legged on the floor. "Oh, hello," she said with a bit of surprise in her voice.

"Tracy, this is my neighbor, Lucas Green. He's a real estate investor. He came over for some help and got roped into helping me instead."

"Oh, well, it's nice to meet you, Lucas," Tracy responded, taking in the rest of the home. "Looks like you've made more progress here than you have at the office."

"Just barely. Lucas had to help me get this room finished." Grant walked over to the three empty cabinet drawers arranged on the floor. "So, the one on the left has the oldest files, and then things progress to the right to the newest."

"Find anything yet?" Tracy asked, dropping her bag to the floor.

"Not really," I piped up. "We just started pulling them out."

Tracy took the second folder from the lineup and skimmed through it as Grant worked the third. Grant was right, everything looked normal, nothing but nice, boring, legitimate receipts and checks. Each page was organized by date in the file, ending with the sale statement. It took over an hour to get every folder opened up and shifted through, the papers laid out on the floor around us.

"Any repeat sellers or buyers?" I asked, still skimming through a few of the more recent files.

"No," Grant said. "Unless you count Zillow."

"We should make a map of all of them," Tracy said. "Maybe there's some consistency there."

Practically every home out here had a Las Vegas address, so it was hard to narrow down locations unless you could find the exact address.

"I already logged most of them earlier," Grant said, tapping his legal pad. "Looks pretty random to me."

"You know, I'm surprised there aren't any other quotes for the renovation work in here," I mused. "You'd think you'd get a couple of different opinions if you're doing such big projects."

"Are all of them from the same company?" Tracy asked, pulling the sheets out of her file. "Battle Born Renovations?"

"That's what mine says, too," I replied. "Signed off by Javier Santana, general contractor."

"Let's check that. Grant, write this down as we go." She pulled out the first one. "Battle Born, quote by Javier Santana," she read off. By the end of it, every single file contained a renovation bill from Battle Born, all signed off by Javier Santana. "I think this might be what we're looking for," she continued. "Using the same agent makes sense; they had a good relationship with Paul. But the same contractor for every single job over ten years? They were never busy with another job or made a mistake or got outbid? There's a connection here."

"I agree," I said. "I fight with contractors all the time. It's very messy. What do you think, Grant?"

Grant hesitated. "I dunno, I have to go to the bathroom." He looked sheepish. "I can't think. I've been holding it too long." We both just looked at him skeptically. "I'll be right back." He hurried out of the room.

Tracy kept muttering to herself as she pulled out her own notepad. "I'm going to need to log every single property mentioned in these and the time period they worked on it."

"That's going to be time-consuming," I said, standing up to stretch my legs.

"That's police work," Tracy answered. "It's not all donuts and shootouts."

"Do you read much?" I asked, looking at the bookshelves against the wall.

"Meh, I didn't even make it through the fourth Harry Potter book," she said, looking up at me. "It was so freaking long, the back half of the pages fell out. I gave up."

"I guess you've never read *Dune*, then?" I asked, pulling the dusty tome from its place.

"Nope. What's it about?"

"Betrayal in the desert."

"Figures. Nothing good ever happens in the desert."

"True. Not many romcoms set in the sands filled with psychedelic worm poop."

"I don't even want to know."

"We have our own version of worm poop. The Internet." I returned the book and picked out another one while glancing back at her. "Battle Born looks like a legitimate company. That means there'll be permits and licensing information for every job. A lot easier than writing it all out yourself."

She nodded. "I'll be able to see where else the company has been working. Maybe there are other projects like these."

Three hours later, our little investigative group had worked through every angle we could imagine, with no pattern emerging. Out of ideas, Tracy suggested it was time to eat, and we'd migrated to the patio now that the sun had sunk beneath the western mountains, giving the air a bit of a chill. The pizza had been delivered, so now we were enjoying ourselves.

"I don't think we're going to get any more out of the files tonight," Tracy said, chewing her slice and staring at the cinderblock wall that fenced in the yard.

"I agree," I responded. "I think we've talked it out at this point."

Grant didn't answer at first. He had spent the most time around the files at this point. "It's probably better to just sleep on it and look into the Battle Born stuff tomorrow when you have your work computer."

"Yeah, you're right," she finally agreed, turning to face us. "So what else is going on, then?"

"I have a dog that doesn't like me," I answered, drawing a laugh from Grant and a snort from Tracy.

"I'd get a pet if I wasn't worried about them getting lost in the house," Grant said. "My family always had a dog or a cat around when I was growing up."

"I couldn't handle a dog," Tracy said. "Maybe a fish to start with."

"My sister has fish," said Grant. "She seems to enjoy them, but they just seem kind of boring to me."

"Better fish than snakes or lizards," I said. "I don't understand why people try to keep those as pets."

"Snakes don't belong in houses," Tracy said firmly.

"I thought I'd see more out here," Grant said.

"There are snakes all over in Georgia. I thought it'd be the same out here."

"I've never seen one in the city the whole time I've lived here," Tracy said. "Only out hiking a few times I have seen them sunning themselves."

"You've been here a long time?" Grant asked her.

"Yeah. My dad and I moved here in 2002 when I was twelve to get away from my mom."

"Have you seen a lot of the shows here?"

"No, not really. Dad used to take me to shows for my birthday when I was younger, but I haven't been to any in a long time."

"I know most of the locals avoid the Strip, but I want to make the most of living in Vegas. I don't know how long I'll be out here. Every comedian in the world comes here pretty much every year."

"That's true. I always see the faces on the billboards when I'm downtown," Tracy said.

"Tom Segura's playing down there now at the Metro."

Finally, my chance. "Oh, he's hilarious. I love his podcast."

"You listen to his podcast?" Grant asked me, looking surprised that someone else might enjoy the same thing he liked.

"My mom's actually a waitress for his shows," Tracy said, drifting off a bit as she said it.

"It must be fun to see him every night."

"I guess you didn't escape your mom, then?" Lucas asked.

"Nope. She showed up after my dad died, sniffing for scraps. I see her sometimes, but lately she's more concerned about her boss framing her for stealing."

"What?" I asked.

"Oh, yeah," Tracy said with a laugh. "She kept calling me and calling me about it, so I met her for lunch the other day. She has this crazy theory that her boss is hiding them in the production gear and getting it out of the building when the shows change over. Oh yeah, and he's apparently also stealing credit cards."

"Well, if you need help, Grant and I volunteer to go to the show."

"For sure," Grant said, enthused for the first time in this conversation. "We'll go every night this week if you need us to."

Tracy shrugged. "Yeah, maybe. I haven't really thought anything through yet. I told my mom I'd call her back when I got an idea together. That'd make two off-the-books investigations I'm running this week."

"So this G Inc. stuff isn't anything official?" I asked. Interesting.

"It's sorta just a hobby of mine at the moment. I got an idea and I'm seeing where it leads, but so far it's just led to folders and folders of gas bills and property taxes."

"And pizza!" Grant added.

"That's true. The pizza's the best part so far." She smiled, looking at both of us. "Well, and the company."

Day 6, 1:34 am

TIM "TIMBO" CYRUS

"You shoulda heard this guy. He was just fucking asking for it," Timbo said, crumbling the empty beer can in his hand to accentuate the point.

"I dunno, man," Ray demurred. "We have a system already. It works."

"The system isn't working. TVs aren't worth shit anymore. A couple of last-model iPads aren't cutting it." Timbo snatched the iPad from their latest score off the table, the extra thick childish looking protective case still on it. After Timbo had encountered the mouthy asshole by the recycling bins, he had road-raged his way through the rest of his route, nearly taking out several bins on the way. After that, he got back to his home in North Las Vegas and started drinking and fuming. By the time Ray had gotten off work and made it to the small house, Timbo was fully loaded and ready to fight the world.

"I know it's not working like it used to, but going in there while someone's home is dangerous."

"It's more dangerous, but there's more reward. When we get in there we can make him show us where the good shit is—guns, cash, the safe. Instead of just grabbing what we can see, we'll get the real load."

"You want to hold this guy hostage?"

"Fuck that. Just in and out. We should be doing this on all our jobs from now on. There's lots of expensive shit in those houses we hit that we're missing because no one's there to show us where it's at." Timbo cracked the next can open and took a long pull. "You said you were with me the whole way. This is the whole way. Are you bailing on me?" He glared at Ray.

"Nah, man, I'm not bailing on you. It's just…"

"It's just what?"

"It's just that I like my job."

"I KNEW IT, MOTHERFUCKER!" Timbo threw the half-full beer can against the wall.

"Dude, it's a sweet gig. I just drive around all day, and they hand me a paycheck at the end of the week. It's not that bad."

"You're such a pussy. Bezos gives you fifteen bucks an hour and now you're sucking his dick. You know how much he makes? How much money he has? He isn't paying you shit. He wouldn't throw you a crumb from his dog's dish if you were starving. But fuck me, right, you're a company man now." He finished off with a sarcastic salute.

"Man, fuck the Man. I'm on your side," Ray pleaded.

"I got news for you, Ray. You *are* the Man."

Ray got up from the sofa, grabbing his Amazon hat from where he had set it on the table and throwing it on the ground. "I'm not bailing on you. It's just that we get hard time if we get caught in those houses pressing those people. That's why we always hit them while they're empty."

"It's time to take some risks. This douchebag today disrespected us. They disrespect us, we got to start taking what's ours, or they're always just gonna treat you like their delivery boy."

Ray grabbed the vodka bottle from the counter and poured a healthy helping into a cracked cup from the counter, following it up with a cold can of Mountain Dew from the fridge. The pale yellow concoction fizzled as he drank it. "They disrespecting you, they disrespecting both of us, homie. I got you."

"Good man." Timbo nodded. That fuckboy from this morning was going to regret running his mouth tonight when he got ahold of him. Not going to be so brave when they're having a conversation in his bedroom instead of out on the street.

* * *

"Pull in here, pull in here," Timbo ordered. It was a 24-hour 7-Eleven.

"What for?"

"I need a Monster. I've been up all day!"

"They have cameras in there," Ray protested.

"So what? I'm not robbing the place."

"Yeah, but they might look at the cameras around

here if they're looking for us. That happens on *48 Hours* all the time."

"Fine, I'll wear this." Timbo snatched a hat off the car's floor and stuck it on his head. "Now I'm a secret agent."

"Better than nothing," Ray muttered. He had pulled the van into the parking lot, but it was still sitting a distance away in the shadows.

"Do you want anything?" Timbo asked, cracking the door open.

"Yeah, get me one of them Coke Coffee things."

"A coffee?"

"Yes, a Coke Coffee."

"A Coke and a coffee?"

"No, one of those Coke Coffees." Timbo just stared back. "I'll just come in with you." Ray flipped the hood up on his hoodie. "Yeah, nothing suspicious about a black man wearing a hoodie in a gas station," he moaned as he turned the ignition off.

Since Timbo had talked Ray into going along with his plan, they had been drinking and scheming at the house. The biggest disagreement had come over what weapons they were going to bring. Timbo wanted to bring his shotgun with them; it was sawed-off and therefore badass and hadn't been used for much more than blowing up cans out in the desert. He also argued for carrying his chrome-plated Colt M1911 pistol. He'd been very proud of it ever since he'd spotted it sitting in a kitchen cabinet of one of their marks about six months ago. Ray had finally vetoed it all, based on the potential legal ramifications of carrying a firearm during the commission of a felony. They'd settled on

Timbo carrying his baseball bat and Ray bringing a length of pipe. He figured it'd be effective, and also something easily discarded if need be.

Back in the van after their snack break, they were rolling once again towards the target. The neighborhood was clearly asleep when they arrived; it was nearly 2 am on a weeknight at this point, so that was to be expected.

"Which one is it?" Ray whispered as he crept through the streets.

"That one!" Timbo pointed at the house on the corner. "Turn your headlights off."

"No, that would look sus," Ray argued back. "I'm gonna check the other streets."

Ray kept the van rolling past the corner house and turned down the next street. That one was as empty as the first one. Finally, after checking all the surrounding streets, he ended back on the right one, coasting to a stop several houses down and flipping the lights off. "I think we should watch it for a bit," he said.

"Yep, but not too long," Timbo replied. He was already gripping the baseball bat like he was on deck in a major league stadium.

"What's the plan now?"

"I brought my lockpicks. I'll pick the lock and we'll go in quiet, head upstairs and grab the fucker. After that, he gives us the shit and we get out of here."

"You can pick the lock?" Ray questioned him. None of Timbo's previous attempts to use the lockpicks Ray had stolen from Amazon had gone well, and usually resulted in them cutting through the door anyway.

"I've been practicing. I'm good now," Timbo insisted.

"The saw's still in the back, though, right?"

"No!" Timbo scolded. "We can't use it. It'll wake the whole street before we're inside."

The minutes crawled past slowly, but time was still the only thing moving on the street. "It's been long enough," Timbo finally said. "No one's around. Let's do this."

Ray dropped the van into gear and slid forward, not even touching the gas but just letting gravity and inertia carry them to the house. Easing his foot onto the brake, they stopped. "Should we leave it running?" he asked.

Timbo paused. "Yeah," he finally said. "Just in case we got to jet."

Both doors opened and the friends climbed out of their vehicle. "Put your mask on!" Ray hissed. They'd brought ski masks just for this purpose.

Timbo pulled it on as he walked around the front of the van, bat in one hand and lockpicks in the other. "Come on."

At the front door, Timbo reached out and tested the doorknob. It was locked. "Just had to check." He laughed.

"Hurry up," Ray said, his back to the door, keeping an eye on the street.

Timbo had thought ahead enough to bring a small flashlight doused with red film to dampen the light that lit his workspace as he started on the doorknob. That one came unlocked surprisingly easy, only about twenty seconds of tinkering before it clicked open. He eased the handle down and put pressure against the door. It held firm, which meant the deadbolt above it had been locked, too.

"Oh God, hurry up!" Ray urged, jumping behind the front porch pillar on his left.

"What is it?" Timbo asked, turning around at the sudden motion.

"I saw someone watching us. He's in the window across the street."

Timbo stared hard. The front of the opposite house was bathed in shadows, compounding the darkness. "I don't see anything."

"I swear I saw someone over there."

"Even if there was someone there, you'd never be able to see them. It's too dark over there."

"I know what I saw."

"Whatever. Tell me if you see anything again." Timbo turned back to the door, then turned back and said, "Wait. Do you think we need something to tie this guy up?"

"I thought you brought tape."

"There's some in the back of the van."

"You didn't bring it with you?"

"No, I brought the lockpicks," Timbo said, holding the pick up as proof. "Go get the tape. It's in the back."

Ray peered around the pillar again. The coast was still clear the best he could tell but stepping back into the open seemed needlessly dangerous. "What if we just used a belt or something?"

"Do you have a belt?"

Ray paused. "Fine, just keep working on the door,"

he said as he finally slipped off the porch and back to their running vehicle. Climbing through his driver side door, he found the tape where it had rolled in the back.

"I got it open!" Timbo said as Ray returned.

"Seriously?"

"Yeah, look." He swung the door open slightly and it moved, revealing the black slit of the interior along the edge. "Okay, are you ready?" He slipped his picks back into his pocket.

"Do you hear that?" Ray asked. Suddenly, he thought he heard a TV from inside the house.

"No! Stop imagining things! Now let's go!" Timbo pushed the door the rest of the way open and stepped inside, Ray following hesitantly behind.

The inside of the house was pitch black. Even the moonlight coming through the windows offered no help. "Where do you think he is?" Ray whispered.

Timbo pointed up. Above them was the second-floor landing. The closed double doors there were barely visible through the dark. Upstairs would be the most likely place for the master bedroom, and the double doors suggested it as well.

Ray nodded as Timbo shined his red tinted light around, looking for the staircase as they crept farther into the house. "There," Ray whispered again. The stairs were just ahead of them to the left. This far into the house, things got a little brighter because of the moonlight shining through the sliding glass back doors, lighting up what looked like the kitchen, dining room and living room in front of them.

The noise of a door opening caught Ray's attention. He was turning toward it when suddenly a bright light was shining in his face. A high-powered flashlight was being focused on them from the far end of the living room. Ray froze for a moment. They were too far away from their blunt instruments to have any effect on the person holding the flashlight. Retreat was the only option, but Ray couldn't move.

"Agh!" Timbo yelled, shielding his eyes as the light centered on him. "Fucking get him!"

The light beam turned, shifting onto Ray. Twenty feet separated him from the source, a man's body just visible behind the flashlight. Instinctively, he reached back with the pipe, flinging it forward as hard as he possibly could toward the other end of the room. The holder of the flashlight reacted and dodged the projectile as it bounced off the wall. Before it hit the ground, the room was flooded with the flash and bang of a gunshot. The bullet skipped harmlessly across the kitchen tile, a reactive discharge as the gunman dodged the pipe.

"*Fuck!*" Timbo screamed. The light beam caught him again. He had dropped the bat and was pulling his chrome-plated gun from his belt. The second flash of the gun reflected off the chrome for a moment, before the bullet punched through his throat. "Ulghrgh!" Timbo gurgled before collapsing to the floor, his hands trying to stop the fountain of blood shooting out of his neck.

"*Tim!!!*" Ray screamed over the crescendo of gunfire, their opponent emptying the gun at them. Ray took a step toward the thrashing form of his friend before a bullet caught him squarely in the side of the head, causing the other side of his skull to blow out, sending matter across the whole kitchen as his body collapsed to the ground. He landed in the expanding pool of blood from Timbo, who was still writhing on the floor.

Day 6, 3:00 am

TRACY COOK

The buzzing was in her dreams again, the noise coming for her like a helicopter that couldn't be seen. Spinning around, she looked for it, but everything was just getting darker…

Tracy jumped awake in her bed, the confusion of the dream replaced by the confusion of being awakened suddenly. It was her phone making the sound, glowing and shaking on the bedside table. It took three tries to answer it. "Hello?" she finally mumbled when she found the correct buttons.

"Detective Cook?" the voice on the other end asked.

"Yeah, that's me."

"Detective, this is Officer Arcia. We responded a little earlier to a report of gunshots at a home on Anadarko Valley Road. We have two fatalities. It looks like they were attempting a robbery using a white van.

You have a notice out for suspects fitting that description."

"That's right." The details of her job were flooding back to her awakened mind. "Wait, what street did you say?"

"Ah, yes, ma'am. The witnesses also say they know you. Apparently, you were visiting them earlier in the evening?"

"Grant?"

"Yes, and his neighbor, Lucas Green."

"That's right. I'll be there as soon as I can." Tracy flipped her lamp on and the phone off.

It only took a few minutes before she was in her car and on the way. Each night before she went to bed, Tracy made sure her next day's work clothes were laid out and ready to go. That made things easy and fast if she got one of these calls like she'd just received. The drive to Anadarko Valley was a simple one, only three turns; and at this time of night, there wasn't any traffic. Tracy was going through what she knew so far, but it didn't seem to connect. If Paul'd been involved with money laundering or drug trafficking, it was possible they'd be keeping tabs on his nephew as he took over the business, in case he stumbled onto anything. However, if the perps on the site were the same people who robbed Lisa's house, it'd be hard to make that leap. There was nothing about the Smith robbery that'd suggest a cartel was involved in any way. So one of these things didn't connect to the other.

The corner that Grant's house sat on was a hive of activity in contrast to the rest of the quiet night. The flashing blue and red lights reflected off every home in sight, and yellow police line tape fluttered in the night breeze. She pulled over at the entrance and walked the last block to stay out of the way of the ambulances and crime scene trucks that were packed onto the street. Flashing her badge at the line, she pushed past. Because of the time, most of the neighbors were watching from their front porches or driveways. The normal cluster of people at the edge of the tape didn't exist in the middle of the night.

Weaving her way through the emergency vehicles, she stopped at the sight of Grant and Lucas, sitting on the curb of his driveway, standard-issue blankets draped around their shoulders. "What happened?" she asked.

Lucas looked up and gave her a grimace. Grant was still staring at the ground. "He's still kinda in shock," Lucas offered.

"Was he hurt?"

"No, not a scratch on him." Lucas stood up and put his hand on Tracy's shoulder, leading her away from Grant. "The shots woke me up and I went to the window. I called the police, and then went in and found him just standing there with the gun."

"Has he said anything?"

"He was able to give a statement to that detective." He nodded toward the guy standing at the open doorway of the house. The man gave her a half-wave. Tracy vaguely recognized him.

"I'll be back in a few," she said to Lucas, climbing up the two steps to the porch.

"I don't know why the officer called you in," the

man said as she approached him. "There's a million white vans out there."

"Better safe than sorry, I guess."

The detective just grunted, turning back inside the house. "Anyways, I'm Dan Shannon, Homicide." He held out a pair of rubber gloves to her.

"I'm Tracy Cook, Robbery." She slipped her hands into the rubber.

"Watch your step. These guys are splattered everywhere."

The inside of Grant's house had changed considerably since she'd left a few hours ago. The space where they'd laid out all of the G Inc. files was now obstructed by two gurneys waiting to carry the bodies out. Two CSI techs were photographing the bodies from various angles where they laid on the floor. The once bright red blood had turned nearly brown and clumpy by now.

"These two picked the lock," Shannon explained. "He had a kit in his pocket. They got this far when they were confronted by the homeowner." He pointed to the two bodies. "They each caught a bullet, as did the microwave and the rest of the kitchen." He gestured behind him.

"He didn't get a shot off?" She pointed to a shiny pistol laying on the ground with a numbered flag next to it.

"Nope, got hit trying to draw it. Though he did throw a pipe at him first. Hit the wall and the homeowner let loose everything he had. I can't believe he actually got lucky enough to hit both of them."

Tracy nodded. She'd been to a lot of crime scenes

during her time on the force, but never to one that was so familiar. She had just walked through this space a dozen times a few hours earlier.

"Does the homeowner have any enemies or anything?" Shannon asked. "The neighbor said he was helping you with an investigation or something?"

"Sorta. His late uncle did some real estate transactions I was interested in digging through, but there wasn't anything to it. A very vague connection to the cartels."

"Ha. If these guys are connected like that then I'm the King of Atlantis." He sneered. "Just two bozos with a lockpick set and a gun."

"So just a robbery gone wrong?" Tracy asked.

"That's what I'm calling it, unless you have something better to suggest than a foiled cartel hit."

"I don't."

Day 6, 4:10 am

GRANT ANDERSON

Grant hadn't moved in over an hour. The emergency vehicles were starting to move on. The excitement had died off as the bodies were rolled into the coroner's van and the police received new calls for their attention. His entire mental capacity was focused on his right hand, the one that had held the gun and fired the shots. It felt like it'd left his body, like it was still sitting on the carpet in the house where he had dropped his gun. The hand that killed was now the hand that couldn't be moved.

"Mr. Anderson." The voice was faint, but the shake brought him back to his current situation. Grant recognized the officer trying to speak to him. He'd been the first on the scene. Officer Arcia, he'd called himself.

"What?" Grant mumbled.

"You can't stay here tonight," the man explained

gently. "It's a crime scene right now."

"But nothing happened here," Grant protested, looking at the ground around him.

"No, not here. The house. You can't stay in the house."

"I'll just stay here. Thanks."

"Okay." The officer walked away.

Grant's mind swam back into the fog it'd been living in since Lucas had pulled him out through the garage. He'd have to disclose what happened here if he was going to sell the house. A house with a double murder in it didn't sell well, even in this market, though it probably wouldn't matter to a professional investor. Maybe G Inc. would be interested in buying the house. Grant smiled to himself. That would be ironic. But how would he get ahold of G Inc.? His uncle paid for everything in the files with checks from them, but there weren't any more in the cabinet. No phone numbers or contact information, not even an email address. Maybe they'd reach out to him if they noticed a house they wanted. His right hand twitched. The feeling was returning now; his hand was reattaching itself.

"He's incoherent still," Officer Arcia said to Lucas and Tracy, standing just behind him.

"I have a couch he can sleep on," Lucas volunteered.

"My guest room is made up, but I've got to work in a couple hours, so he'd just be there by himself," Tracy said.

"I can keep an eye on him tomorrow. I only need to run a few errands. I can leave the TV on for him and let Deputy watch him." Officer Arcia shot him a look, and he explained, "That's my dog."

"That'd probably be the best option. Hopefully they can get this scene cleared pretty soon and he can get back in there."

"That's a problem for tomorrow," Tracy said. "In the meantime, I'll grab some stuff out of his bedroom. He'll need his phone, toothbrush, underwear."

"Alright. I'll take him over to my place now."

Lucas and Arcia helped Grant up from the curb, holding him gently but firmly until they were sure his legs functioned well enough to walk the distance himself. "Is the TV on?" Grant muttered. "I can still hear the TV."

"We can watch TV if you want," Lucas answered, steering him through the doorway.

Day 6, 8:02 am

TRACY COOK

This morning was a two Ding Dong kinda morning. After Tracy had finished at Grant's, she went home and tried to sleep for the two hours she had left of the night. That failed, so instead she took a shower and went to work early. It was catching up with her now that she was at her desk. Out in the field it was easier to deal with being tired; the constant movement helped keep the body and mind awake. However, staring at a computer screen had the opposite effect.

"I hear you had an eventful night," Bill greeted her as he joined her at their desk.

"Yep." She crunched into the second frozen treat.

"What do you have so far?"

Tracy got Bill up to speed on what had happened last night and the information she had pulled about the suspects, both deceased. Detective Shannon's paperwork hadn't been logged yet, so it wasn't computer official yet. "A white van registered to Tim was recovered on the scene. But nothing incriminating was found in the vehicle."

"Residencies?"

"Both have the same listed address out on the east side. Looks like a little shitbox from what I can tell. I have a call in to the landlord to get us in. Cellphones are still being processed."

Bill typed the names into the search bar. Each of them had a rap sheet, though nothing very interesting. Drunk and disorderly a couple of times, Timothy with a DUI, and Ray with a domestic disturbance call a couple of years ago. "Their records are fairly clean, considering they were breaking and entering with a deadly weapon."

"Yeah, that's what I thought, too. If they are our guys from Tropical, it seems odd that they went in during the night with the owner there. They seemed to prioritize avoiding people at the last one."

"Maybe they aren't our guys."

Tracy's phone started vibrating. It was a 702 number, the same one she'd dialed earlier this morning when she'd left a message with the landlord. The conversation didn't last long; he was very eager to help the police out and also concerned with collecting their late payment for the month, which despite Tracy's insistence that she couldn't help him with that, he kept pressing. At this point she would pay the rent just to get him to shut up about it. "One hour! We'll be there in one hour!" she finished firmly.

"Yes, yes, one hour, but who is going to get his stuff?"

He just kept on talking as she hung up the call. "This guy's going to be fun to deal with," she commented.

"Uh-huh," Bill answered back.

* * *

"Timbo was always late with his rent. I should have known he was up to no good." The landlord, one Mr. Louis, had been rambling from the moment Tracy and Bill had arrived at the ramshackle house listed as Tim and Ray's residence. In most areas of the country, a house that had a front yard of just dirt was a sure sign that some type of criminal lived there. In Vegas, it was more accepted. If you wanted grass, you had to have a watering system to keep it alive. That was an extra expense that not many landlords were going to deal with, hence why they would opt for decorative rocks or desert palms to pretty up the space. However, the closest this home got to landscape features was an old bicycle and glittering glass from smashed beer bottles.

"Did you bring any trash bags?" Louis continued as the group stood outside the front door.

"Excuse me?" Tracy asked back.

"You're here to clean this place out, right?"

"Mr. Louis, we're the police, not a cleaning crew," Bill answered. "We're here to look for evidence. That's it."

"But someone is going to need to clean this out. They are very messy people." He pointed to the two-foot-high mound of crushed-up cans piled up next to the door. "Who does this? You write this down, add it to his crimes."

"Could you unlock the door, please?" Tracy responded curtly.

Mr. Louis produced a huge ring of keys from his pocket. It appeared he either owned hundreds of properties or had never thrown a key away in his life, though he had the right key picked out surprisingly quick. He popped the door and was starting to lead them in when Bill reached out and grabbed his shoulder. "Actually, you're going to need to wait outside while we conduct our search. Protocol."

"I know where everything is, though."

"Even so, it's legally required for you to remain outside," Bill said firmly, stepping past him. Tracy followed him in.

"If you see any money, that's mine! Tim owes it to me for rent!"

"Will do," Bill responded, shutting the door behind them.

"Good idea with the legal requirements," Tracy noted, flicking on the overhead light.

"I would've probably killed him and then framed Timbo for the murder if he came in here."

Louis hadn't been lying about the two thieves being messy. Tracy had been getting used to seeing a mess after visiting Paul's old haunts, but this one was different, less hoarder and more just pure pigsty. Beer bottles and takeout containers were strewn about everywhere, clothing wadded up on the shelves, and dried food stuck to everything. It had a smell, but it was manageable for the short term, a mix of locker room and stale McDonald's.

"I see an iPad there," Bill called out, pointing to the couch. A tablet protected in a bright blue rubber case was sticking out of the cushions.

"Looks like a match," Tracy said as she pulled it out. Drawn in black sharpie on the bottom of it was the name "Max Smith," with his mother's phone number below it. She held it out for Bill to read.

"Case closed," Bill declared, fishing his phone out of his pocket. If there was evidence from one robbery in here, there was probably more for cases that weren't theirs. Time to call in some help for sorting through all of this.

Tracy kept pushing through the house. First, she came across a bathroom. A single glance told her all she wanted to know about that room. If there was any evidence in there, someone else was going to have to fetch and disinfect it, since it was probably covered in pee. Next was a bedroom: saggy mattress, clothes everywhere, and a couple of bongs next to the bed. Across from that was another bedroom in similar shape. Finally in the back of the house was what would've been the spare bedroom, but it had become a storage space for stolen goods. Several TVs were stacked against the wall, while the rest of the room was filled with laptops, game consoles, and two tricked-out-looking bikes. In the center of all of it was a charging station for Makita power tools and two batteries sitting on it. The drill, grinder, and Sawzall laid on the floor next to it. Everything a modern thief needed to break through a door. "Hey, Bill, we got the motherlode back here," she called.

Bill hung up the phone and joined her in the room.

"You think they ever thought about stealing stuff that wasn't electronic? Jewelry or something would have a much better resale value and would be easier to move."

"I don't think those two could tell the difference between a real diamond or a plastic one. But they know what an Xbox is, so they were just stealing the stuff they could use."

"Something tells me they weren't going to be using these bikes." Bill spun the wheel on one of them.

"Maybe you'll get to call your new friends back and tell them you've recovered their stolen goods."

"That's a good idea. In the meantime, you should go tell Mr. Louis that we're going to be a while and he should just leave us the key."

"That sounds like a job for the senior detective," Tracy shot back. But Bill already had the phone up to his ear and was miming not being able to talk because he was on a very important call. "Fine." She stomped back toward the front door. Maybe she could call in a uniformed officer to keep him busy with statements if he wouldn't leave.

Day 6, 8:45 am

LUCAS GREEN

"Let's go for a walk," I said to Grant. I had put him to bed on my couch around 4:30 am, then gone to bed myself. Considering the traumatic event he'd just gone through, I assumed he'd sleep most of the day. Instead, I was awakened a couple hours later to him pawing through the kitchen. Cereal and orange juice was all I could offer him, which he refused on account of his canker sores. After his dry cereal breakfast, he was just staring out the window, so it was time to get him outside. Deputy had pointedly ignored all the excitement of last night, but he did seem interested in the house guest.

"I don't have any shoes," Grant said, after I directed him toward the pile of his clothes Tracy had retrieved from his closet last night.

"Yeah, I guess she forgot those." I'd offer him a pair of mine, but I didn't have any extra. Shoes took up a lot of luggage space. "I'll go get you yours. What's your garage code? And is there anything else you want me to grab?" We weren't supposed to go back into the house until the police released it back to Grant. But Grant needed shoes, which gave me as good an excuse to go over there as any.

"No, just my shoes. They're in my room."

Outside, everything was back to normal, the activity of the night gone, only the "Do Not Cross" tape plastered across the door suggesting anything unusual had happened. The garage door creaked open. It wasn't used to moving since it was impossible to get a car inside it, and even walking through the junk piles was difficult. Last night I had to practically drag Grant through the mess to get him out of the house as the police approached.

"Lucas!" Grant was shouting from my front door now.

"Yes!" I yelled back across the street.

"Could you get my headphones? I think they're on the dresser in my room!"

"Anything else?"

"Yeah, my buttwipes from the bathroom!" he yelled into the void.

"What?" I yelled back.

"Buttwipes! They're on the back of the toilet!"

"Alright." I turned back to the garage. Shoes, buttwipes, and headphones, oh my. The air out here could be painfully dry. My first night in the house, I slept with a wet washcloth across my face just to get some moisture in my breath. I guess other parts of Grant were affected by the dryness as well.

His house already had a warm, dry sensation to it. The police had shut off the HVAC systems before they left. I'd never really understood why cops did this—it wasn't like the house systems were going to suck up any key evidence or blow something away—but they always did it anyway. Even though it was still morning, the sun had already started to do its work, so the house was noticeably warmer than you would expect.

Grant's headphones and buttwipes were where he said they'd be, and his tennis shoes were piled in the corner with the rest of his shoes. My short visits to his house hadn't given me a chance to survey the layout from the vantage point of his bedroom. It was really set up well for Grant to ambush the would-be assailants. They had to expose themselves as they neared the stairs, and the light coming through the front and back doors highlighted them while hiding Grant in the shadows. The two robbers had been in over their head from the start, in a bad tactical spot and outgunned. So Grant would live another day.

The question was, when would I hear from Carlos and Javy about the failed attempt? I'm sure Javy would have some pleasant insights into what could've been done better. But now was the time to figure out a new plan, complicated by the fact that the target was now living with me. That would be hard to explain to Carlos and Javy, and they'd have a point; the fact that the target was living on my couch would make it a lot harder to finish him off and not arouse suspicion. The strange new neighbor from out of town would make a perfect suspect.

Day 6, 3:00 pm

TRACY COOK

Tracy and Bill were finally back at their desks. It had taken several hours to catalogue the treasure discovered in the back bedroom. Bill had lost his cool with the landlord by the end of the search. Louis had refused to leave and was badgering everyone arriving about what was still owed to him, and who would deal with the stuff the police left behind. Finally, it had been enough for Bill, and Louis had been forced to accept that he wasn't going to get his way. He stalked off and spent the rest of the afternoon waiting in his car.

So far they'd found stuff connected with ten different unsolved break-ins throughout the valley, and goods totaling nearly $10,000. During their unearthing of evidence, they had discovered that the chrome M1911 recovered from the scene last night was also stolen. It had escaped notice the night before since the serial numbers were filed off, but an exact match to the gun had been reported missing, along with the two bikes that were sitting in there. A bike-riding gun enthusiast was an odd combination, but in Vegas it seemed like everyone had a gun of some sorts.

"All that for maybe 10K, probably less on the street," Bill muttered, going over the pictures. If the tech department ended up being able to access the phones found in the van, maybe they'd have some further leads to work on. Considering how much merchandise had been discovered in the home, there had to have been plenty that'd already been sold to finance their regal lifestyle of beer and weed. Maybe the phone would have some clues as to who they were selling the goods to and what other robberies they could be involved in.

They had found everything reported missing from Lisa Smith's house. Her boys would be happy, though the TV mount was still sawed off, and the garage door that Lisa had totaled would cost a bit to replace. Hopefully her homeowner's insurance would see fit to cover that expense, even if it was self-inflicted.

"You say we never solve any crimes," Tracy said proudly. "This is the second case we've closed this week."

"That's true. It only took these guys getting murdered to help us out. You going to call Lisa about all of this?"

"Yeah, I can, unless you want to."

"No, I need to go get my lunch. I left my salad in the fridge." He stood up from the desk. Tracy had run out and got food for herself while they were waiting around Timbo's house. Of course, Bill wouldn't stoop so low as to eat at the taco shop Tracy had picked, so he had been left hungry.

Lisa was very appreciative, which was nice. These types of calls were pretty rare, a welcome relief from the usual slog of calls to be made bearing bad or no news. She even invited Tracy and Bill over for dinner whenever they wanted, which Tracy politely declined. She had managed to avoid telling Lisa how the break in the case had occurred, but that would definitely come up during a dinner, and might put a bit of a sour spin on things if Lisa knew what fate had befallen the men who'd sawed through her front door. Most people didn't like knowing that they were connected in any way to violent deaths, no matter how indirectly. Messes with the sleeping patterns.

Tracy's mind drifted back to Grant. He was probably going to need some therapy. Not only had he witnessed violence, he'd been the perpetrator of that violence. Hopefully Lucas was taking good care of him. On a whim she typed Lucas's name into the database. Nothing came back; his record was as clean as could possibly be. Guess Grant was in good hands, then.

Her phone buzzed, "Mom" flashing across the screen. "Hi, Mom," she said after picking up.

"Tracy, it's getting worse! I need help now!" Shelly was practically screaming into the phone.

"What's going on?" she answered with a sigh. The sky was always falling.

"Garrett had me hand out the credit card readers for the show tonight! If some of them are fake, they'll blame me!"

Tracy groaned, climbing to her feet. She needed a stiff shot, but a Coke would have to suffice. "Mom, I don't think he has a bunch of rigged credit card machines."

"Why don't you believe me!!!" Shelly screeched into the phone as Tracy reached the break room and the vending machines.

"You don't have any proof the machines are different. You're just paranoid."

"No, I have proof now."

"What do you mean?" Tracy was trying to work the vending machine even while her mom rambled in her ear, which almost caused her to punch in the number for a Diet Coke, which would've been catastrophic.

"We're supposed to pick up our credit card readers downstairs, one hour before the doors open. But he met me up in the lobby and gave me a bunch to hand out. He said he was walking past and grabbed them so we didn't have to go down there."

"Alright." The Coke bottle was on its way.

"Which he's never done before, but then I started looking at them and it didn't have the casino's barcode sticker on the back of it. It had a different one that looks like an official one, but it isn't. It's fake."

"Maybe they just changed the stickers, Mom."

"Your dad never believed me either," Shelly snapped. Tracy bit her tongue. If there was one person who had a right to not trust Shelly, it was her late father.

Tracy unscrewed the bottle cap and the refreshing hiss of carbonation escaped. She did appreciate this vending machine; it kept the bottles very cold in there. There was no worse feeling in the entire world than getting a warm bottle of Coke when you expected it to be cold. The first sip was always magical.

"Are you there?" Shelly demanded, unaware of Tracy's physical activities on the other end of the line.

"Yeah, I'm thinking about it."

"Well, think faster. I'm on my break, but I have to go back in soon."

"You're working tonight?"

"Yes, we have a show tonight, and then tomorrow's the last one for two weeks. That's why I need you right now. The case with all the stolen stuff will leave tomorrow."

"Do you think he'll put the fake readers in there, too?"

"I didn't even think of that! You have to stop him!"

"Okay, I'll come up with a plan for tomorrow night. We'll figure out a way to track what's going on."

"I thought you already came up with a plan!" Shelly shouted. "You said you were thinking of one!"

"Yes, *thinking* of one!" Tracy raised her voice back. "There's a lot going on right now."

"Tracy, this is really important. I can lose my job just from the stolen liquor, and now with this credit card thing, it's way more serious. I ran off two thousand dollars on it last night. If they think it was me doing it, they'll arrest me!"

She was right—stealing some bottles of liquor or a few lost phones would probably just get someone of her stature fired. But credit card fraud was a much bigger offense, and the casino might press charges to make an example out of her. Ever since the casinos started becoming owned by corporations instead of mobsters and were now shying away from dropping thieves into Lake Mead, they had become very vindictive in the courts.

"I understand what's going on, Mom. I work for the police."

"Then you know how urgent this is," Shelly shot back.

"Yeah, I'll call you in the morning and let you know what I figured out."

"Not too early. I'll be at Ethan's tonight."

Tracy sighed again. "Okay, not too early."

Day 6, 3:30 pm

LUCAS GREEN

"Grant, is your phone ringing?" I called into the living room. Grant had remained motionless most of the day. I hadn't even noticed him making any trips to the bathroom, which was disturbing. Even Deputy had relieved himself a few times.

He didn't answer. He was about twenty episodes deep into *Seinfeld* at this point of the day. Walking into the room, I saw that he was still curled under his blankets, his phone vibrating on the table next to him. I answered it for him. "This is Grant's phone."

"This is Detective Shannon," the voice on the other end announced.

"Hey, this is Lucas, Grant's neighbor. Grant's resting." "Resting" was a polite term for what he was doing, since he hadn't even flinched when the phone rang.

"Alright, I just wanted to let you know we're

releasing the house back to him. The techs just picked up the last of their equipment, so it's all yours now." I walked over to the window and peered through the blinds, revealing that the police tape had indeed been removed from the door. Apparently there had been some visitors we'd missed.

"That's faster than I expected," I said back.

"Yeah, it's an open-and-shut case. We found a bunch of stolen goods in the perps' home. Just a classic case of picking the wrong house. Someone will probably be in contact with Grant in the near future for follow-ups, but as of now, everything's settled."

"Okay, I'll let him know and see what he wants to do."

"Thank you." The detective clicked off the line.

"You're allowed back in your house now," I said, turning back to Grant. He just muttered something unintelligible. Grabbing the controller from where it had been sitting on the floor, I paused the Judaic antics happening on the screen. "Grant, are you with me here?"

"Yeah. What's up?" He rubbed his eyes and started speaking rather clearly for the first time.

"Your house has been released, so what do you want to do?"

"I dunno. It's pretty far away." He craned his head to look toward it out the window.

"Okay, I'm going to call some cleaners and see what they say about getting out here." I handed the remote back to him. He instantly unpaused the show and burrowed back into the couch.

Back upstairs, I fired up the search engine and

started looking through crime scene clean-up crews. I wondered if Grant could file a claim on his homeowner's insurance policy. Must be something in there about splattering two people all over the kitchen floor. Either way, we were going to need the cleaners, whether covered or not. Grant wasn't going to be able to clean it up, considering he was having trouble even getting off the couch; and I was one hundred percent sure I was not getting involved. I was already more involved than I should be, considering my objectives.

I'd been struggling all day with deciding on the next course of action and if I should loop in Carlos on what happened last night. On the one hand, he'd appreciate that an action was attempted, however defunct it ended up being. But he'd probably be more bothered by the fact that it failed, and that the target was now watching sitcoms on my couch with my dog. I decided to wait and see if they contacted me about it. I was interested in seeing what kind of information they had access to, and how closely they were monitoring the situation here.

I typed the number of the cleaners into my phone. Hopefully they could get the place cleaned up quickly before it really got bad in there. With the AC off, it was bound to be very hot in there by this time of day. We should at least go open the windows to get the breeze flowing through. You didn't want that smell baked into your house.

Day 6, 6:30 pm

GRANT ANDERSON

"Grant. Grant!" Tracy's voice cut through the TV dialogue once again.

"What?" he answered back as he paused the show.

"Do you think you could handle going to the Tom Segura show tomorrow night?"

"Yeah, why wouldn't I?" he asked back, drawing questioning looks from both Tracy and Lucas. The reason was clear to them, but apparently not to Grant.

"Could you come in here so we can plan it out?" she asked.

Throwing the blanket off of him, Grant trooped into the kitchen. Tracy and Lucas were both sitting on the bar stools around the island, eating their food. A third plate waited for him in front of the last stool. Taking his seat, he absentmindedly took a bite from the chicken tenders. Tracy smiled and continued the discussion. "The last show is tomorrow night, and my mom thinks they'll move all the stolen stuff after the show when they load everything out."

"Any idea where it goes?" Lucas asked.

"No. Her source says it depends on which truck it gets loaded onto. There are several different companies that have equipment down there."

"So if we go to the show, what are we looking for?" Grant asked, finally showing some interest in something today that wasn't on Netflix.

"I was thinking we could leave a phone or something. We could track it and see where it goes."

"That's a good idea."

"Do you have any extra phones?" Lucas asked. They both shook their heads. "How about a tracker?"

Grant shook his head again. Tracy said, "Not personally. We have ones at work, but I can't use them for something like this."

"Okay, I can get us some burner phones tomorrow for cheap. I think I have a tracker that'll work. My company uses them for their work computers and things."

"That'd be great," Tracy said. "I'll call my mom and see if she knows what section she's going to be working tonight, so she can find them and make sure they get turned in. It would suck if they just end up kicked under some seat at the end of the night."

"So we leave the phones and then what happens? We wait there and follow it?" Grant asked.

"No, I think just come home. With the trackers we can just wait and see what happens. If it goes somewhere else, we'll have enough proof to go to the hotel security team, I think."

"Not the police?"

"It depends. Doing some off-the-books work like this might interfere with being able to prosecute them. But the hotel won't care about due process."

"And besides," Lucas cut in, "the point isn't to get someone thrown in jail. It's just to make sure your mom doesn't take the fall."

"Exactly," Tracy agreed.

"What should we wear?" Grant asked.

"I think you can wear whatever you want," Lucas answered. "What would you normally wear to a comedy show?"

"Probably something nice, but this is all I have," Grant said, looking down at his mismatched clothes that Tracy had grabbed for him.

"We can go back over and get you something else to wear from your closet," Tracy answered.

"No. The police said we can't go back in there. They want it left alone."

"Grant," Lucas said. "I told you before, the police are done with your house. We're free to go back there."

"You didn't tell me that."

"Yes, I did. By tomorrow night, everything will be cleaned up and it'll be as good as new."

Grant picked up another piece of chicken, silently dipped it, and started chewing on it. Going to see the show and helping out Tracy was a great opportunity; having to go back into that house was a non-starter, though. He'd almost died last time he was in there. The flash of the metal pipe flying toward him kept running through his mind all day long. A little better aim and it would've hit him squarely in the head. The two men would've been on him in an instant and beaten him to death before he could stand up. Instead, it missed, and they were the ones who were dead. There were just too many variables to feel comfortable in that house again. Every time he walked through that door he'd see the shadowy figures, standing at the base of the stairs.

"Maybe we can buy some new clothes for the show," he suggested.

"That is an option," Lucas conceded.

"I think I'm gonna go back and finish that episode I was on." Grant picked up his plate and walked back to the living room.

"At least he took his food with him," he heard Lucas say as he left the room.

Day 7, 8:45 am

TRACY COOK

After leaving Lucas's last night, Tracy went home and dialed her mom. After Shelly didn't answer, Tracy realized it was still showtime down at the theater. She called back around eleven when her mom was off of work and she answered. Shelly was less manic than usual; Tracy could clearly tell that Ethan was sitting right next to her, and that Shelly was putting on a good act for him. Shelly confirmed which rows were hers to cover as a waitress, which sent Tracy hunting online for two tickets in that section for Grant and Lucas. As long as Lucas could get the phones and tracking device he said he had access to, they were ready for this evening. Shelly was very keyed up, which could be an issue if she got too talkative and started blabbing about the caper to her co-workers. Tracy issued strict instructions to keep her mouth shut if she wanted the plan to work. She was to serve Grant and Lucas like normal, run their credit cards if she had the reader she thought was corrupted, and be sure to deliver the lost phones to the boss like she had every other night.

That had been last night. Now Tracy was sitting at her desk and going through everything she could find on Battle Born Renovations. The company was legitimate, and all its licenses and tax filings were up to date. The legal owner of the company was Miguel Guerra. His record was clean other than a few traffic citations, speeding and using a cellphone while driving. Pretty basic stuff. Tracy pushed deeper into the documentation. Because of the nature of the work, there were plenty of permits filed under the company's name, which gave a glimpse into their business. A lot of the permits lined up with the G Inc. records were as would be expected, since they seemed to be the preferred client, but there were some permits for work not connected to the files, so that's where Tracy started. Maybe some of these side jobs would reveal something noteworthy. But it was a dead end from a paperwork side. Everything seemed to be on the up-and-up; the clients were real homeowners who didn't have any connection to known criminals, just people who needed their kitchens remodeled. Cross-referencing even showed that a lot of those customers were the ones quoted in the reviews on their website. Just happy people all around. Well, if there wasn't anything to find in their business dealings, Tracy would look into their employees.

"How's it going over there?" Bill's voice broke her concentration.

"What's that?" she asked, looking up.

"I asked how it's going. You're muttering up a

storm over there."

"It's fine. I'm looking through this company, but there doesn't seem to be anything fishy with them so far. Just standard contractors."

"You want to hear about my night?" he asked.

"Sure, I could use a break."

"At some point there were bushes that went around the edge of our front yard. The previous owner had decided they didn't like them and ripped them out, but they didn't really do anything to fix the holes. So when we bought it, the yard was rough-looking around the edges. But I've been throwing dirt into the divots and trying to get the grass to grow in since we moved in. A week ago, Becky decided she can't take it anymore."

"She can't take the yard anymore?"

"Exactly. It's been this way for three years, but all of a sudden it's a problem. So she decides she's going to plant flowers along the edge of the yard. She went to the nursery and bought like ten bags of mulch and a bunch of flowers and started tearing the yard all up again."

"That seems like a lot of mulch."

"It's way too much mulch. She used two and a half bags and now there are seven full bags sitting in the garage I have to climb around to get into my car. She plants all these flowers and it looks great, except we live in a fucking desert. If you plant a flower in like Florida or something, you only need to water it the first day and then it's just part of nature, there to live a full life under the sun. You try and give someone a flower out here, it's like giving them a cancer-riddled child to care for. Oh, it's certainly going to die very soon; no matter how much effort you expend, it's going to shrivel up like a witch's tit. But here, have fun with it while it lasts."

"That seems like kind of an aggressive analogy," Tracy offered. Most times when you bring cancer and children into an argument, the other side is going to focus on that detail instead of the larger point.

"That's what Becky said, but what do you think happened? I came home last night and they're all dead, because she forgot to water them for two days and the sun cooked them like a fried egg."

"Makes sense."

"Now Becky wants to get more sprinklers for the front yard and plant new ones. Maybe these ones will last longer than a week."

"I thought you already have sprinklers."

"We do. With the grass we have to have them, but they run just far enough to keep the grass alive, not the flowers, so we'd have to dig up the entire yard to run specific sprinklers right to where each flower is planted to make sure it gets enough to drink."

"Do you need a shovel?" Tracy offered in an overly serious tone.

Bill grimaced. "No, I have a shovel, thank you, Tracy. What I need is for you to talk some sense into my wife. Why does the front yard need flowers? It looked fine before."

"You need me to talk to her?"

"I need someone. She won't listen to anything else I say, ever since I brought up the cancer-riddled children."

They got back to work, but after a few minutes of

silence, Tracy said, "Maybe you should try planting cactuses in the yard instead of the flowers." The thought had occurred to her while looking up all the known employees of Battle Born Renovations.

"Isn't the plural 'cacti?'" he argued.

"Yeah, proper grammar is what you should be focusing on right now."

"It seems like it'd be hard to plant a cactus. They don't like being touched."

"That's a Becky problem. She's the one doing the planting, isn't she?"

"You don't know anything about marriage," he huffed, turning back to his screen.

He was right about that. Her parents' marriage hadn't taught her much about anything other than that sleeping with the neighbor's husband, who also happened to be Tracy's math teacher, was frowned upon, which she figured was commonly known, not something that had to be taught to married people. But what she lacked in knowledge about being married, she was making up for in knowledge about a certain renovation company operating in the Las Vegas valley.

So far she had found Carlos Guerra, the brother of the owner and seemingly his unofficial partner. His name wasn't listed anywhere official, but his face kept popping up in pictures from the company's Facebook page, and his name in customer reviews. After that there were several long-term employees who showed up in permit filings, tax documents, and the same social media postings. It appeared it was a family-run business with a lot of loyalty shown to its staff. Most of them had been there for years. At the start of the company's history, nearly every permit was filed under Miguel's name. He was a certified general contractor and appeared very hands-on in the running of the company. That lasted a few years until the name Javy Santana showed up as the new general contractor. Every permit for the past six years had been handled by him. His face was also in some of the pictures posted, though always looking disgruntled that his picture was being taken.

After him was one more name that showed up on the permits, and that was Juan Heredia. He had an electrical license and, as you guessed, was the resident electrician. He was noticeably older than the rest of the crew. Tracy typed his name into the police database and his driver's license popped up. Born in 1965; that confirmed him being nearly twenty years older than the rest of the crew, but it wasn't uncommon for an electrician to be that age. Most of them probably skewed older than younger at this point.

Tracy scrolled through his information. The same address had been listed for him for over a decade now. It looked like he'd bought a house near the bottom of the market in Las Vegas after the housing crash. The Zillow search showed that he had made a good investment so far; the house listed was worth 150K more than he paid for it. It took a couple of windows to find, but she tracked down the closing statement that had been filed with the state. Listed as the buyer's agent was the familiar name Paul Sherman. Was that suspicious? If Paul was handling the renovation work on behalf of G Inc. and Juan was doing a lot of that work, it could be naturally assumed that they'd crossed paths fairly often; and that when Juan wanted to buy a house, he asked the only agent he knew. She marked it down on her notepad: *See if Grant has any documents pertaining to Juan Heredia.*

His criminal history was next. His record was perfectly clean for the past ten years, not even any of the speeding tickets or parking citations people are prone to get even when they're trying to obey the law. But that hadn't always been the case for Juan. His record as a young man showed someone who'd been going down a bad path: breaking and entering, possession of stolen goods, and several counts of possession of a controlled substance. Stealing and drugs could be indicators of a troublemaker, but it was the charge in the middle of all those that Tracy fixated on: "Aiming a Gun at a Human Being."

That was an interesting crime to be charged with. It was one that Tracy was familiar with as a member of law enforcement, though people were rarely charged with it, because it really only covered accidental or careless pointing or firing of a gun. If you were pointing a gun at someone to cause fear of death, that became a felony, assault with a deadly weapon; and that was far more common, since not many people point guns at other people for nice reasons. Tracy clicked open the files on the charge and found that it had been a plea deal. Juan had actually been arrested for a multitude of crimes one night in June of 2008, including assault with a deadly weapon. But his lawyers had worked a miracle and got it all reduced to a gross misdemeanor, $5,000 in fines, and six months in jail.

Tracy started skimming through the police report. Juan and a man named Hector Camargo had been apprehended after a panicked 911 call reporting men with guns outside of a bar in the Sunrise Manor area of town. Tracy noted the bar and area. A police report never signaled anything good, but it went double for the Sunrise Manor area of town. It was close to Nellis Air Force Base and one of the rougher parts of the city. But since it couldn't be seen from the Strip, it didn't bother the tourists, so it was tolerated.

The rest of the report was vague. Whatever reason they'd shown up with guns had been resolved by the time the police showed up. Some witnesses reported several gunshots having been fired. However, there was no physical evidence supporting that, and none of the people directly involved would admit to anything. According to them it was all just a misunderstanding; "these two guys showed up and started waving guns around as a joke," they claimed. The cops on the scene brought them in for the more serious charges they believed them guilty of, but it left enough room that the DA didn't have a strong enough case to make them stick. She scrolled back and typed "Hector Camargo" into the search field. It took a minute to load all of his history. The past few years had been clean, but that was because he was serving a five-year sentence for transportation of a controlled substance.

At the top of the page was the name that jumped out to her; known associates, Edger Mencia. The kingpin of the valley was a known associate of this man. An hour later, Tracy had his life mapped out. Hector had been in the business since he was a teenager. The juvenile stuff was sealed, but it was clear he'd been working his entire life. First it was street dealing, and then more serious charges as he moved up the ladder. By 2008, he appeared to be one of the Mencia organization's enforcers. Multiple charges for varying types of threats and violence, most of them dismissed or pled way down, as had happened with the one at the bar in Sunrise. He finally got hit with a large amount of methamphetamine in the trunk of his car and a judge who wouldn't play ball. That accounted for his current residence in a cell block.

Tracy flipped back to Juan Heredia. His record was pristine in comparison, but the link showed through; he was one person removed from Mencia himself. A reasonable person could assume that since he and Hector had had the same charges brought against them and shared the same lawyer, they'd been working together at the time of the gun charges. The cops on the scene were probably right; this was the delivery of a threat to someone who had defied Edger Mencia, instead of just some casual gunplay in the middle of the night.

Tracy leaned back in her chair and looked over to Bill. "I think I got something you should look at."

Day 7, 10:00 am

LUCAS GREEN

We had finished another walk around the neighborhood. I hadn't expected I'd be so active while I was in Las Vegas—not many people plan on getting into exercise when they're visiting the desert—but here I was. Deputy was part of the cover, and he needed to be walked to an extent, though he probably would've argued against it, being as resigned to the world as he was. Grant, on the other hand, needed the exercise, but had to be coerced into doing it. After Tracy had left last night, he had spent the rest of the night on the couch, plowing through another half season of *Seinfeld*. It could've been worse; he could be one of those people who watched the Kardashians or *Real Housewives*, although their audience was mostly women. If Grant had chosen to watch that, I probably would've killed him myself yesterday and been completely justified.

This morning the TV was back on before I had even woken up, as if we were just living through yesterday once again. So I forced him to get his shoes on and we were out on the street. It really didn't matter to me if Grant drank himself to death or gave everything up and moved back home. What did matter was that as long as he was hiding on my couch, there couldn't be any more attempts on his life; and if that didn't happen, then I couldn't leave. Every day I spent babysitting him was a day of my life that I could never get back, so pushing him forward was the best path for the both of us. But mostly for me.

"The show starts at 9 pm tonight," I said, walking back into the house.

"Okay," he answered, trudging along behind me.

"Do you want to get dinner first?"

"Guess so." He made a bee line for the couch again.

"What about clothes?"

"You said we could go shopping." He looked back at me. So I had. Apparently the Xbox, the clothes he was wearing, and the rest of the stuff I'd salvaged from his house were good enough to keep using, but not the rest of his clothes.

"Where do you want to go shopping?" There's a Target a couple of blocks away; that should suffice.

"We should go to the mall."

"The mall?"

"Yeah, the outlet mall downtown is really nice."

"Alright. Let's get going, then."

* * *

Thirty-three minutes later, we were pulling into the parking garage at Las Vegas North Premium Outlets. Even though it was 11 am, the parking garage was practically full, causing us to keep climbing higher and higher until we ended up on the top deck. "Where do you think we should start?" Grant asked once we were parked and walking toward the elevator.

"I don't know. What are you looking for?" I hadn't brought any going-out clothes to Vegas. However, I suspected that jeans and a nice shirt would suffice for a comedy show on the Strip. In my experience down there, if you were attending an event, you'd come across people who were elegantly dressed and people wearing the same stuff they wore to the pool. So landing in the middle wasn't the worst thing you could do.

"Have you ever shopped at Brooks Brothers?" he asked as we arrived at the elevator doors.

"A suit? You want to get a suit?" I responded, while pushing the button on the wall.

"You think that's too much?"

"Is Tom Segura wearing a suit on stage?"

"No, probably not."

"If the guy on stage isn't that dressed up, you probably don't need to be." I hit the button again. The faded, weathered plastic made it hard to tell if it had lit up or not.

"I don't want to wear my usual stuff. That's why I was thinking of something nicer."

"That's fine. How about a pair of slacks and a nice sweater?"

He wrinkled his nose. "It's Vegas, though. A sweater seems like a bit much."

"It's going to be cold in the theater. And if you want to dress nicely, you can't have your bare arms hanging out."

"That's true."

"Okay, how about jeans and a sport coat?" I pitched back, jamming the elevator button again.

"That'd be nice. You know, I've never owned a sport coat."

"We can check Brooks Brothers for one."

"Okay. I don't think the elevator works here." He pointed down the elevator shaft. The exterior sides were glass-paneled so you could watch the car rise and fall. "Last time I was here it didn't work either, and it looks like it's just stuck on the floor below us."

"I guess we're taking the stairs, then." Just what this day needed, more walking.

Twenty minutes later, Grant was modeling jackets with a kindly elderly gentleman who was helping him make his decision. I'm not much for fashion montages, so I slipped out the doors and was sitting in the shade outside. Pulling out my job phone, I dialed the number. A few moments later, Javy's distinctive voice ground into my ears. "What?"

"I need two phones. iPhones, recent models."

"You already have a phone."

"This isn't my letter to Santa. I need two iPhones, today."

"Why today?"

"Because I said so."

Silence came from the other end. For all his

blustering, Javy knew his place in the hierarchy, which was to facilitate my work. Ever since Carlos had floated the idea of me moving against Miguel, it should've been clear to him why his boss had made the decision to hire me. It was to field-test my abilities and then unleash it on his own brother, at less risk to himself. Sending Javy against Miguel would cause a civil war, which the Guerra crew would be lucky to survive. But a heart attack or a car crash, like I was known to cause, would be the perfect opportunity for Carlos to make his move. Javy knew that now.

"I'm busy for the next two hours," I continued. "I can meet at 2:30 at the Home Depot if you'll be ready by then."

"2:30." His voice echoed through the phone as the call ended.

Grant burst out of the store right as I was sliding the phone back into my pocket. "I think this jacket looks amazing," he chortled, joining me on the bench.

"That's good. Are we all done now?"

"I think I still need some shoes. What do you think?"

"It would look funny if you showed up in your socks."

He laughed as he stood up. "Let's go find the directory."

Day 7, 1:00 pm

BILL STRIDER

Bill was driving this time. He and Tracy were heading to a pawn shop. One of the snowboards from the Dupree robbery had been reported at a shop on Charleston. It was the very first hint of anything turning up from that case.

Tracy was busily skimming through the case file as Bill guided the car through the traffic. It was the middle of the day so it wasn't too bad, but there wasn't a direct route to the shop, so he was winding through the surface streets.

"A pawn shop is a weird place to shop for a snowboard, isn't it?" Tracy asked, still looking at the files.

"What do you go shopping for at pawn shops?"

"I've never actually shopped at a pawn shop."

"Well, aren't you the sophisticate."

The pawn shop wasn't much, even by the

standards of a shop that deals in things people wanted to get rid of. However, they did stock a surprisingly large amount of ammunition. The rest of the shop was the usual assorted junk being passed off as merchandise—old musical instruments, prehistoric power tools, and rusty workout equipment, which was extra-strange since the dry desert climate didn't promote rusting.

"Do you need any bullets?" Tracy asked Bill quietly, nodding to the large Ziploc bags of ammo sitting on the shelves.

"I buy ammo at these places sometimes."

"Really?"

"Yeah. It's mostly reloads from all the gun ranges on the Strip. It's cheap and good enough for target shooting." While Tracy had completed all of her weapons training and dutifully visited the police firing range as often as was required, she didn't have much interest in guns for fun. She had her service weapon that she carried during business hours, and a smaller version of the weapon she carried while off-duty.

"Most cops only fire their weapon twice a year during their required range time," he continued. "That's insane. If you have to draw your weapon, your life is going to depend on how prepared you are to use that gun and if the answer is, 'Six months ago I shot a couple mags,' you better hope the other guy hasn't shot in seven months."

Tracy nodded. Her last session on the range had been three months ago. And that reminded her, she hadn't cleaned her personal gun after that trip. She had cleaned the service pistol as expected, but set the other gun aside for later, and never got back to it once she started moving into the new house.

"I'll take you out to the range I shoot at. It's down in Boulder, but it's a lot of fun." She'd spent enough time with Bill now to know that this was his polite way of suggesting that Tracy needed to become more active with her firearm training.

"Why do you drive all the way out there to shoot? There are plenty of ranges in town."

"It's outside, and you can set up your own courses and practice different scenarios. It's better than just shooting at paper." He pulled out his badge and flashed it at the man behind the cash register. "Detective Strider. I believe we spoke on the phone earlier."

"I'll go get it," the man answered, looking rather annoyed that someone was bothering him at work. A minute later he returned from the back room, the bright red board gleaming in the light. "Someone brought this in yesterday." He dropped it onto the counter.

"Have you ever snowboarded?" Bill asked as he took the board, starting to inspect it.

"Me?" Tracy responded, slightly surprised. But he could only be talking to her; the man behind the counter looked like he had trouble just standing on flat ground.

"Yes, you."

"I've been up to Mount Charleston once. My dad used to ski back in Michigan. He tried to teach me, but I didn't like it."

"Hand me the page for this board."

Flipping the folder open, Tracy scrolled through until a page with a picture of a red Burton board showed up, handing it over to Bill.

"This isn't the one we're looking for," he announced, handing the paper back to Tracy.

"Really?" Tracy and the employee said in unison.

"Yep. This is a 162 wide board." He jabbed his finger at the marking near the center of the board. "The one we want is just a 162."

"So I can put it back up?" the man asked.

"It's yours. You can do as you please," Bill responded simply. "Thanks for calling us." He gave the man a nod and turned away to leave.

Back in the car, Tracy stuffed the item page back into its proper spot in the file. "It did seem weird that they'd steal all that stuff just for one piece to end up in a pawn shop like that," she said once they were rolling again.

"Yeah, I figured if it was the one we wanted, it would've changed hands a few times before it got here." He pulled the car back onto Charleston Boulevard. "What are you going to do about Juan Heredia?" They were done with their assigned mission of snowboard recovery and could now slip back into the conversation they wanted to have.

"I haven't thought about it yet."

"Pull him over."

"You think so?"

"Yep. Track him down and pull him over for something, and see how it goes."

"I'm not really a traffic cop." A detective pulling someone over for a busted taillight or improper lane shift wasn't that common.

"He won't know that. Just get a feel for him and see how he reacts. He used to work for a cartel member. Now he's an electrician. Is that all he is, or did he just get reassigned to a different section of the cartel?"

Tracy nodded. It wasn't her style to be pulling people over to further her off-the-books investigation into a company that hadn't committed a crime that she was aware of. However, looking through the database and Grant's file cabinet was only going to get her so far.

"Alright, I'll see if I can track him down when we get back."

Day 7, 2:47 pm

CARLOS GUERRA

Carlos drummed his fingers on the new granite countertop. They had just been installed the day before, so the protective plastic layer still clung to the cold rock. Since his brother was out of town dealing with the money-laundering side of things offshore, he was running the day-to-day operations here in town, which surprisingly was boring.

Miguel had built a high-functioning system that didn't need much hands-on leadership day to day. The product was picked up from Mencia's randomized drop points outside of the city. It was normally Carlos or Javy who carried out that duty. They drove it the rest of the way into town and brought it to a renovation project. In there the team chopped it up, sorted it into retail-sized amounts, and bagged it. Doing the work in different places every month was complicated—the equipment had to be transportable—but it wasn't that

212

hard. The different locations meant that the product was kept away from anything legally owned by BBR; since the houses were owned by G Inc. on paper, that would require a separate warrant if the police ever got tipped off.

Getting a judge to sign off on searching a third party's property would be more complicated, which was why Miguel set it up that way. The more difficult an investigation into their activities was, the less likely they'd ever be targeted. The police were very careful about spending taxpayer money when it came to things that didn't directly benefit the department. A helicopter, a missile-shooting drone, or a tank for their SWAT team, they'd spend money on those new toys like a lotto winner placing bets at the Bellagio. Spending money on overtime for surveillance, chasing warrants, and cracking international banking records, then they're suddenly fiscally conservative. *It's just not worth the public's money for us to be worrying about stuff like that, but check out our new Bluetooth-compatible surface-to-air rocket launchers!*

Once the product was divided up, it was delivered to the street dealers. This was the most dangerous part of the operation. Sure, getting caught coming back from the desert with a trunk full of gak would result in some serious time, but everyone involved was a professional who was serious about precautions. However, the street dealers were by definition not careful. They were young, dumb, and probably partaking in their product as well. They were basically the foot soldiers of drug dealing, and foot soldiers existed to be sacrificed.

Miguel's system had worked out dead drops for the

drugs. The actual dealers never saw who they were buying from, and they received instructions on delivering the money weekly from random phone numbers. Several of the dealers had been picked up over the years, but the only information they could provide about their suppliers was so scant that the detectives could never work up the chain. It was as if they were dealing with a ghost. It helped that Miguel kept obsessive track of the dealers, issuing them detailed instructions on how to corner their markets and provide a better customer experience. That was backed by the strong arm of Carlos and Javy. If a dealer was slipping, they'd find themselves face-to-face with them in the most unexpected locations. They only had to teach a few lessons before everyone caught on that the suppliers were not to be trifled with if you wanted to retain all of your body parts in working order.

A few times an outside party had made trouble with the dealers and that was Carlos's favorite part of the job. Once in Green Valley, a couple frat boy types had thought that the local dealer, a younger kid named Ernesto, was an easy mark. They'd been used to pushing kids like him around their entire life and figured the same thing would work on Ernesto. They roughed him up one night and spent the entire next day running through the entire supply they had gotten off of him. Ernesto was smarter than he looked, though, and once he was able, he followed the protocol and called in a Code X-Ray. The two gap-year boys were partying at the Mandalay Bay pool when Javy tracked them down. A short while later, two beautiful women approached them and they became fast friends. Ninety minutes later, both boys were fast asleep in the back of Carlos's truck. They wandered into Indian Springs, Nevada a couple days later, fifty miles outside the city, both missing a finger and a hefty sum from their bank accounts. The money had been willingly given after they woke up in the desert, but the fingers had been taken anyway.

So there was excitement to be had in the business, but that was the exception. The usual was boring routine work like scouting drop locations, organizing burner phones, and checking boxes in the complicated spreadsheets that Miguel had designed.

The rumble of Javy's truck pulled Carlos out of his daze in the new kitchen. He knew far more about installing cabinetry than he ever wished to. He and Lucas walked in a moment later. "Looks like you all have been busy," Lucas commented, looking around at the renovations.

"Unlike you," Carlos answered back evenly.

"Art can't be rushed, I've explained that to you several times."

"I've heard that excuse every time you've come here. And now you need phones to get your job done?" Carlos slid the two phones across the countertop toward Lucas.

"You didn't hear about the two burglars Grant shot dead in his house the other night?" Lucas said cooly, picking the phones up and slipping them into his pocket. "I thought a development like that wouldn't have escaped your notice."

Carlos looked back at Javy, who shrugged unknowingly at him. "Either way, he's still alive."

"That's true, but it's not my fault the thieves I sent in there are so slow on the draw." Lucas looked back at Javy. "But sometimes you don't get to pick who you work with."

"So what now?" Javy shot back. "Someone tried to kill him. Another attack will look suspicious."

"Very insightful," Lucas answered.

"He's right," Carlos said. "He gets shot now and it looks like he was a target. We're paying you to make sure no one looks into it."

"I'm aware of the difficulties. I'm handling it."

"With phones?" Javy sneered.

"With whatever I believe needs to be done. You know, your intimidation tactics would work a lot better if you weren't also begging me to take on more work for you."

"Fuck you," Javy said.

"You want your brother dead," Lucas continued, directing his comments straight at Carlos. "That's not something that should be multi-tasked. One at a time is enough. I finish Grant and then we can talk about what needs to happen to go that far up the chain, and how much more it'll cost."

"You're right," Carlos said. "You should focus on the task at hand, since so far it appears to be too much for you to handle. And since you're so distracted by costs, let me assure you the cost of us having to intervene would be much greater."

"Duly noted. Are we done?"

Carlos nodded slowly as Javy stepped forward. "Let's go," he ordered.

* * *

I climbed back into Javy's truck, currently carrying four phones. I already had the tracking devices we'd use; they were part of the shopping list I'd given Harold the other day. At the time I didn't have a specific purpose in mind; they were just useful to have around. It was always better to have one and not need it than need one and not have it, as the saying goes.

"I'm going to need something else as well," I said as Javy drove us back to my car. Javy just glared at me. "A couple of Xanaxes."

"Xanax?"

"Yes. Grant just shot two people in his living room, and believe it or not, he's running a little off-kilter at the moment. A perfect reason for him to take pills to mellow him out and let him sleep through the night."

"So you feel sorry for him and his sleep schedule?"

"It also has the side effect of slowing reaction times and mental dexterity. I'm sure you can see how that would benefit our side of the equation."

"I know plenty of people on Xanax. They seem perfectly normal."

"That's because they're used to taking them. Grant's an Advil kinda person. Get some real drugs in his mouth and he won't be able to walk."

"Fine, I can get you some."

"When?" I demanded. I was talking to a drug dealer, after all.

"I don't know, tomorrow."

"You don't have any on you?"

"No, I sleep fine, even though I've shot more

people than your boyfriend."

"That's a sign of a psychopath."

"You're one to talk."

"Just get me the pills tomorrow."

Day 7, 5:05 pm

TRACY COOK

Back in front of her computer, Tracy had dug into Juan and the information they had on him. He personally owned a Honda Civic and a Honda CRV, seemingly his wife's vehicle. He was also listed on the BBR insurance as a primary driver of the company's 2009 Chevy Express cargo van. Bill agreed it was the perfect vehicle for an electrician; white vans had become something of a common target for their investigations.

The current electrical permits under his name were for a property on the northish side of town, the most recent property filed in the G Inc. cabinet. Those were the only facts available to her; the rest was just assumption that he'd still be there and would be leaving the job site around 5 pm.

Tracy got there around 4:40, and the van was sitting in the driveway. So far so good. She drove out of the neighborhood and set up position on the street, waiting for him to head home for the night. It didn't take long. Even if BBR was a front for illegal activities, you could at least commend them for treating their employees right.

Juan and his white van were heading directly west, not in the direction of the BBR office but toward his home. Tracy trailed after him, for a while on the smaller cross streets that bisected the subdivision part of the town and finally onto a bigger commercialized street as he stayed westbound. It was hard to tell if he was driving carefully to avoid attracting attention, or if he was just a boring driver. Las Vegas had the reputation for hosting some very aggressive drivers, but Juan was not one of them. He slowed on yellows and cruised at the speed limit the entire way home. He was making it hard to pull him over, even with a cop watching his every move.

Finally, as Juan shifted into the left lane, he failed to use his blinker. Tracy breathed a sigh of relief. Pulling him over just because she wanted to get a look at him for her own personal investigation was pushing the limits of acceptable behavior enough, so making up an infraction to justify the stop was more than she wanted to do. She followed him on through the turn, flipping her lights on once they were safely on the side street he'd led them down. Juan responded immediately, his hazards coming on, and he drifted to a stop along the sidewalk.

With both cars stopped, Tracy climbed out and made her approach. It'd been awhile since she'd conducted a traffic stop. Her biggest fear doing them was getting hit by a passing vehicle while on the side of the road. Luckily, they were on a smaller street and there shouldn't be any reckless driving going on in the middle of the day. Juan already had his window rolled down and his license and registration waiting for her. "Hello," she greeted him, staying back just far enough that the door frame provided some shielding if he was planning on shooting at her, as had been drilled into her at the academy. But there was nothing threatening in sight, just Juan and his paperwork. "License and registration, please." Juan handed them over without comment. "I'll run these and be back," she said, stepping back toward her car. There wasn't any need to run the checks on him. She'd already done that at the office and knew what they showed. Still, it would've looked weird if she didn't follow standard procedure.

After spending a few minutes waiting in her car, she returned to Juan's window. "Here you go, sir." He nodded and took the documents back. "I pulled you over for not signaling your lane shift back there."

"Sorry about that, officer." He spoke in clear English. Tracy had wondered if he wasn't particularly fluent in English and that was why he was remaining silent, but apparently, he spoke it well, so he was choosing to remain quiet on purpose.

"Is there somewhere you are trying to go in a hurry?"

"Just heading home from work."

"Oh, yeah? What do you do?"

"I'm a residential electrician."

"So you repair lights, fix outlets, that kind of stuff?" So far he wasn't revealing much at all. He was clearly older than most people who got caught in the drug business, which tended to attract a younger crowd. By the time they were Juan's age, they were either in prison or at the top administrative level, driving Lamborghinis and wearing too much cologne.

"I work for a renovation company, so I handle the electrical work for that." He gestured toward the company logo on the side of the door.

"Interesting. How long have you worked for them?"

"About ten years now."

"That's impressive. What did you do before that?"

Juan gave her a hard look. Clearly, his past wasn't something he wanted to discuss with the police. "Mostly odd jobs, nothing serious."

"You had some run-ins with the law back then, huh?"

"I was young and grew up in a bad neighborhood."

"You've left that all behind now?"

"I learned my lesson, officer. I'm just an electrician now, and that's all I do."

"So you never do any work for Edgar Mencia?"

He bristled at that charge. "I haven't seen Mencia in over a decade. I grew up in a bad neighborhood. Not everyone gets out right away." He gave Tracy a long look. "You're a detective, aren't you?"

"I am, and I know you worked as an enforcer for the cartel."

"Like I said, I've learned my lesson," he said stiffly, turning his head forward so he didn't have to look at her anymore.

"Juan, if there's anything you want to talk about,

I'm happy to listen. Things going on at the renovations, your old friends dropping by once in a while for favors. I could help you."

"I'm an electrician. Unless you know how to get new lights in a ceiling without going into the attic, I don't need any help." He continued staring forward.

"Very good, then. I'll just give you a warning about not using your blinkers. Have a nice day, sir." Her voice was menacingly warm.

"You, too," he answered as the window rolled up. He drove away before Tracy was even back to her own car.

Day 7, 8:03 pm

GRANT ANDERSON

"I haven't been to this casino before," Lucas said as they walked through the doors from the parking garage into the brand new building, housing the Strip's newest casino.

"Me neither. I've heard it's really nice," Grant answered.

Most of the casinos were meticulously maintained; the shine was part of the experience. Of course, this particular mega-center sat on the ground that used to be covered by one of the originals; that wasn't so shiny anymore. The first wave of casinos that had formed the Las Vegas Strip were being replaced by behemoths. The low-slung neon-covered buildings that had made Vegas famous weren't worth the space they were taking up anymore. The same spot of coveted ground could house a gambling floor twice the size, plus a nightclub and a day spa, with a lavish pool and a spacious theater thrown in. That was what this building housed; everything you could possibly want from a Vegas vacation was located in this complex. If the casino had it their way, you'd never leave the premises until your flight back to whatever dull land from whence you came.

"Do you gamble much?" Grant asked as the pair walked across the glittering marble floors. The interior was as pristine as could be, every window streak-free and not a fleck of gunk on the floors, yet it was missing something. Personality. The charm of the older themed resorts was lacking. In the buildings that had made Las Vegas famous, you had a feeling the decor had been picked out because it was unique or cool in a sense. In the stark modern ones, you could tell that every detail had been a consensus decision to be the least offensive and most soothing choice possible. The goal wasn't to be bold or interesting in their designs, but purposefully forgettable. The worst fear of the executives wasn't that their casinos were boring, but that they could be mocked. No one wanted to stay in a Medieval-themed resort anymore, or pirate-themed. There was too much money involved to risk becoming part of a humiliating social media trend. It was a safer bet to blend in than stand out, and casinos only made safe bets. So every new resort that went up became indistinguishable from each other, a glamorous reminder that the entire structure was built with the sole purpose of getting your money. They couldn't even be bothered to make the experience memorable.

"No, I'm not much of a gambler," Lucas answered.

"I don't understand the people who play the slot machines. It doesn't look fun at all." Grant pointed over to the rows of machines, entertaining their users as they poured money into it.

"Yeah, me, either. The fun wears off pretty quickly." After their shopping trip, Grant and Lucas had returned to the house. Lucas had slipped off for his meeting to collect the decoy phones for tonight, making it back just in time to deal with the cleaning crew that had arrived. They had toured the house and set to work scrubbing out the blood stains while Grant relaxed on the couch watching another season of *Seinfeld*. They had finished their cleaning just before it was time to leave for the Strip, but they said the house needed to air out for about a day to diffuse all the chemicals they'd sprayed in there. Grant would be spending another night on the couch either way. Perhaps tomorrow he'd feel recovered enough to enter his own house.

After a few minutes of walking, the two roommates had found the entrance to the theater. It was hard to miss with the giant line of people shuffling forward slowly toward the doors. Inside the lobby, it was more of the same—carpet designed to disgust people so that they stay focused on the gambling, walls that were painted bland neutral colors, and artwork hung on the walls that looked like they'd been painted to purposefully be unappealing to look at.

"Do you want a drink?" Grant asked, once they'd both made it out of the bathroom.

"Sure, but we need to find Tracy's mom," Lucas reminded him. If her credit card reader was dishonest, they needed to test it out.

"Do you know what she looks like?" Grant asked, scanning the crowd for waitresses.

"No, but we're supposed to be sitting in her section. It's over there." He pointed toward the far left side of the lobby.

The usher at the door checked their tickets and sent them through into the actual theater. It was much bigger than you'd expect for something attached to a casino. Lucas had been expecting a glorified nightclub, but instead it was a full-sized auditorium with a balcony and stadium seating. The resort looked massive from the outside, but he'd missed whatever part housed this spectacle.

"These are them," Grant said, pointing to the two seats on the end, only four rows from the stage.

"I hope this isn't one of those shows where they smash watermelons, because we're in the splash zone," Lucas remarked, nodding toward the curtained stage.

"No, Tom's just a regular standup. You know that, you've heard his podcasts."

"Yeah, I was just joking," Lucas said, taking his seat. "Keep an eye out for the waitress. Her name's Shelly."

"Okay." Grant said he was watching for Shelly to appear, but his attention seemed wholly focused on the curtain covering the stage, as if Tom Segura was just going to jump through it any moment and start the show. "Have you seen any of his shows before?" Grant asked over his shoulder.

"No, I haven't been to many live shows," Lucas answered. It was his belief that almost every live performance was better watched from the comfort of his own couch than in the confines of plastic seats and unruly strangers pressing against him.

"I went and saw Bill Burr in Atlanta last year and it was terrible. The guy behind me talked the entire time, then started screaming things at him from the balcony. The guy in front of me got so drunk, he was on the phone with his Uber driver in the middle of the show."

"I'm sure the Vegas crowd will behave better," Lucas commented, even though looking around at the mass of people, he didn't believe it. Most of them looked like they'd already been drinking for a while and were lucky to have stumbled into the show they'd bought tickets for.

"There's a waitress," Grant said, pointing across the section of seats to the middle aisle. The woman he was pointing at was definitely younger than Tracy.

"I don't think that's Tracy's mom."

"Yeah, probably not. She has blond hair." He turned back to the still-covered stage.

Before Lucas could dig into that thought, he spotted someone who could be old enough to be Tracy's mother, even if she was doing her best to hide that fact. "I think I see her. Give me your credit card and wait here."

Grant did as he was told, distractedly fumbling with his wallet to produce his Visa. Lucas took it from him and left him there, still staring at the stage. Walking back up the aisle, he approached the waitress. "Hi, Shelly?" He asked it like a question, but her name tag had already confirmed the fact before he spoke.

"Hi, can I help you?" Her voice was welcoming, even though her eyes didn't seem to agree.

"Yes, I'm Lucas, a friend of Tracy's."

Her eyes got wide. "Oh."

"I think I should buy a drink from you," Lucas said, holding out Grant's credit card.

"Of course. What would you like?"

"Two Jack and Cokes, please." He wasn't sure if it was a good idea for Grant to be drinking, considering he was acting pretty drunk on his own, but at this point it couldn't hurt.

Shelly took his card and swiped it through the machine. "There's something different about this one, I know it," she whispered as she worked the device.

"You know where our seats are at?" Nodding, she handed the card back to him. "There will be two iPhones under the seats at the end of the night." He slipped the card back into his wallet.

"I'll go get you your drinks and bring them to your seat," she said.

Day 7, 11:15 pm

TRACY COOK

Tracy hung up the phone. It was her mother, confirming that she'd retrieved the two phones Lucas and Grant had left and had deposited them with her boss, just like she'd done with the other lost items. Her mother had then rambled for another ten minutes about all the other stuff Garrett had done that made her mad—rude comments, correcting her grammar, and forcing her to cover up her tattoos when she was working. None of it constituted a crime, but offended her mother, nonetheless. She believed this guy was setting her up to take the fall for an impressive amount of theft, yet she was angrier that he made her wear a long-sleeve shirt at work.

Looking back at the corkboard she'd erected, she pinned the blown-up mugshot of Juan Heredia to it. It had finally reached the point where there were so many details, the case was starting to blur together in her mind so a visual representation had to be created. The colored strings stretched from Mencia to Heredia, and from his picture to BBR's logo, and then to a piece of paper she had scrawled "G Inc." across. There was no logo to be found for that company, so handwriting would have to do. The lines connected, or "dots" if you preferred that popular phrase; however, the connection didn't amount to anything yet, just coincidence or happenstance at this point. But Tracy knew there was something going on with these companies.

Flipping through her phone, she found Lucas's name and dialed it. He answered on the first ring. "Hey, how did it go?" she asked.

"Good. We ran the card and left the phones, like we talked about."

"Alright. My mom said she found them and delivered them like the others."

"Good. I'll check the tracker website when I get home. We're still driving back."

"I don't think they'll move until the middle of the night. Depending on how long the loadout takes, my mom's friend says it'll take several hours before everything's loaded up."

"Okay. I'll send you the link to it in a little bit."

"Sounds good. I'll check in with you in the morning."

"Will do. Have a good night."

Tracy responded the same and ended the call. She hoped she wouldn't need a board for that investigation as well. Hopefully if there actually was someone stealing things from the theater, they'd take it home with them tonight and the case would wrap itself up nicely.

Tracy picked up the picture of Grant and looked at it. If he was involved, he wouldn't have been so helpful with the G Inc. files. She hadn't known they existed until he told her about them and helped her sort through all the papers. Yet if G Inc. was laundering money through their real estate investments, they'd need an agent to help them with it.

She tacked the photo up next to his uncle.

Day 8, 8:05 am

TRACY COOK

It was a forty-minute drive out of the city to get to High Desert State Prison. Tracy had made the drive plenty of times before. It was easy, just get on I-95 north and cruise through the barren wastelands until you arrived. The valley was the limit of Las Vegas; as soon as you crossed out of its perimeter, there was nothing but open country.

Finally, the turn arrived. It wasn't even a traditional highway exit, just a road intersecting with the highway. Turn left and head towards the only buildings visible for miles. There were two other correctional facilities clustered out there you had to drive past before you got to High Desert, the one housing the more serious criminals and where Hector Camargo had been spending his time for the past two years.

There was no gate to drive through; just find a parking spot and walk in. Tracy showed her badge, signed the proper forms, and left her belongings and service weapon in the lockers before being escorted to the interview rooms. She had called ahead this morning so Hector was already waiting for her when she arrived. He was handcuffed to the table in his orange jumpsuit, looking impatient, as if this interview was keeping him from something important. His eyes glared with anger as Tracy entered the room, his shaved skull glistening in the florescent lighting.

"Mr. Camargo, I'm Detective Tracy Cook with the LVMPD Robbery division," she greeted him, taking her seat across the steel table.

"I don't give a fuck. Why'd you drag me down here this early?" he growled back in slightly accented English.

"I'm here to talk about this incident." She spread the folder open. It was the "Aiming a Gun at a Human Being" case Juan Heredia had been involved in.

Hector's eyes didn't leave Tracy's face as she showed him the papers. "It was a misunderstanding," he answered evenly.

"I don't think you even looked at this report."

"Don't need to. Anything you guys got with my name on it was a misunderstanding."

"I see." Tracy pulled out a paper from the back of the folder. It was the summary of the case that had resulted in the current conviction which sent Hector here. "Was this a misunderstanding as well? Several pounds of methamphetamine sitting in the back seat of your car?" Hector didn't answer. "Maybe you were just holding it for a friend. Or maybe you didn't know it was meth. It does look like rock candy, after all. Did you think you'd made a big score of dessert?"

"Mis-un-der-stand-ing," he said in a slow, drawn-out manner.

"Be that as it may," Tracy continued, sliding the paper back into the folder, "I think you misunderstand me."

"You? Really? So you aren't just some bitch come up to shake me down over some shit from years ago?"

"Actually, I'm not here about you at all. I'm here about someone you used to work with, Juan Heredia."

Hector scoffed. "There ain't anything to know about Juan Heredia."

"He was arrested with you during this misunderstanding. Had the same lawyer, got the same deal as you. Seems like you two were friends, or you at least had one friend in common."

"Juan's a good guy. He just got caught in the wrong place at the wrong time and some confusion happened."

"Confusion that involved pointing guns at people? He'd have to be carrying a gun for a mistake like this to happen, and I've never seen his name appearing on any concealed carry permits."

"You really think I got anything to say about Juan? Is this your first day on the job, honey? Juan was just a guy in the neighborhood, and that's it." More annoyance was showing through.

"What's Juan been up to lately?"

"I don't know. We don't get too many visitors in this corner of the desert."

"I'm just trying to understand what happened. You work for Edgar Mencia, enforcing his will around town, and one day you bring this Juan guy with you and then he just retires? I didn't think the cartel offered early retirement."

"They can arrange a retirement for you if you want one," he sneered.

"I see we've reached the 'groundless threats' phase of the conversation. If Juan's out of the business, why can't you talk about him?"

"We don't talk about people, period, bitch. Juan was around and then he went to work for Miguel. Got him doing electrical work or something."

Tracy jumped back slightly. "You know Miguel Guerra?"

Hector looked toward the window, slamming his fists on the table. "I don't know shit. I don't even know this Juan guy. It was one night, years ago."

"But you do know Miguel Guerra, the owner of Battle Born Renovations. How do you know him?" Tracy said, pressing harder.

"I want my lawyer," Hector answered.

"Is that the same lawyer Mencia has on retainer? The one who got you and Juan the sweet deal?"

"None of that matters. I want him here. Go call him and tell him you got questions for me and see what he says."

"That's alright, I think I got what I came for. It was nice meeting you, Mr. Camargo."

"Fuck off."

"I hope you enjoy the rest of your stay here," she said with a smile, standing up and collecting the folder. "I hear this part of the desert is really lovely this time of year. And the next year, and the year after that."

Hector didn't answer, just purposefully stared out the window as she exited. Hector Camargo had been as uncooperative as expected, but he'd let one piece of useful information slip. Miguel Guerra wasn't just a small business owner, renovating the out-of-date homes in the Las Vegas valley. He was also somehow connected to the Mencia operation. If your name was known in those circles, it meant you were important in some kind of way.

The drive back from High Desert had gone pretty quickly, mostly because Tracy was reliving the conversation over in her head the entire way. Hector knowing Miguel suggested that Miguel had been involved in some way with the Mencia organization, although his record had come up clean. Tracy had double-checked when she had gotten back to the car, pulling out her laptop and combing through his name. Just like she'd remembered, his history was clear of anything serious, just traffic violations, which had been paid promptly and without incident. His name didn't come up in any cross-reference with Mencia or Hector. If anyone who'd investigated those two had ever encountered Miguel in their search, they'd never made a note of it. As far as the public record was concerned, Miguel was nothing more than a small business owner who kept busy renovating single-family homes.

Tracy guided her car off the highway and onto Sahara Avenue. The trackers Lucas had installed on the two phones they had "lost" at the Tom Segura show were still reporting that they had barely moved since last night. Lucas had sent over the link to the app that followed them, and Tracy had been checking it ever since. At first, they pinged on the map inside the resort, but sometime during the night that had moved to the very edge of the property. Looking at the map view of it, it would suggest the phones had been tossed into the dirt lot that separated the resort's property from the strip club behind it. That was what Tracy had driven down here to investigate.

The back lot of the casino was still pretty rough-looking. When they'd leveled the old casino, they'd turned the entire lot into a dirt pad before rebuilding the new structure. The new buildings didn't use the entire plot of land, so the back edges of it had been left to the wild, which in Vegas meant homeless encampments and trash blown by the harsh desert wind. It was this scene she drove past, keeping an eye on her phone as it showed her creeping closer to the blinking light that represented the tracking device. Weaving around a couple of dumpsters, she found what she was looking for, three semi-trailers lined up at the edge of the driveway. The app blinked faster as she neared them, until it told her she was only a few feet away from the missing phones as she glided to a stop behind the trailers. The back doors were padlocked shut; she could see them from her seat. The phones had indeed been loaded up last night like Shelly had said they'd be, but they hadn't left the property, at least not yet. Since they were still on casino property, there was surely a surveillance camera pointed in this direction. If someone came and removed the case from the trucks here, it'd be caught on video; otherwise, all she could do was wait for the trailers to be moved. Presumably there was someone expecting this gear to be returned.

Tracy checked the time; she was due back at the

station for another meeting of the famous Task Force X. Dean Wilson had been threatening them with forced overtime if they didn't find something incriminating in the mounds of paperwork soon.

She nudged the gas pedal and steered around the trailers. It felt like Shelly and Dean were conspiring to suck up every available free moment she had. Hopefully something would happen soon with this trailer and let her wrap up one of these side investigations.

Day 8, 2:00 pm

LUCAS GREEN

Our adventure at the comedy show last night had gone spectacularly. Grant laughed himself into a fit in the first ten minutes and hadn't stopped talking about his favorite jokes the entire ride home. He seemingly had no memory of why we'd actually bought the tickets to the show or that Tracy's mom was even there. Once we got home, he parked himself right on the couch and re-watched Tom's older comedy specials on Netflix for the rest of the night. However, this morning he'd suffered a relapse and was just cranking through *Seinfeld* episodes once again.

"Hey, Grant. Want to try going on a walk?" I offered.

"No," he answered swiftly, even clicking the volume up a few notches on the TV.

"You know, your house should be all cleaned out and ready to go back into by now. The cleaners said it'd be ready this morning."

He couldn't be bothered to answer that question, but just kept staring at the TV from his curled-up position on the couch. Good thing I didn't actually own that couch; I doubted the smell of him living on it for this many days would ever come out of it.

I left him there as I headed out the door and crossed the street. Several of the windows had been left open by the cleaners, and they'd installed a temporary screen across the openings to keep the bugs out and still let the air flow. The house had a peculiar smell when I'd visited before the deaths, an odd mixture of Paul's junk, the fungus that was surely growing beneath the mess, and Grant's air freshener that he sprayed around there compulsively. It masked the former stench, but just created a new stench of its own.

Now the house smelled of industrial-strength cleaners. The airflow and fans had pushed out enough of the fumes that it wasn't hard to breathe, but the chemical smell remained, which was probably a little better than the original smell. The carpet in the front room had been nearly fully removed, except for the part underneath the bookshelves along the wall. I imagined it wasn't in their contract to move heavy things if there wasn't any gore on them. The blood that ran off the kitchen tile into the front room had seeped all the way through to the concrete slab underneath. The bare concrete nearest to where the bodies had fallen had clearly been scrubbed intensely; the surface of it practically gleamed in comparison to the rest of the bare floor, showing stains scattered across the entire length. The carpet on the stairs and been removed as well, leaving just the bare wooden steps. In the kitchen, all of the tile on the floor, the countertop, and the back splash had been scrubbed so thoroughly that it looked almost brand-new, if you overlooked the tiles shattered by the ricocheting bullets.

On the countertop was a detailed list of the items that'd been thrown away by the cleaners. Most notable was the toaster and microwave; they'd apparently been splattered with some human remains which rendered them unsalvageable. The list included a bunch of other kitchen accessories but all were easily replaced with a trip to Target. This space was now the cleanest part of the entire house by a long shot. It might be a good housekeeping trick to shoot people in some of the other rooms in order to justify calling in the professionals.

Either way, Grant was going to have to make some decisions. He'd been looking to replace the carpet in the entire house previously, but now needed to pull the trigger on what remained. He probably wasn't in the mood to hear that quality joke, but I bet Tom Segura would appreciate it. Standing in his way was the considerable mess that existed in the carpeted rooms upstairs. If you were going to bring people out to install it in the living room and stairs, you might as well do the entire house, but the entire house needed to be relieved of its debris. It was probably time to call in a dumpster to handle the rest of the mess. Grant's methodical and slow approach to the problem wasn't going to work any longer.

My phone rang. Javy. "What?" I said, answering it.

"Your pill bottle is in the bushes out front."

"Quite the delivery service you're operating."

He didn't answer, just ended the call.

I locked Grant's door behind me. There were several bushes in my front yard, and after a quick survey I spotted the pill bottle, a little less than half full. Still, it'd be enough for Grant. He probably couldn't even handle a full dose. Going back in, I found Grant where I'd left him, knee-deep in '90s neuroticism. Pulling the remote out of his reach, I paused the show. "Grant, you need to look at me." He already was, since I was standing between him and the television. "We need to talk about your house."

"I don't want to." He broke his gaze and stared at the ceiling.

"You can't live on my couch watching TV for much longer. You're going to need to go home."

"I'm not going back over there," he stated firmly.

"Then what are you going to do?"

He didn't answer, just stared blankly while stroking Deputy's ears, who was curled up on the floor next to him.

"Grant, do you need to call your family or something? Maybe someone can come out and help you."

"No, I'm not calling them."

"Okay, then you're going to have to make some decisions."

"I can't spend the night in that house. I saw them die in there!" he shouted out, throwing the blankets off of him and jumping to his feet.

"Grant, that's in your mind. What happened in your house has passed. It's over. What you're dealing with is what's in your memory, and I promise you, you'll see those images regardless of what space you find yourself."

"That doesn't make any sense. It happened over there. Right at the stairs."

"You're right, it happened over there, but it's over now. Now it's happening up here." I tapped the side of my head.

"I'm not going back over there."

"So you're going to live on my couch?"

"I'll live in the office if I have to!" he shouted over his shoulder as he retreated to the bathroom.

He hid in there for about an hour. Maybe he was on the toilet the whole time; considering he'd been eating pretty much nothing other than junk food the past couple of days, it'd make sense that he was backed up. Either way, he finally crept out of the bathroom, heading back toward the TV. "Grant, come in here," I called to him from the kitchen.

He sulked in, trying not to make eye contact. "What?"

"Take this." I held out a single Xanax tablet and a glass of water.

"What is it?" he asked, but instinctively accepted the glass.

"It's a Xanax. It'll help you calm down."

"I don't think I need anything. I feel calm."

"Grant." I held the pill up for him to get a better look at it. "Take this. You need a break from whatever's going on in that head of yours. It'll just relax you." He took the pill without further comment and swallowed it down with a sip from the glass.

"Alright, I got some work to take care of, but after that I have an idea for something to do tonight. I think you'll enjoy it." I gave him a pat on the shoulder.

"What is it?"

"It's a surprise. Go back and watch TV and I'll get you when it's time to leave."

Day 8, 3:06 pm

TRACY COOK

Tracy checked the numbers on the side of the house. 7856—that was the one she was looking for. She'd been working her way down the list of homes worked on by Battle Born Renovations. This was the fifth one she'd seen. The records showed that the work had finished in October the previous year and sold only a month later, to a single man named John Matzek. The previous four homes had looked normal from the outside, though no one had answered when she knocked on the doors. So maybe the fifth time was the charm. The exterior looked normal. The national trends in home renovations hadn't caught on in Las Vegas when it came to exterior design. In other areas the farmhouse style was all the rage, with people looking to upgrade their house; but that style was focused on siding, wood accents, and big windows, none of which worked in the desert.

The vast majority of homes here were stucco, and they were all painted some bland color. Wooden porches were beautiful, but not practical in an area when the temperature remained in the nineties even after dark. And large windows were a quick path to having your furniture melt or blowing out your air conditioner. So out here, the updating happened inside. The outsides got an occasional new coat of paint and maybe some adjustments to the landscaping. Besides, even if you wanted to go all-out, having the only house in the neighborhood that looked radically different was a turn-off for most people. These subdivisions were purposefully conformist.

Tracy knocked on the front door and only had to wait a moment before it opened up. "Oh, hello," the man who opened the door greeted her. He was middle-aged and a bit overweight, with the kind of bright brown hair that could only come from a bottle.

"Hello. Mr. Matzek?"

"Yeah, that's me," he answered, his voice falling a bit as he assumed he was getting roped into some kind of sales pitch.

"My name is Tracy Cook. I'm a detective with Las Vegas Metro." She flashed her badge at him.

"A detective?" he asked, looking past her to scan the street.

"Yes, sir. Is everything okay?"

"Yeah," he replied a little distractedly. "I'm expecting a package. I thought that's who you were."

"Oh, sorry to interrupt that. I was wondering if you could answer a few questions for me."

"About what?"

"I'm actually interested in your home. You bought it last year?"

"Yes, I did."

"Did you ever meet the sellers?"

"No, they moved out long before I moved in."

"How about the people who renovated the house? Did you meet any of them?"

"No, I didn't."

"How about the quality of the work? Have you noticed anything that doesn't seem right with the house?"

"What do you mean? Are you investigating my house?" he asked, giving Tracy an annoyed look.

"No, I'm looking into the company that handled the work. It seems they're skipping a lot of corners and charging a lot. That's a form of fraud." It wasn't really the truth, but telling him the truth would probably take an hour to explain, and even Tracy didn't fully understand it all.

"Oh," the man answered, looking a little relieved. "To be honest, there's some things that could use some work. And actually, a week after I moved in, I was having trouble with the outlets in the kitchen. I called my agent and he made some calls, and a guy came out and got it figured out."

"Who did he call?"

"I'm not sure."

"Did they leave a card or anything?"

"No, nothing like that. They didn't have uniforms or anything. Even their truck was blank, no company name on it."

"Was it this man?" Tracy pulled up a picture of

Juan on her phone and showed it to him.

"Yeah, that was him. There was another guy with him, but that guy did most of the work."

Tracy flipped through the photos of the other BBR employees until John stopped her at the last one, the picture of Carlos. "That's the guy. He just kinda stood around while the other guy worked on the outlets. I don't know what he was doing here, since he wasn't dressed for doing any physical work."

"Was there anything else noteworthy? Did they say anything that seemed weird, or talk about something you remember?" Tracy asked.

"Nope, not really. They kept to themselves."

Tracy thanked him for his time and pressed her card into his hand. Walking back to her car, she focused on what he had just told her. None of it was stand-out weird, though in her experience, once a house was sold, the sellers were pretty adamant about not repairing anything. The fact that Juan and Carlos came back out free of charge would suggest they were very sensitive about any questions about their work.

"Detective!" John's voice called out as she was about to sink into the driver's seat.

"Yes?" she answered, jumping back onto the sidewalk. John had followed her down the walkway.

"I just thought of something. I don't know if it's important, though."

"I'll listen to anything."

"Well, the listing for the house said they'd put in new all-wood cabinets. But I wasn't sure about it when I looked at the house, so before I bought it, I had a home inspection done, and specifically asked him to check the cabinets and see if they were all wood. Which he said they were, top of the line."

"Uh-huh." Tracy nodded along.

"But, I still don't think they are." He looked a little ashamed that he had decided to air his grievances about his cabinetry to a police detective.

"Could I look at them?" Tracy asked.

"Sure." He led them back toward the front door and through the house to the kitchen in the rear of it. The cabinets looked nice, painted a solid color that complemented the rest of the room; however, the design and texture of them did give off an aged vibe instead of the sleeker look most modern styles followed.

"I really liked the kitchen, but after I moved in, I made friends with the people who live across the street, and their kitchen looks exactly like mine. The cabinets are identical, just different colors." He reached for the refrigerator. "And look at this." He grabbed either side of the fridge and pulled it forward. It rolled easily across the tile until there was a big enough gap to get behind it. "Look at the side of the cabinets down there." He pointed to the bottom of them. On either side of the hole the fridge lived in, the bases of the cabinets were significantly warped. Not warped like wood, though; bulged out like what happens when composite boards get wet.

"Wood wouldn't do that," Tracy muttered as she ran her hand over them. Grant had talked about this during the tour of the house when she first met him.

"Yeah. And when did they get that wet, if they're brand new?"

Tracy stepped out of the opening and they both rolled the fridge back into place. "So they didn't replace the cabinets, but they claimed they did and your inspector backed them up on it?"

"Yep. That's weird, right?"

"It is. Do you have the name of the inspector you used?"

"Um, yeah. I'll have to go find his card. That stuff is upstairs." He answered without moving.

"I can wait here," Tracy answered firmly.

"Right." He hurried out of the kitchen toward the stairwell they'd passed on their way in.

Day 8, 6:59 pm

LUCAS GREEN

"You want another pill?" I asked as we crossed the street from my house to Grant's driveway.

"Sure," he muttered, trying to avoid looking at the front door of his house. He'd been relaxed for the past few hours, even though he'd just remained sitting on the couch. There was a discernible change to his voice; no one who didn't know him well would've noticed, but having gotten to know him pretty well while he lived on my couch, I did. The Xanax Effect.

I climbed into the driver's seat of his car and had a pill waiting for him once he got situated. I'd told him that my car was technically a company car and shouldn't be used for a trip that was just sightseeing, and he agreed to donate his car to the venture, though it was also clear that he didn't want to drive. Which was perfectly fine, since I wouldn't have ridden in a car he was driving anyway.

"So where are we going?" he asked, once we had made it to the 215 on the far west side of town, heading south.

"I was thinking we could go 'over the hump to Pahrump,' as they say."

"Oh," he answered. Nevada has four congressional districts, and three of them encompass parts of the Las Vegas valley. That should tell you about every other city in the state that isn't Las Vegas. They would barely even appear on a map in a lot of other states. But in Nevada, they get their names on the highway signs and regularly mentioned in the news because of their one claim to fame—legalized prostitution.

"Look, Tracy's calling." Grant held up his phone for me to see.

"Let's just keep this a guys' trip, whaddya think?" I answered.

"She probably just wants to talk about her mom and phones," Grant replied, looking a little confused.

"We'll talk to her later about it," I said, gently pulling the ringing phone out of his grasp and declining the call. A conversation with her would sorta derail the plan already in motion. "Have you thought about what comedy shows you want to see next?" I asked, changing the subject.

"No, not yet. I need to look and see who else is coming to town. I've always wanted to see Dave Chappelle, but I don't think he really tours much."

"Man, everyone was obsessed with his show when I was a kid. Even when I was in Iraq, people wouldn't stop talking about it." It was true; there was a period in my life when entire conversations were had just in

Chappelle quotes.

"You were in the Army?" Grant asked.

"Oh, not really. I was more of a contractor." That was also the truth. I never had enlisted, even though I'd been close to the fighting. But a different, far more lucrative opportunity had opened up and brought me where I was now.

"What did you do over there?" His words made it seem like he was pressing me, but his voice still carried a Xanny slur. Even if I told him, he wouldn't remember.

"Nothing very interesting. Just guarding certain people while they had business over there."

He just nodded. The second dose was kicking in at this point, which was slowing him down like construction on the highway.

What I had told him was true; it was protection for visitors to the active warzone that was Baghdad. But those visitors came from Mexico, Colombia, and Miami, and their business was the drug business. After all, Coca-Cola used World War Two to expand its business across the globe, too. They made a commitment to bring an ice-cold glass of Coke to every GI, regardless of where they were deployed. That expansion model worked like a charm; by the time the atomic clouds dissipated, the Coca-Cola company was firmly entrenched in every corner of the world as the official soft drink of the new American Empire.

That trick didn't escape the notice of the next generation of entrepreneurs. Every time some new frontier was opened up by the great American war machine, it created a new market of customers and suppliers for every kind of merchandise. Afghanistan was a windfall for the cartels, with routine military flights straight from the majestic poppy fields of the Hindu Kush into American bases around the world. Iraq didn't offer the same advantages, but it had its own unique features—customers who had previously been out of reach, and more importantly, easy access to the underworld of the Middle East. Huge amounts of oil-rich Arabs looking to diversify their investments that could be used to finance operations all around the world, often with sovereign protection if the right prince was involved. Plenty of laboratories and factories could be put into production that also received active US military protection after some money got passed around. Even better for the cartels was the literal buffet of American military equipment, all available to the highest bidder, and sometimes not even the highest; there was plenty to go around. Small arms had never been a problem for the cartels; but now the military was "losing" surface-to-air rockets, armored vehicles, and every other type of military hardware, chalked up to being "destroyed" in IED attacks, only to show up again where the cartel needed them the most.

Of course, these emissaries couldn't just show up with a bunch of South American muscle and blend in, so they hired people like me. A typical American of military age who looked the right way and breezed through the cursory background checks. That was my Iraq experience, riding around in G-Wagens and standing guard while two representatives argued about how hard it would be to steal an M1 Abrams main battle tank and ship it to Caracas.

"Grant, why don't you tell me about your family?" I asked once we were on Blue Diamond, with just desert ahead of us.

Day 8, 9:04 pm

GRANT ANDERSON

"What did you say your name was?" she asked as she closed the door behind her.

"Grant," he answered thickly. The second Xanax dose Lucas had given him was dulling his clarity pretty well by this point. He hid his hands in his pockets, his fingers pulling aggressively at the thread he had worked out of the stitching. He was grateful for the dullness induced by the last pill, because this was one of the most anxiety-ridden moments in Grant's life. He was alone with a prostitute in a bedroom.

"Do you want to get comfortable?" she asked, crossing the room toward the bed. Grant watched from his stationary spot just inside the door. When Lucas had led him into the building, he tried to continue forward one step at a time. That brought him to where he was now, with one final step ahead of him.

"What was your name again?" he asked back. He'd

always thought that hearing him talk was a surefire way to kill a woman's interest in sex, so maybe it would work this time.

"It's Violet. Remember, you said that's the name of your sister's cat," she answered softly, taking his hand and pulling him toward the bed.

"Oh, yeah." That actually was the name of his sister's cat, but he didn't remember the conversation. Everything since they had arrived in Pahrump was blurry. He thought back and tried to remember it all.

Lucas had driven them into town and straight here, to the Silk House. "A strip club?" Grant mumbled once they'd found a spot in the parking lot. Las Vegas had plenty of strip clubs to pick from that would've been a much shorter drive.

"It's a little better than a strip club," Lucas answered, leading him up the steps. Grant had been to a few clubs in his time. They were fun, but never as much fun as you hoped for.

Lucas went to the front desk and got them checked in, before another woman guided them through the gift shop into the lounge. This room was surrounded by plush couches and low tables. Against the back wall was the bar with a few patrons sitting at it, scantily-clad women artificially enjoying the conversation. "Grab a seat, I'll get drinks," Lucas ordered.

"None for me," Grant answered, sliding into the nearest couch. There was a small stage and pole in the corner of the room, but it wasn't the focal point of the room. In fact, it looked like it was there more as decoration.

"Hello." The voice of the woman suddenly

standing next to him sounded loud in his ear.

"Hey," he answered.

"I'm Violet." She extended her hand. She had short blond hair, and the right side of her head was shaved nearly to the scalp. She smiled widely as he looked at her, though it was the kind of smile that didn't extend past the corners of her lips.

"My sister's cat is named Violet," Grant answered. She nodded as if that was an appropriate response.

"Here you go, buddy!" Lucas thrust the glass into his hands. "I see you're working fast." He extended his hand to Violet. "I'm his friend, Lucas."

"Nice to meet you both."

"We were in Vegas and kind of bored, and I thought, hey, let's go to Pahrump and see what's happening at the Silk House." Lucas spoke louder than he usually did, sitting down on the couch.

"We're always ready to party out here," she answered rather formally.

"So you like Grant, huh?" He grabbed his friend by the shoulders and rocked him a bit. "He's pretty shy, though. Might have to talk him into it."

"I'm very good with shy guys. They're my favorite."

"Then I guess we won't get along very well!" Lucas blurted out. "I haven't been shy since I was fourteen and my mom called me in the middle of the night to come pick her up from Mr. Mike's house. He was my English teacher. I guess my mom was getting some extra credit lessons as well."

"Oh," Violet answered. "Do you see any of the girls in here that you like?" she asked, changing the subject from whatever trauma Lucas was working through.

"I like that one over there." He pointed to the black woman talking to the bartender. "Call me Stevie Wonder, 'cause I got jungle fever tonight, baby!"

"I'll go get her. Her name is Chloe." Violet got up and walked over to her.

"What's the deal with this place? Why aren't they dancing?" Grant asked thickly, looking around the room again. All the girls were dressed provocatively, but they were still covered up. Even the worst strip clubs featured pasties at the very least.

"This is a brothel, dude."

"A brothel?"

"Yeah, what did you think this was?"

"I dunno." Grant took a sip of his drink. "This is really cold."

"I think that Violet really likes you. Is that what she said her name was?" Lucas kept talking, mostly to himself. "I think she's a good one for you. A shaved head means she's a little freaky, and that's exactly what you can use right now, someone to fuck that shit out of your head."

"I'm not banging a hooker," Grant groaned, looking away from Violet and Chloe as they walked back to them. Lucas jumped up and intercepted them before they got all the way back, wrapping his arms around Chloe who responded in kind while he spoke to Violet. A moment later, Lucas and Chloe, were gone and it was just Violet approaching the couch.

"Come on, I want to show you something," she said gently, pulling him up.

"That's okay, I think I'll stay here. I didn't know what this place is until just now."

"Grant, please come with me. It'll be okay." Her voice coaxed life into his legs, and before he knew it they were in this room.

Back in the present, Violet yanked a little harder and Grant tumbled into the bed with her. "So, what do you feel like doing?" she asked, running her fingers along his chest.

"I'm not really in the mood."

"Your friend said you needed some coaxing. That you'd be scared," she said, keeping her hands busy crawling around his body.

"He doesn't know what I need," Grant replied.

"We can just talk if you want, but I don't think *he* wants to listen to us." She grabbed ahold of the bulge in Grant's pants as she spoke. His mind may have been trying to get out of the situation, but his anatomy was less philosophical and more instinctively driven.

"No." Grant pushed her hand away from there. "I don't want to do this."

"Oh, I'm sorry to hear that," Violet answered, putting on a pouty face.

"I killed someone. Two people, in fact," he blurted out, pushing Violet farther away. She just looked at him confused, trying to decipher if she should be afraid or not. "He didn't tell you that, did he?" Grant raised his voice, pointing out toward where he'd last seen Lucas. "He doesn't understand. He wants me to just go back to living life like normal and get out of his house, but I can't do that. Every time I close my eyes…"

He drifted for a moment and Violet reached out, resting her hand on his upper arm. "It's okay, we can just talk," she said softly.

"I could barely see what they were doing, but I saw them when the gun flashed. That's burned into my eyes, them looking at me, and then them on the floor." He trailed off again.

"That's okay," Violet said soothingly, rubbing his arm. "I'm sure they deserved it."

Grant jumped up. "Deserved it?" he yelled, looking around wildly. "If they deserved it, then what do I deserve?"

"I just mean—"

"None of us deserved what happened, but I'm the one who has to deal with it, not you! Not Lucas! Me!" Spinning around, he bolted for the door and back down the hallway Violet had led him through. The walls of the corridor were melting into the floor as Grant stumbled down them. At the front desk he swiped the keys from the basket the clerk held out. He tried to grasp his phone and wallet that were in there as well, but they slipped through his fingers and landed on the floor, which was too far away from Grant to worry about. He couldn't breathe inside, the air wasn't right.

Slumping through the doors, the fresh air of the night wrapped around him and let him finally catch his breath. The confusion swirling around him took a step back, leaving Grant in the middle of a bubble. The rest of the world was spinning around him like a tornado, but inside the perimeter he was safe. The red blur of his car glowed through the swirling mass of reality that surrounded him. Fumbling with his keys, he clicked the unlock button and slid into the driver's seat. The prescription bottle of Xanax was waiting there for him, perfectly still in the chaos. Lucas had left it sitting on the dashboard behind the steering wheel. It was impossible to miss. So Grant did what it commanded and slipped another pill into his mouth. The roar of the tornado faded out slightly as he jammed the key into the ignition.

Day 8, 9:34 pm

LUCAS GREEN

Chloe led me down the hallway to her room. It looked like it would smell bad, but it didn't; it actually smelled like a hospital. They took their cleaning seriously here at the Silk House.

"Where do you want to start?" Chloe asked as she dropped herself back onto the bed invitingly and I started to undo my belt. When we'd entered the establishment, we'd been patted down and sent through a metal detector. Our phones were detained and held at the front desk, along with our IDs and keys. Only our wallets were allowed to make it deeper into the sex hive, and even those had been peeked into. The occasional weirdo might try to slip a razor blade into the room, but more likely was drugs; and if there's one thing management wanted to keep away from their girls, it was controlled substances. Brothels are always under scrutiny, and adding drug possession to the mix is a quick way to get shut down. So only money is allowed into the building, but management also prefers plastic money, because that way they're sure to get their cut. My wallet only had about a hundred dollars cash, which the security guard counted quickly. That wasn't enough to buy any off-the-books special favors, so it passed through.

I had prepared for that eventuality. Attached perfectly underneath my oversized belt were several vacuum-sealed bags. They were small enough that they'd escaped the casual pat-down. I held the belt up and Chloe noticed the packages. "What are those?" she asked hesitantly.

"How much do you make a night?"

"Depends on the night."

"Your best night?"

"Here? My best night's a couple of grand."

Pulling the first package off of the belt, I ripped the end of it off and it instantly doubled in size as the air flowed in. Sticking my fingers in, I pulled out the freshly expanded crisp hundred-dollar bills. "That's two grand." I tossed the bills toward her and pulled two more packages off their hiding spots. "Four and six," I counted out, holding them out in her direction.

"What are you trying to buy?" she asked, her voice heavy with suspicion and a little bit of fear creeping in.

"Just your help. I need to know exactly what happens with my friend when Violet gets him back here. Plus, I'll probably need a ride back to Las Vegas." She reached for the other two packages in my hand, but I withdrew them. "You'll get these later, once this business is settled." I slipped them into my pocket.

Chloe thought for a moment, her hands absentmindedly stroking the cash already in her possession. "Yeah, I can do that," she finally answered, tucking her new cash into her gaudy clutch purse next to the assorted condoms she carried. "Wanting to watch a friend have sex isn't as rare a request as you'd think it is." She walked to the door. "Wait here. I'll make sure they go into the room next to us."

She left me alone in the room. I would have sat down on the bed, but despite the heavy scent of cleaning products, it still didn't seem clean enough to me.

Day 8, 10:12 pm

GRANT ANDERSON

The adrenaline of fleeing the brothel focused Grant's mind enough for him to get the car out of the small city and onto the highway back toward Vegas. But it wasn't enough to last him the entire drive, and the swirling wall closed back in around him. Reaching for the radio dial, he cranked the music up louder. On this side of the mountains, none of the presets worked, so the radio had scanned through until he stopped it on the clearest station he could find. He didn't recognize any of the music that came through, but the noise was better than driving in silence. But the louder it got, the more it just faded into the background.

"Stay awake, stay awake," Grant repeated to himself. His eyelids were getting heavier as he sped through the darkness of this desert roadway. There wasn't even a gas station to light the way home, just empty road until you passed through the mountains.

His mind raced through everything that had happened since he'd decided to move into his uncle's house. Cleaning up what was left of his existence, meeting Tracy, angry clients, then Lucas moving in across the street, finally a person who seemed like he could be a friend. But it wasn't the Lucas he knew who'd dragged him out here tonight. He seemed completely different. No matter how hard Grant tried to focus on his different thoughts, they were eventually swept away by the storm in his own head. What had happened at the foot of the stairs was always lurking in there, the images of the slowly trickling blood along the grout lines toward the carpet. Watching TV dulled it by turning his mind off. The excursions he'd done with Lucas, shopping or going to the comedy show, forced him to find new things to think about, letting the present moment control his mind. But the entire time, the darkness lingered in there, slowing his mind, obscuring his thoughts, and locking him into this mental paralysis. Even when it wasn't dominating his thoughts, he lived with the knowledge that it was in there, just watching like a predator in the night.

He had pills for that, though, to calm his thoughts and dull their sharpness. Reaching for the bottle between his legs, he found another one of the bitter pills and slipped it into his mouth. He couldn't remember the last time he'd taken one, but it must have been awhile. Choking it down, he smiled. Once it hit he'd feel better.

His headlights illuminated the road ahead of him, though their yellow glow couldn't break through the wall of confusion that he drove towards. It was just the bubble around him that was clear; the rest of the world was hazy. Out of the edges of the fuzziness came a solid image—a rabbit, hopping into the middle of the road, as if it too was trapped in a bubble that kept it from seeing the speeding vehicle. The entirety of the surroundings was empty—the only things that existed for miles were Grant and the rabbit—and yet it had decided that it could wait no longer on the side of the road and must cross paths with him at that precise moment. Grant's reaction time was so slowed that he didn't even utter a sound as he yanked the steering wheel to the left, to veer away from the collision. His voice didn't work, nor did his feet, as his right foot remained glued to the accelerator. The car lurched into the opposite lane, the tires skidding across the road until they left the asphalt and gripped only dust. Grant's eyes couldn't make sense of the changing scenery—he was just along for the ride—but the desert floor gave way to a gully, the crack in the earth that centuries of flash floods had created. These cracks in the barren tundra stretched across the entire state, and it accepted Grant and his vehicle without comment. The front passenger wheel was the first to leave the solid earth. The Yaris pitched in that direction instantly, sending it corkscrewing into the void. The drop was only about ten feet, but the car had time to flip completely over before it came to a stop. Upside down and crunched against the rock wall, it lost all its momentum.

The dirt and earth that had been disturbed was still raining down around the car as Grant lost consciousness and went limp inside the confines of the seatbelt.

Day 9, 8:05 am

TRACY COOK

Grant's phone rang until it went to voicemail. Tracy didn't bother to leave a message. Instead, she just typed out a quick text message: *Give me a call. Do you know of a home inspector named Josh Davidson?* The business card John Matzek had supplied her listed that name as the sole proprietor of "Sure Check," a home inspection company. Tracy's own Google search and database check had supported everything the business card claimed. He had an average of four stars in his Google reviews and only the standard type of complaints: didn't return a phone call, disagreement about his fees, and one very articulate customer who felt that his website's billing system was too complicated. Those issues might dissuade her from hiring him to inspect any new real estate purchases, but none of it suggested the outright fraud that Matzek had alleged. Tracy had been racking her brain to try and remember if Josh

Davidson was mentioned in any of the files they'd sorted through a couple of nights ago, but it didn't jog any memories. If his name or invoices were in the files, they weren't obvious enough to attract attention the first time they'd sorted through them.

Tracy selected Lucas from her contacts list and dialed his number. Grant might still be living on his couch-bound schedule, which could explain why he wasn't answering his phone first thing in the morning, but Lucas seemed to be a punctual riser. His phone went to voicemail as well, and Tracy ended the call. Maybe they were busy or something. She slipped the phone back in her pocket and entered the precinct building. Hopefully Grant would call her back by lunchtime and he could look through the files; or better yet, he might know Davidson off the top of his head. It was usual practice for agents and home inspectors to work together pretty often.

Bill sat at his desk, bouncing his knee as she approached. "Morning," she greeted him, dropping her bag onto the desk.

"Don't get comfortable," he replied.

"We got a call already?"

"Sorta. The captain would like to see both of us," he answered evenly.

"Something going on?"

"Did you go up and talk to Hector Camargo yesterday?"

"Yeah?" She looked even more confused.

"Well, he called his overpriced attorney, who was in here at 7 am to let the captain know what Mencia and he thought about that little visit."

"Oh. I was just asking about Juan Heredia. I wanted to know if he still had any connection to them." The sudden shock of trouble caused her voice to drop to a near-whisper.

"I get that, but we talked about this being an off-the-books, in-your-spare-time kind of investigation. Going to a prison and talking to a very well-connected enforcer for the Mencia cartel is not very low-key." Tracy didn't have a response for that. It hadn't occurred to her that she might be overreaching. "Come on, let's go."

Captain Snitker's office was at the far end of the building from their desk. Obviously an older hand at police work, he was pretty detached from the day-to-day activity of his detectives. He let them do their thing and only wanted to be involved if he absolutely had to be. It gave the squad plenty of room to work without anyone breathing down their necks; however, it also meant a lack of support if someone needed it. This was a different situation; hearing from defense lawyers and probably the district attorney wasn't something he was going to appreciate.

Bill led his partner through the door of the office. "Close the door," the captain ordered once they'd come in. Tracy pushed the door closed, revealing State Trooper Dean Wilson sitting on the couch in the corner of the room, a smirk across his face. "So I was visited by some friendly fellows from Fried, Morton and Associates this morning," the captain explained dryly. "Any guess what they wanted?" He glared at Tracy.

"I'm sorry, Captain," she replied. "I was just trying to find out if he knew someone I'm looking into."

"Yes, they gave me the whole rundown of your interrogation. Looking into this Heredia guy who hasn't had a case against him in years, and apparently is just an electrician now." Tracy didn't answer, since there wasn't really a question in the statement. "Why is my newest Robbery detective looking into this guy? Did he steal some electrical wire? Hijack a delivery of light bulbs?"

"I think I know what's going on," Dean interjected, standing up from the couch behind them and moving around toward the captain's desk. "You saw the picture of your friend Paul on the wall and started trying to sabotage my investigation to protect him."

"That doesn't make any sense," Tracy shot back. "You said yourself you aren't even looking into him."

"But he was on the board, meaning he's part of my investigation!" Dean roared. "Thanks to your snooping around, Mencia's lawyers are going to be fighting us over everything just for fun!"

"Investigate Paul all you want! He's dead!"

Dean looked flustered for a moment at that revelation. "It doesn't matter who's alive or dead. You're ruining Task Force X with your nonsense. You're fired! Turn in your badge and gun!"

"Alright, calm down," Captain Snitker cut in.

"No, you need to fire her right now!" Dean shouted. "She's clearly working for the cartel to undermine my work!"

The other three people in the room just stared at him for a few moments once he finished ranting. "I'll assign someone else to the task force in her place," the captain said.

"No!" Dean shrieked. "I don't want anyone else from your bullshit department." He shook his finger at the captain. "Obviously you're all a bunch of amateurs." Whirling around, he glared at Tracy and Bill. "If I see you anywhere near my investigations, I'll have you arrested," he snarled before barging out the door, slamming it behind him.

"And I thought this was going to be unpleasant," Bill remarked once the dust settled.

"I don't want to hear any more about this," the captain finally said.

"There's something going on with the renovation company," Tracy said.

"I don't want to hear any more about this!"

Tracy started to respond but caught herself. "Yes, sir."

"Good. Now go do the work you're actually being paid to do and stay away from anyone connected to the cartel lawyers. Because if they end up back in here, you're going to be solving crimes for Animal Control."

"Yes sir," they both answered, Bill leading the way out of the office.

Day 9, 8:06 am

LUCAS GREEN

"Yeah, turn there," I directed. We were coming up on the last turns on the way to my house.

"At the stop sign?" Chloe asked.

"Yes." My phone buzzed and I saw Tracy's name on the screen. That was unexpected, but probably not an issue. I let it keep ringing until the voicemail kicked in.

Chloe swung the car down the left turn and my neighborhood appeared before us. She was a good driver and had earned her money so far. Being a lady of the evening came with certain skills. Most of those skills were useless to me in the project at hand, but some of them had more practical applications. We had watched as Grant had spun out of control while visiting with Violet, and then she'd set me up on the couch in her apartment while I waited the night out. If my cover story was that I'd spent the night with a hooker, then I might as well do that. My work in Pahrump had been over the moment Grant sped off in a drug-fueled haze; however, my cover story needed some depth, so I talked Chloe into an early morning drive into Vegas. That way I actually lived through the details of the story, no holes to find if someone started digging into it.

Harold had supplied me with a few tracking devices; two of them were stuck to the phones we'd used as bait at the comedy show, and another was buried in the decaying remains of a cheeseburger in the back seat of Grant's car. I'd bought the meal a few days ago and let it ferment in the backyard until last night, when I shoved it under the passenger seat. It smelled a little bit, so I sprayed the car with some air freshener before I let Grant get in. Even if someone tried to search the car for evidence, they'd never peel apart the congealed buns of some forgotten food under the seat. If Tracy was that persistent, the tracker featured a self-destruct option as well. It was very simple, but when I was done with it, I could send a command remotely and the tiny motherboard would start running as many processes as it possibly could until it overheated and burned out. They might be able to figure out that it was a piece of electronics, but there'd be no evidence to prove it was anything other than just a slightly melted piece of circuitry and plastic.

I had watched the tracker from my phone the entire night. Forty-two minutes after Grant had left the brothel, the tracker stopped moving, slightly off the edge of Highway 160, and it hadn't moved since. Either the smell had gotten to Grant and he'd tossed the bag, which I doubted since Grant was so Xannied out by that time he couldn't have smelled a buffalo herd, or he'd driven his car off the road.

At 6:30 am, Chloe had awakened from her room and we were ready to get on the road. I had impressed upon her before she went to sleep that our activities were to remain a secret forever. If anyone ever asked, we hooked up in her official capacity and then arranged a friendly visit to her own place, where the rules were a little less stringent and we could explore my desires deeper. After that she had given me a ride home, since my friend had abandoned me. It was pretty much the truth, except for the sex part. The irony struck me on the drive back; most people would create elaborate lies to deny sleeping with a hooker, and here I was, creating a lie that I *had* been hooking up with her.

"That one there," I said, pointing out my driveway. Chloe guided the car into the empty space and put it into park. I pulled out my last vacuum-sealed package. "You remember everything we talked about last night?" I said, holding it up.

"I do," she answered cautiously.

"Then this is yours." I dropped it into her lap. "And I know I can trust you to remember the correct parts of this night."

"I will."

"Good. Have a nice drive back." I hopped out of the car.

She backed out slowly, heading back the way we'd come in. She had managed a ten-thousand-dollar night without even taking her top off; not bad, considering how she usually made her money. I walked through my front door and saw that my couch was empty. That was my final fear, that somehow Grant would've escaped it all and just be waiting for me to join him as he powered through Season Eight of *Seinfeld*. Larry David had left the show by that point, and it was noticeable in the style and tempo of the show, but it did feature some classic episodes. The house was silent, though. Deputy wasn't even making noise, just staring at me as I entered before dropping his head back down to his paws.

"Long night?" I asked him. He didn't answer, but it couldn't have been longer than mine, I thought as I climbed the stairs.

Day 9, 3:10 pm

TRACY COOK

Tracy was sitting quietly at her desk. She was supposed to be logging information into the computer from a robbery two weeks ago at a baseball card store. Apparently baseball cards have made a comeback and people are getting pretty aggressive over them. But today was turning out to be a lot harder than she'd expected. After the morning meeting with the captain, she hadn't been able to make progress on anything all day. She kept praying for dispatch to call and send them out on something new; that would get her out of the office and let her think about something else. But it hadn't happened; so far it was just trying to slog through reports and case files.

Bill had done his best to deflect the fallout, pointing out that getting the department away from the task force was in everyone's best interest. Even without catching the full wrath, though, it'd been a deflating meeting. The captain and Bill were right; she hadn't uncovered anything of actual value to the investigation, or even proved that there should be an investigation. The biggest thing she'd uncovered was that Paul Sherman was dead, but that wasn't really a mystery. It was public record.

"You doing alright?" Bill asked across the desk. Even though he couldn't read Tracy's mind, it was clear from the slow pace of her fingers on the keys that she wasn't very invested in her work at the moment.

"Yeah," she muttered, refocusing on the page in her hand. Several minutes of typing followed before she couldn't take it anymore. "Hector Camargo knows Miguel Guerra," she blurted out toward Bill.

He leaned back from his computer and looked at her. "What's that?"

"Camargo said that Juan Heredia went to work for Miguel. If Miguel is just some guy who owns a renovation company, why would a guy like Camargo even know his name? Juan was supposedly barely involved in the cartel's business, but Hector knows who employs him now?"

Bill nodded. "That's not much, but it does feel like something."

"I know. What if Juan just shifted jobs in the organization? Enforcing wasn't what he was cut out to do, so they shifted him over to Miguel's side of things."

"To be an electrician?"

"An electrician for a company that's actually a front for money laundering." Tracy related the story John Matzek had told her the day before about the cabinets. On the face of it, it seemed like typical cheap contractor nonsense, but the home inspector looking the other way added another layer of mystery.

"Interesting," Bill answered. "But it's still a jump to connect that to the cartel. More like a real estate agent just being shady."

Before Tracy could protest, her cellphone pinged. Unlocking the screen, she saw that she had an email notification. It was from the tracking website Lucas had sent her for the trackers on the lost cellphones. They were on the move. The map showed them having left the Strip and heading north, in the general direction of Tracy.

"What's up?" Bill asked.

"It's the thing with my mom. Can you cover for me for a while?" she asked, grabbing her bag.

"Is this your other off-the-books investigation?" he asked sarcastically.

"Yes, but it's for my mother. What am I supposed to do?"

"Fair enough. I'll call you if anything comes up."

Tracy hurried for the exit. Maybe she could wrap this side project up in a hurry and get back to her actual job soon.

Day 9, 3:40 pm

LUCAS GREEN

I finally pushed the covers off me. Deputy was standing in the doorway looking at me. He probably needed to pee. "Me first," I croaked, making my way to the master bathroom. I hadn't bothered undressing when I'd gotten back from the long night with Chloe, just kicked my shoes off and peeled my socks into a ball on the floor. My phones had stayed silent the entire day; so far, no news was good news. Swiping through my phone to the tracker page, it showed Grant's tracker to be in the same place it'd been since last night. Maybe he was just sightseeing in the desert.

"Let's go." I ordered Deputy down the stairs and let him out the back door. He went through the door quicker than I had ever seen him move before. Then again, he'd been inside for a very long time. "Good dog," I encouraged him as he eventually trotted past me back into the house. Even though he'd been cooped up, he was too smart to stay outside for longer than he had to.

The Guerra burner phone started to ring, and I answered it. "Do you have something to report?" The voice on the other end was Carlos. So Carlos had improved his surveillance of the situation. His spotters had clearly noticed that Grant's car hadn't returned home yet, and that he wasn't at his office, either. It was looking like Carlos was finally starting to run a competent operation.

"Not officially."

"Is he not missing?"

"He is, but nothing's for sure yet, just that he didn't make it home last night and hasn't been seen since then."

"But you have an idea?"

"I do. You want me to come down and catch you up on what's going on?"

Carlos hesitated at first. "Do you have the details?"

"I have a pretty good idea."

"We still have the items we need to deal with," Carlos replied. Whatever items Grant unwittingly had in his possession that incriminated the Guerra organization was still the top priority for Carlos.

"I don't think the time's right yet. Until he's found one way or another, you might get unexpected visitors. And if he does make it back, he'll notice that someone's been in there."

"*Is* he coming back?"

"Anything's possible." Carlos didn't answer this time. "I'll come down to the office and fill you in. Until something official happens, though, I have to recommend waiting."

"Fine." He hung up the call.

Setting the phone down, I looked around the kitchen. It was pretty bare. Looks like I'd be stopping for food on my way down to Battle Born Renovations. If Grant was here, he'd insist on getting chicken fingers, which wasn't a bad idea. Of course, if he was here, I probably wouldn't be taking a trip down to meet with the people who were trying to have him killed. But that was just an inside joke with myself.

Even though my stomach was aching, I still needed a shower because my clothes smelled like Chloe. The amount of perfume she wore was shocking; even her car reeked of the scent. Even for assassins, it wasn't the best business practice to show up to meetings smelling like you were trying to disguise the smell of sex. It was like I'd doused myself in Drakkar Noir.

Day 9, 3:45 pm

TRACY COOK

Most of the streets in Las Vegas were somewhat familiar to Tracy. Granted, most of them looked pretty similar in general, and since mountains loomed over the entire valley, the view blurred together. It wasn't until Tracy was fully into the parking lot that she recognized the buildings she was looking at. She'd been here last week with the stolen cables and laptops. The trackers had led her back to EventRig. It made sense; apparently this company did work on concerts, and the truck was filled with concert equipment.

She cruised past the rear of the building, where she spotted the truck she'd been following backed up to the loading dock. However, the tracker was actually farther away than the truck was, so the case had already been unloaded. Pulling around, she parked in front of the main entrance and walked in. The same receptionist from her previous visit greeted her, and

Tracy asked to speak with the building manager Mark. A few minutes later, Mark came out. "Detective!" he greeted her.

"Hello, Mark. Good to see you again." She held her hand out.

"Is your partner here?"

"No, it's just me today."

"What can I help you with?"

"Actually, could we speak in your office, please?"

"Of course." He motioned for her to follow him down the hallway to the door with his name on it. The office featured a desk and computer as you would expect, a couple of file cabinets and assorted office equipment piled in the corner. His actual desk was covered in papers, and the back of his computer monitor was covered in stickers and printed-out memes, most of them promoting Republican and gun-right causes. Several others were aimed at lazy workers or people who didn't get their work done promptly.

Mark closed the door behind them as Tracy took a seat in front of his desk. He slid the office chair around the monitor so he could see Tracy. "I'm actually here for more of a personal issue," she began.

"I'm very flattered, Detective, but my dogs keep me very busy. Not really any time for dating." He answered with a laugh, gesturing toward the pictures of him and two German shepherds on the wall.

"Ah, yes." Tracy squirmed uncomfortably. "Well, I was wondering about your job here. Do you have any contact with the shows your company does, or the people that work on them?"

"I sit in on the meetings for upcoming jobs, and

sometimes help with ordering parts or equipment that jobs might need. As for the crew, some of them are friends. We go out to eat and stuff like that when they're in town."

"Would you know who was working on the Tom Segura show down at the Strip?"

"Hmm." He gazed at the wall for a moment. "I don't think so, but I could check."

Tracy had been a little guarded in her comments so far. It was entirely possible that Mark himself was connected to all this. But at this point, it seemed unlikely he had any special contacts with the crew down there, so she said, "My mother works at the theater he was playing at and believes there was some theft going on. That the stolen items are being locked in a road case and then shipped out when the show loads out." Mark nodded along. "I had a tracker put on some dummy phones, and they arrived on the truck that's currently out on your loading dock. I believe the case they're in has already been rolled into the building."

"Oh, wow. Do you want to go look for it?"

"Yes, but I'm more interested in who's receiving the case."

"Gotcha. Well, let's go look for it. Maybe it has a name on it or something."

Tracy stood up with him as they went for the door. "Do you really think the person's name will be on the case? In my experience, not many criminals sign their name on the tools of the crime."

"Yeah, but we don't really use your normal road cases here," Mark explained as he led her down the hallway to the warehouse door. "We actually use open-top bins for our cables. You saw them the last time you were here." Tracy made that connection as he spoke. The blue metal bins had been all over the warehouse floor last week. "So most likely if this road case you're looking for is lockable, it has a lid, which means it's not our company's property."

"Is it normal to get cases that don't belong to you?"

"Actually, it is. Most of the crew guys have some kind of work box that belongs to them, and we store them here when they come back from jobs. And often other companies' equipment will end up here for certain projects, waiting to get sent out on another job we're both involved in."

They were out in the warehouse now, heading toward the loading dock. It was a familiar route to Tracy. It looked the same as it had last week, and the door that had been breached then was located right next to the trailer that had brought the case into the building. "This isn't the most organized company," Mark continued, "so things might get offloaded here and just pushed into a corner, and no one knows what it's doing there." They had reached the loading dock and could look into the back of the trailer, which was still open. It was completely empty. "Let me grab Nick," Mark said. "Wait here for a minute."

He returned a few minutes later with a grumpy-looking man following behind. He was also bald and was wearing heavy boots, his clothing smeared with dust. "This is Nick. He's the shipping manager here. This is Tracy." She noticed that he had purposely avoided identifying her as police.

"Yeah, what's going on?" he asked with annoyance.

"There was a case on this truck I'm looking for."

"It was mostly truss and motors. That's all over there." He jerked his thumb back to a collection of gear behind him.

"Yeah, but was there a road case on the truck?" Mark interjected.

"I dunno. I didn't do it all myself."

"Who did?"

"Whoever was here. I can't be chasing down some random case. I got three jobs that have to be pulled before five, and two more trucks coming back in like ten minutes."

"Thank you," Tracy said to his back as he stomped off.

"Sorry about him," Mark said. "He struggles with his job of unloading and loading trucks."

"That's alright," she said, smiling. She fished her phone out of her pocket. "I don't know how accurate this tracker is. It might be able to show exactly which case it's in." She thumbed through the screens until the tracking page came up. "It moved!" she exclaimed. The pulsing blue dot was now down the street several buildings.

"Let me see." Mark examined the screen as Tracy showed it to him. "That's our other building. Most of the work boxes are stored there, so someone must've just driven it down there now on the forklift. We can get to it that way." He pointed out the door to the back side of the building.

A five-minute walk later, they were in another warehouse. "This half is our staging building and that half is automation," Mark explained as they entered, the phone steering them toward the automation side of the building. This building was similar to the other one, featuring blue bins and equipment, but clearly geared to a different side of the business. Instead of trusses, chain motors, and grease, it was a lot more sawdust and machinery.

"That could be it," Mark said, pointing down one of the aisles. There were several cases sitting there, looking like they'd just been rolled off a forklift. The app pointed them straight to them as well. Mark separated the three cases. Two of them had "property of" stickers on them, identifying the owners. Mark said he recognized both of the names as people employed by the company. But the third case was completely unmarked and featured two large locks keeping it shut.

The tracking app went solid blue when Tracy held her phone over it. "We found your case," Mark said.

"Now I need to know who's coming for it," she replied, glancing around the warehouse.

Day 9, 4:25 pm

CARLOS GUERRA

Carlos was in his office when he heard the receptionist welcome Lucas into the building. He had shied away up to now from meeting Lucas on company property, or at least on company property that might be watched. The flips were another matter; there were people coming in and out of there all day long. But here at the office, things needed to stay more subdued; and considering that Lucas was an off-the-books employee of his, it was better to keep him away. But he was sick of driving out to the construction site, so he would tolerate a quick meeting with the guy at the office.

Amy led Lucas into the office, with Javy following behind. "Please shut the door, Amy," he instructed as she left. Amy had an idea that more went on at this business than met the eye, but she kept her suspicions to herself and appreciated the extra money that found its way into her pocket.

"What did you do to this guy?" Javy asked as soon as the door clicked shut.

Lucas answered him, being politer than they'd expected. He gave them a quick rundown on Grant's declining mental stability, and his sudden reliance on prescription drugs that led to him running out of the brothel and speeding off into the night. "So, are you proud of me?" Lucas said, finishing his story.

"Javy, you gave him these drugs?" Carlos asked, ignoring the sarcasm from Lucas.

"Yeah, just some Xanax. Nothing that can be traced back to us."

"I actually put the pills in a bottle I took out of his house," Lucas explained. "They'll just assume he's another victim of the drug epidemic."

"Then why did you tell us to wait on cleaning out the stuff we need?" Javy pressed on.

"Because it's not for sure yet. He hasn't been confirmed as dead yet, even though he is. He's been making friends with a very pretty local detective, so it won't be long before the cops are looking for him, and I suspect they'll check his house and might notice something missing. Or even worse, walk in on you doing your work."

"Why is he friends with a cop?" Carlos snapped.

"I'm not in charge of his social calendar," Lucas answered. "But I've seen her poking around at the office and his house."

Carlos and Javy exchanged glances. It was the type of look from people who could feel the noose tighten ever so slightly.

"That's fine, she's doesn't matter," Carlos finally said. "As long as we eventually get the stuff we need, it'll be easier once they find a body and any interest in his death has moved on."

"What about the other job?" Javy asked pointedly at Lucas.

"I believe I said I'd consider that after this one is concluded, which we just clarified has not happened yet." Lucas looked back to Carlos. "What else do we need to talk about?"

"I don't like knowing there's someone like you out there who's heard us talking about this but hasn't proved yet what side he's on," Javy snapped, stepping between Lucas's chair and the desk.

"That's your fault for talking to me about it, then."

"Maybe I should handle the matter, then."

"Maybe you should."

"Stop it," Carlos cut in again. "It's better to move slowly and surely than leave a loose end because of our haste."

"You sound like Miguel," Javy shot back.

"Miguel's right about how to do things. He just doesn't have the imagination to dream bigger." Javy accepted his chastisement and moved back against the wall. "I'm very happy with your work," Carlos continued, turning directly toward Lucas. "Under-promise and over-deliver. That's a good quality."

"I always over-deliver. That's why people hire me instead of relying on their local street toughs," Lucas responded, purposefully refusing to acknowledge Javy glaring at him from the corner.

"Very well. What else needs to be taken care of?"

Carlos asked.

Lucas went through the extraction protocols he worked by: the house would have to be cleaned, the items in it destroyed, and the final payment delivered. Thankfully, their transaction was almost complete.

Day 9, 4:45 pm

TRACY COOK

Tracy steered her car through the start of rush hour traffic. She had finished at EventRig a bit ago and hadn't had the nerve to go back to the precinct. Mark had promised he could watch the case with the security cameras inside the building. With Tracy keeping an eye on the tracker app, they would know the moment someone came for it. Since then, she'd been driving a little aimlessly around the streets. Nothing but mindless paperwork waited for her back at her desk, and the thought of going back to it was making her depressed. Bill was on her side, though he wasn't as convinced as she was that something nefarious was going on. He was looking at it all as coincidence at this point, which was fair; he was still just an outside observer to the situation.

Even though she wasn't really paying attention to where she was driving, she steered herself closer and closer to the center of it all, the Battle Born Renovations office. It wasn't much; a renovation company didn't really need an impressive office. Most meetings with clients were going to happen at the house that needed work done, not in some glass-framed room with mock-up drawings. The BBR building was simple, with an impressively tall chain-link fence around the perimeter. It looked like there were some supplies lined up along the edges, stacked on the far side. A pile that looked like lumber covered with a tarp on the side was nearest where she'd parked. The whole street contained businesses of a similar level, which meant her car wouldn't be noticed idling across the street. In front of the building were several cars parked in the designated spaces; a 4Runner, a company pickup truck, a recent-model Camry, and a BMW wrapped in a bright blue reflective wrap. It wasn't hard to make a guess about who owned the BMW. Carlos Guerra's lifestyle screamed "drug dealer." It was hard to believe a general contractor type would be driving around in a vehicle that looked like that. Yet there was nothing on Carlos. It seemed like his brother had seen to that; he kept him on the straight and narrow as far as the law was concerned and avoided detection.

Tracy fought the urge to deliver a cliched line about how she was onto him now. It would've been a perfect moment for a cutaway to a commercial break —the dogged detective finally getting her eye on the prize, a quarry that had grown fat and smug over the years but was about to meet swift justice. Tracy would have blurted it out just for the humor of the moment, but she didn't believe it was true. You could fill a book with known criminals who continued to commit crimes even with the police looking at them. Bill was right about that, she'd conceded; being a police officer was more about seeming like you were omnipresent than actually being so. A Wizard of Oz type of situation, she started to imagine who in her orbit would fill out the cast of that movie. She could pass for Dorothy but wasn't sure who Bill would consent to being. Probably the Tin Man; he was brave and smart, but his heart was lacking. Though not in the cardiovascular sense, Bill was very well-circulated.

Tracy's drifting thoughts came to an abrupt end as the front door to BBR opened. Out came Javy Santana, followed by a white man, and then Carlos Guerra. It took her a moment to register who she was looking at. The distance accounted for some of it, but it was mostly the fact that she had never expected to see Lucas Green walking out of that door. Her eyes spun to the 4Runner, which she now recognized as his car. It'd been sitting there the entire time and she hadn't realized it.

The trio spoke for a moment before Lucas departed to the driver-side door, no handshakes or long goodbyes. It couldn't be a business meeting; if Lucas was talking to them for legitimate renovation work, there would've been a handshake, a "thanks for stopping by, looking forward to working with you" type of goodbye, all smiles and shoulder slaps. Instead, they separated like they were associates, people who were accustomed to working with one another.

Tracy's mind came to a crashing stop like a derailed train, the possibilities piling up on top of each other before she could think a single thought. All she could think to do was thumb her phone to Grant's number and dial it. If his neighbor was consorting with the very people he was helping her look into, then he was in danger. Had Lucas been spying on them this entire time?

The call went to voicemail, and Grant's overly pleasant voice offered her the chance to leave a message, but she declined. She realized it was her second call he hadn't answered, and he had never called her back. She sent him a short text message, they had only recently met and he was admittedly going through a tough time in his life, but it had been a day and a half since she had heard anything from him, which felt unusual. She was starting to worry.

Day 9, 9:00 pm

SHELLY LOUIS

Shelly Louis groaned as she stepped back onto the casino floor. Her shoes were digging into her feet, and she knew already she'd have a blister by the end of her shift.

Serving drinks to the mindless gamblers at the slot machines wasn't the worst job she'd ever had, but it was one of the most depressing. The drinks were free, which meant that tips were often forgotten, though not if the machine paid out. Once she had landed a five-hundred-dollar tip on a single Pepsi delivery, by arriving with the drink at the exact same moment the machine started going through its orgasmic noises of announcing a winner. The elderly man lugging an oxygen canister behind him was so happy at the $113,000 he'd won, he'd handed her his bucket of remaining chips. "I did it!" he exclaimed and gave her a hug. His oxygen line got caught on his watch as he pulled away. She tried to hand the bucket back to him, but he pushed it away. "I don't need those anymore!"

But winning big was a rarity, and so were respectable tips, though she did try to learn the method the machines used to issue their rewards. Even if she couldn't be the winner, maybe she could be standing there when it happened and some of the success would land on her.

She delivered the first drinks of the night, two vodka cranberries, to a fat couple from the Midwest who were camped out on the *Wheel of Fortune* machines. The man grunted as she handed him his drink, the woman only offering her trash, her previous drink cup stuffed with used napkins. It wasn't uncommon.

She roamed through the rows of machines. Some people were too distracted by playing to think about drinks, and others were just sitting there wasting time themselves; drink or no drink, they didn't really care one way or another. Working in the theater was much better, even with her boss Garrett being a slimy dirtbag. What else would you expect from middle management at a casino? He'd tried to hook up with her a few times, though he was too much of a pussy to actually push for it. Even as a sexual predator he was disappointing. After the last time was when she started to notice the thievery. She wondered if she had sucked his dick if she'd now be enjoying the loot of lost cellphones and casino liquor. He was a lowlife at everything who couldn't get laid, so busied himself with petty theft.

Even still, working in there was more fun. The customers were excited to be seeing a show, and since they actually had to pay for drinks, they were much more generous with their tips. None of the wait staff in there liked dealing with Garrett, but if you wanted the good money, you had to deal with him and his dick at some point.

She took the next order, a Jack and Shit, which is what she called a Jack with Pepsi instead of Coke. She wouldn't drink it, but the gambler who ordered it was far too drunk to notice the inferior quality of the soda used. He'd be lucky to still be awake by the time she got back. It was still something that was hard to get used to in this city, the blackout drunks who were out while the sun was still shining. It seemed like a waste of nightlife to be too drunk before it even started, but that was on them.

Winding her way back through the machines, she headed for the employees-only corridor that led behind the actual casino bar to collect the drinks. The drinks were made quickly, but Shelly loitered for a few minutes talking with the other waitresses. They weren't supposed to be too fast with the drinks; after all, they were free, and the point of them being free was to keep the patrons in their seat in front of the slot machine. Bring the drinks too quickly and they might get up and leave; but with a drink ordered but not delivered yet, they were going to continue to sit there and wait for it. Time at the screen—that was what the casino bosses were really concerned about.

She took two steps out of the open doorway with the drinks when her path was blocked. Two casino security guards had stepped in front of her in the middle of the walkway that encircled the casino floor. "Miss Louis?" the one on the right asked. He was vaguely familiar to her; she had seen him around but had never met him.

"Yes?"

"You need to come with us."

"I need to deliver these drinks!" she protested, looking wildly around. As two uniformed Las Vegas police officers materialized next to her, she found herself boxed in, as if they expected her to make a run for it. "What's going on?" she exclaimed, taking a half-step back.

"You're being arrested for theft," the guard on the right said.

"I haven't stolen anything!" She was yelling now. "It was Garrett! Ask my daughter! She's a cop! She knows all about this!"

"I'll take those," the guard on the left said, reaching forward and taking the drink tray from her hands.

"I didn't do anything," she continued as the guard took her by the arm.

"Either way, you need to come with us." They spun her around toward the hallway that led into the depths of the hotel.

Day 10, 1:00 am

JOAN LEE

Joan Lee had had her brights clicked on for the past thirty minutes. They kept the road ahead illuminated as she cruised toward the mountains. Her go-to listening habit was true crime podcasts. Her boyfriend hated them, but she loved listening to them. She realized they were always hosted by women. Must be like *Gilmore Girls*. That was a show her and all her girlfriends loved, though she'd never been able to get Terrence to watch more than ten minutes of it before he started making fun of it. Some things truly are gendered, it doesn't matter what the prevailing social theories say; girls like *Gilmore Girls* and guys don't.

However, riding alone in the car through the darkness made the story of the Maine truck-stop killings ring a little closer to home, hence the extra bright lights to ward off whatever might be hiding in the dark ahead of her. It was interesting that on this side of the mountains it should be so dark, while just over the crests ahead shone a city that could be seen from space. Just another hour or so before she made it to her friend's house.

Ali always let her crash on the couch when she came in for work. There was a ceiling on how successful you could be in Pahrump as a dancer. She didn't mind picking up a shift at Last Chance Johnnies during the week, and she wasn't ready to completely sell herself over to the world-famous houses the city contained. So she was stuck making the commute every weekend into the city to make the real money. She had an in at a couple of the clubs near the Strip, and they always needed extra girls during the weekend. Joan made enough in two nights to make it worth the drive, and living in Pahrump was a fraction of the cost of living in the city. So as long as you didn't mind the hours-long commutes, it made sense. Joan had finished her shift early at Johnnies and decided to drive over during the night instead of in the morning. Ali would be getting home about the time she arrived, and she could sleep in tomorrow before it was time to get ready for work.

Joan eased her foot off of the accelerator and the cruise control assumed the responsibility. Her legs were already tired from the routine she had perfected on the pole, and keeping her foot in the same position for the entire drive had caused her leg to cramp up. Reaching down to take a sip of her Coke, her eyes came off the road for just a moment. She focused them back and let out a little scream. Her foot kicked back into action and slammed on the brake pedal, releasing the cruise control and burning rubber in the process. Ahead of her, now well within the limits of her headlights, was a terrifying sight. The longer she looked at it, the more the image came together. At first it looked like a demon waiting for her on the side of the road, then a disfigured animal, before her mind translated the images. It was actually a man, half-standing and half-dragging his body along. In his right hand he carried a tree branch of some kind that he was using as a cane. He was waving his other hand limply in her direction, beckoning her onwards.

Reaching into the glove compartment, she pulled out her Smith and Wesson. She might be a woman, but Nevada women learned early on how to scare off rattlers and men. Both wanted the same thing, and both got dealt with the same way. Easing her foot off the brake, the car continued rolling forward until she was within fifty feet of the person. She checked her surroundings carefully. There weren't any signs of there being anyone else out there other than the two of them. She wasn't about to get jumped in some scheme designed expressly to surprise her. Opening the driver's door, she stepped onto the running board. "What are you doing out here?" she demanded of the stranger.

He coughed, croaked, and stumbled to the ground. His face finally came fully up toward her, the bright lights revealing a face covered in dried blood and dirt, the glitter of glass still embedded in his skin.

Carefully, Joan approached him, the gun cocked and loaded at her side. "What happened to you?"

The man tried to speak again. This time his raspy voice came through. "Help." He held out his limp left hand, his wrist clearly broken beneath the swollen bruised skin.

"What happened to you?" she asked again.

"Crash," he sputtered, pointing his right hand off into the darkness, as his improvised cane fell to the ground. "Water."

Joan clicked the safety back on. Leaning down, she grabbed the man and dragged him back toward her car.

Day 10, 9:30 am

BILL STRIDER

Bill was driving this time; Tracy was a little too on-edge to handle the wheel. She was instead in the passenger seat, nervously drumming her fingers on her knee.

"You need to be calm when we go in there," he said.

"I will be," she answered sharply. She had called him in a near-panic last night after she witnessed Lucas meeting with Carlos Guerra. Or, maybe "panic" was the wrong word; more like a tizzy, talking a million miles an hour and jumping subjects in mid-sentence. She had tailed Lucas after he left. He stopped for a couple of seemingly normal errands at the grocery store and the gas station. Meanwhile, Bill had detoured over to Grant's house and looked for him. He didn't answer the door and there was no sign of him through the windows. After that, Bill had driven to the Port

Harvest office, but there was no sign of him there either, and the establishments on either side said they hadn't seen Grant in days.

The partners had met back at the office that night and dug through everything they could possibly find. There was no evidence of Grant anywhere for the past few days. They'd sent out a preliminary missing person report to every law enforcement agency in the state, as well as all the hospitals in the valley. Nothing had come back by morning. Apparently Grant had vanished. That brought them here, pulling into Lucas's driveway. As far as could be determined, Grant hadn't been seen since the comedy show, which was nearly fifty hours ago.

"You ready?" Bill asked once they were parked next to the 4Runner.

"I am."

"Go knock on the door," Bill ordered. He backtracked and did a careful lap around Lucas's vehicle. It looked the average amount of dirty. No signs of having been offroading or being washed recently. That, at least, suggested that Grant wasn't buried out in the desert somewhere.

"Hey, Tracy!" Lucas's voice welcomed her as he opened the door.

"Hi, Lucas," she answered. "This is my partner, Detective Bill Strider." She waved back toward him.

"Hello," Lucas answered cheerfully.

"Could we come in and talk for a few minutes?"

"Of course, come on in." He threw the door open wide and led them into the living room. The space was perfectly clean, with an Xbox and its accessories piled neatly on the coffee table. "What can I do for you?"

"We're looking for your neighbor, Grant Anderson," Bill answered him.

"Oh, did something else happen to him?"

"What do you mean 'something else?'" Bill asked quickly.

"Well, he shot those two guys the other day."

Bill nodded along. Tracy had briefed him on this guy, and her assessment of him seemed confused, like she hadn't been able to get a good read on him. Bill had to agree so far. Based on their limited conversation, he was personable but somehow distant at the same time.

"When was the last time you saw him? He was staying here, wasn't he?" Tracy asked this time.

"Yeah, sorta. He was just crashing on the couch while his house got sorted out from the crime scene stuff."

"When did you see him last?" Bill asked the question again.

"Two nights ago."

"So you saw him after you got back from Tom Segura?" Tracy asked.

"Yes. We came back here after the show and then he was here the entire next day."

"And what happened?" Bill pressed.

"It's kinda embarrassing," Lucas demurred.

"We've heard a lot of embarrassing stories in our line of work."

"Alright. Well." Lucas shifted around uncomfortably in his seat. "He was being really mopey, and I'd tried everything I could to get him going again, but nothing was working. I thought maybe some girls could cheer him up."

"So a strip club?" Tracy asked. Grant didn't seem like a strip club kind of guy, but it was hard to argue with boobs.

"No, we went to Pahrump." Lucas sighed.

"Oh," Tracy responded. The implication was clear as day.

"Did you leave him there?" Bill asked. It wouldn't be the first time a guy disappeared with a lady of the evening.

"No, he left me."

"And yet here you are."

"Yeah, I was with my lady in a room, and I paid another girl to take care of him. But I guess he freaked out and ran off. He had the keys and just disappeared."

Neither of the detectives spoke at first, trying to think through the situation as Lucas had described it. "When exactly was this?" Tracy finally asked, flipping her notebook open for the first time.

"It was around 10 pm. I didn't know for a while that he'd left, because I was…you know, busy. When I got out, his girl told me what happened, and he wouldn't pick up his phone when I tried calling him."

"How did you get home? That's a long taxi drive."

"The girl I was with invited me over to her place and then gave me a ride back in the morning."

"You went home with a prostitute, and then she gave you a ride from Pahrump to Las Vegas?" Tracy asked rather incredulously.

"Yes."

"That seems unlikely."

"I mean, I paid for the entire thing. And it wasn't cheap."

"And when you got home, was there any sign of Grant?" Bill interjected.

"No, he wasn't here. He kept talking about not going back into his house, so I figured he was at a hotel or something because he didn't want to deal with me anymore."

"So your depressed friend runs off in the night and hasn't been seen for an extended period of time, and you just write it off to awkwardness?" Bill pressed.

"Look, we aren't really friends. We only met a few days ago. I'm just here for work and he happens to be my neighbor, and then all this stuff has happened. She knows him as well as I do." He pointed at Tracy. "He needed a place to stay, so I felt bad and let him sleep here. He was depressed so I tried to get him laid." He shrugged his shoulders. "What else am I supposed to do? Put up fliers with his face on it?"

"If you wanted to get him laid, I can think of several options before going to a whorehouse a couple of hours away," Bill answered.

"Yeah, he wasn't really in a 'picking up girls at the bar' kinda headspace," Lucas countered. "He was depressing even the paid girls."

"So you have no idea where he is?" Tracy asked again.

"No, I haven't seen him since the other night."

"How about Carlos Guerra?" Bill asked.

"What about him?"

"You saw him?"

"Yes, I was at his office yesterday," Lucas

answered, as if that was the most obvious thing to be doing in the world.

"What brought you to his office?" Tracy asked.

"I was there for you?" Lucas answered with a look of confusion on his face.

"I don't need any renovation work done."

"You were looking into them because of the files Grant has, and my company will need renovation work done when we buy properties out here. So it seemed like the perfect excuse to meet with him and let you know what I found," he answered earnestly.

"You were investigating him?" Bill asked, disbelievingly.

"Sorta, I guess. We just talked about normal work stuff. They all seemed like the real deal when it comes to renovations."

"You just took it upon yourself to start investigating these people?" Tracy pressed him.

"Well, we've already been doing that, haven't we? We went through all those records, then planted those trackers on those phones for you. Why wouldn't I go talk to him if I had a valid reason?"

"What about the phones?" Bill cut in.

Tracy cut him off. "It's something to do with my mom." She looked back at Bill, who seemed annoyed that Lucas knew more than he did.

The conversation stalled for a moment before Bill asked the next question. "Did you notice anything unusual at BBR?"

"Nope. They seemed legit, knew what they were talking about, and were excited to work with us."

"Who exactly is it that you work for?" Tracy asked,

but her buzzing phone took her attention. Lucas started to answer, but halted while she dug her phone out. The caller ID showed it was coming from Las Vegas Metro PD. "Detective Cook," she answered. "Really? You're sure? Yeah, I'll come down. Thanks, Officer." She hung up and began gathering her things. "I guess I need to go. We can pick this back up later."

Both the men stood up with her. "Is everything okay?" Lucas asked. "Is it something with Grant?"

"No, it's my mother." She sighed.

"Thanks for your time, Mr. Green," Bill said. "Let us know if you think of anything new about Grant, or if you see any signs of him."

"Of course, of course." He followed them to the door and showed them out.

"What's going on?" Bill demanded once Lucas had shut the front door behind them.

"My mother got arrested last night for stealing from the casino," Tracy answered, slamming her bag into the back seat of the car.

"Oh."

"Can you take us back to the office? I'll take my car downtown where she's being held."

"Sure thing."

Day 10, 10:30 am

GRANT ANDERSON

"Can you open your eyes, sir?" The voice echoed through Grant's mind for a few moments before he snapped awake. The image of the two men dying on his kitchen floor had been replaced with the image of the moon hovering about him in the night sky through the broken window of his car.

"Yes," he blurted out before his eyes were even open. The bright starkness of the hospital was shocking. It was a far cry from the cold, dirty darkness of his last memories.

"Do you know where you are?" the man standing at the foot of his bed asked.

"Um, it looks like I'm in a hospital." Grant groaned. It was clearly the right answer, he felt sure of that. Most of his body was covered with a blanket, though his left arm was sticking out of the covers with a large cast wrapped around his wrist.

314

"Do you know how you got here?" the man continued, shining the light into Grant's eyes.

"Um, I remember a lady on the side of the road," he said slowly. The events of the previous night were starting to uncoil themselves in his mind.

"That's right, Ms. Lee found you walking down the highway."

"Now, do you know your name?" This question came from a uniformed police officer who'd been sitting on the opposite side of the room. Grant hadn't noticed him there.

"Yes, I'm Grant, Grant Anderson."

"Ms. Lee found you on the side of the road last night, but we just located your car. It was about fifty feet off the side and down a gully. Pretty hard to find." The officer stood up. "We didn't know who you were until we found the car, but we assumed you were the owner of the vehicle. Was there anyone else involved in this accident?"

"Huh?"

"Was there anyone in the car with you or on the road when it happened?"

"No, it was just me. There was a rabbit and I swerved." That part of his memory was still pretty foggy.

"Okay, you look fine at this point," the doctor cut in. Whatever questions the cop had, the doctor didn't want to stick around and wait through them. "You have a broken wrist on your left arm. Your left leg is pretty badly bruised, but no serious damage. You suffered a concussion and some mild head trauma. Probably explains why you were out of it for a full day.

That and the Xanax." He flicked the chart slightly. "Because of that, you were dehydrated and suffering from exhaustion when you came in. We got you full of fluids and put this on." He tapped the cast. "You're ready to be discharged at this point. All you need is some rest, and it's better to do that at home. Any questions?"

"I can go home?" Grant asked, looking at the tubes and wires still curled all around him.

"Yep. Just go on bed rest for the rest of the week, contact your personal physician for a follow up." The doctor removed his gloves. "Some people will be in soon to discharge you." He left.

"Okay, I'm going to need a statement," the police officer said, stepping forward. "Everything you remember since you got in that car."

Grant looked at him and his uniform. The patch on his shoulder read *Pahrump*. "Am I in Pahrump?"

"Yep. After Ms. Lee found you, she drove you back here."

"I can't be discharged. I don't know how to get home. And you said my car's in a gully."

"We do have taxis here, or you can call someone to come get you."

Day 10, 10:32 am

TRACY COOK

Tracy had checked in at the desk and it only took a few minutes before she was escorted back to the room her mother was being held in. Professional courtesy, she guessed. They had put Shelly into an interrogation room for the visit and she was looking rough, Tracy thought as she caught a glimpse of her before entering the room. She had spent nearly twelve hours down here and probably hadn't slept at all the entire night. "Hi, Mom," she said once the door was open. Shelly didn't respond with words, but instead just burst into tears with her head on the table. "Mom, it's okay. Please stop crying." Tracy consoled her stiffly, stepping forward and patting her back. It could have been a sweet moment if it wasn't for the awkwardness.

Lifting her head, Shelly tried to talk, but it just came out all blubbery and with no discernible words. "Uh-huh," Tracy answered before walking back to the door and retrieving some Kleenex from outside the room. Talking to her mom was always an ordeal; she didn't want to have to deal with snot pouring from her face as well.

Finally after a few minutes, Shelly had regained her composure enough to sit upright in her chair. "Tell me what happened," Tracy prodded her. That was all it took, as Shelly launched into a very descriptive account of everything that'd happened in the past twenty-four hours, even though she had only been arrested twelve hours before. She also covered yesterday's breakfast and her trip to Verizon and the very unhelpful associate there. "Mom, tell me about getting arrested," Tracy finally cut in.

"It was horrible!" she shrieked. She picked up the story at about the same place Tracy had interrupted. Finally, she got to the important parts. Theft was what she was being charged with. There were several witness statements that blamed her for the stolen cellphones, as well as selling drinks for cash and pocketing the money. None of the charges were particularly serious; the whole thing could probably get pled down to probation. However, something like that on your record would prevent Shelly from getting any more work at the casinos in town. More importantly, she hadn't actually committed the crimes. Tracy knew the phones in question were locked up in a road case at EventRig.

"I thought you were dealing with this!" Shelly said. "That's why I came to you. If I knew you weren't going to do anything about it, I would've found someone who could actually help me."

"Mom, calm down."

"No! I'm in here because of you! You were supposed to stop this from happening!" she shrieked.

"I'm working on it, but no one's come for the phones yet."

"But they came for me. Clearly, you messed up!"

She had a point. Something had happened to cause Garrett or whoever had decided to pin the blame onto Shelly to want to get ahead of the issue. Whoever was supposed to retrieve the loot at EventRig must've been tipped off about her visit, or actually saw her poking around the road case. She was going to call Mark when she got out of here and see if anything had changed with the case since yesterday. Maybe he could make a list of all the people they'd seen when they'd been walking through the buildings and discussing the case. There could be a connection to make there.

"Mom, I'm still working on it."

"Oh, good, I'll just wait here for you to finish, then," she said defiantly.

"Let me get your bail set up and you can get out of here and we'll figure this out."

"What's the point? They fired me. I'm going to lose everything. I might as well just stay here."

"Really? You'd rather just stay in jail?"

"Why not? I'm getting used to it," she answered forlornly.

"Alright, Mom, listen. Just stay calm. I'll get you out soon and we'll get a lawyer and figure everything out." Tracy stood up from her chair. "Can you handle being in here a little longer?"

"Do I have a choice?"

"Love you. I'll see you in a bit." Tracy turned back

toward the door as her phone started buzzing. "Desert Plains Hospital" identified the caller. She wondered to herself where exactly that was as she answered the call.

Day 10, 10:35 am

CARLOS GUERRA

"Are you sure?" Carlos demanded.

"Yeah, look," Javy answered, handing his phone over. The text read, *Grant located in Pahrump hospital, alive and well.*

"He's supposed to be dead by now," Carlos growled.

"The cops apparently put out an alert for him last night, then he showed up at a hospital this morning."

Carlos took the coffee mug that'd been on his desk and smashed it against the wall. "That little shit was in here yesterday acting all fucking high and mighty, and the job still wasn't done!"

"I've been telling you, he's just dicking around. This guy was sleeping on his fucking couch, and he still couldn't manage to kill him."

"He was *what?!*" Carlos roared.

"After he killed those two guys, Lucas was letting

him sleep on his couch while his house got cleaned up."

"Why didn't you tell me that?"

"I thought you'd get mad."

"Of course, I'd get mad." Carlos was pacing the room now. "The man I'm trying to have killed is sleeping on the couch of the man I'm paying to kill him."

"You've been paying for a slumber party," Javy joked.

"Shut the fuck up." Javy fell silent and let his boss continue to pace. "This has to be resolved. Miguel's going to be back any day, and once he is, this is all going to get a lot harder."

"If this guy can't even kill Grant the nerd, how's he going to do anything against Miguel?"

"Get him on the phone. I want to hear his excuse."

Javy flipped his phone out and dialed the number. Lucas's voice sounded out quickly. "Yes?"

"Anderson was found last night on the road to Pahrump," Carlos said, trying desperately to keep his voice even.

"Okay."

"He's being treated at the hospital in Pahrump as we speak. Apparently he's just a little dehydrated."

"Lucky him."

"Is that all you have to say?"

"There isn't anything else to say. This is how it works."

"*No!* You were here yesterday assuring us he was dead, that we just needed to wait for the body to be found."

"That's not how I remember it."

Carlos reached out and squeezed his hands as if they were locked around Lucas's neck. If he'd been in the office right now instead of hiding across the phone lines, he'd already be dead. "You said he was dead."

"I did *not* say that. But I understand you might have trouble understanding English words since it's not your native tongue."

"Fuck you!" Carlos screamed into the phone. "Did I say that right?!"

"If Grant's really alive, I'll just start another project. That's how it works."

"We don't have time for another one of your half-baked schemes. He was supposed to be dead already!"

"I've already explained, that isn't how it works. Now, I have work to do. Is there anything else you'd like to discuss?"

Carlos scooped the phone up and launched it into the wet spot on the wall where the coffee had splattered a few minutes before.

Day 10, 12:05 pm

TRACY COOK

Tracy eased her car around the ambulance in the loading zone and came to a stop directly in front of Grant. He was sitting in a wheelchair and looked exceptionally uncomfortable with his hospital gown whipping in the breeze. His feet were covered in flimsy hospital slippers and a plastic shopping bag sat on his lap, looking like it contained all his worldly possessions.

"I got it," he protested through the open window as she started to get out. "I can walk fine." He pushed himself out of the chair while fighting with the edges of the gown to keep them together in the back. Leaning across the seat, Tracy popped the passenger side door handle and swung it open for him. He slid in at an awkward angle, trying to keep his butt pointed away from everyone. "Sorry about this," he said. "They cut my clothes off and I didn't have any money to get something from the gift shop."

"Don't worry about it."

"I'm really sorry. I don't want to ruin your seat."

"It's fine, really. It's a seat. You're sitting on it." She put the car back into drive.

"There's another thing, too. I need to go get my phone and wallet. It's at the Silk House." He said this meekly, looking at the ground.

"Alright." She tapped the name into her phone. It was only a couple of minutes away.

"Maybe after I get my wallet, we could stop at a Walmart or something and I could get some clothes."

"Yeah, no problem," she replied, turning out of the hospital complex.

They remained silent as she drove them to the Silk House. It was unimpressive-looking in the daylight, the rough spots showing through in its upkeep. Grant waddled through the doors in his hospital slippers and came back out in only a few minutes.

Next, Tracy drove them to the Walmart which was just down the street. He handed over his credit card and went to wait by the bathrooms while she collected and paid for his new clothing—a medium t-shirt, one pair of chinos size 32/32, a pack of socks, a pack of underwear, and size 10 basic sneakers. She had tried to convince him it was okay with her if he rode back in the gown, but he refused. It didn't bother her that he was partly exposed; her eyes were on the road. But it seemed to be making him exceedingly on edge; and considering he had just been in the hospital, she agreed with him.

Finally, he stumbled out of the bathroom dressed

in Walmart's finest. He was clearly still having trouble working with his cast-bound left arm. "How about lunch?" Tracy asked once they were back in the car.

"Oh, it's okay. You need to get back," he protested.

"I need to eat as well. Sonic or Panda Express?"

"Sonic. I could use a shake."

The chit-chat on the drive home had been kept to a minimum. Grant was still struggling with the physical pain of his accident, as well as the emotional trauma of having to call Tracy to pick him up. "I'm sorry about all of this," he offered again, once her car pulled into the driveway.

"Grant, it's okay. We're friends and you needed help. I'm happy to do it."

"Look, it wasn't my idea to go out there. That's not what I do, and I was all messed up from the Xanax—"

"Xanax?" she interrupted.

"Yeah, Lucas got me some Xanax the other day. He said it'd help with my anxiety."

"Where did he get it from?"

He thought for a moment. "I don't know."

"Do you have it with you?"

"No. It's probably still in the car, or in the gully."

"You should be careful taking drugs from strangers."

"I know. I wasn't thinking straight."

Tracy eyed her rearview mirror, reflecting Lucas's house back at her. There weren't any signs of him, but his car was parked in the driveway. "Let's go inside and talk for a few minutes."

"Alright." Grant sighed and went for the keypad that would open the garage door. He had no idea where his house keys were; probably still attached to the key in the ignition of his totaled car. The inside was a lot different than he remembered. The faint smell of the cleaners still existed and large parts of the kitchen had been professionally cleaned. You might actually confuse it for a different house for a few minutes before you looked around the living room.

"Do you need stuff for the house?" she asked once they were inside. "Food or anything?"

"I don't know. Let me look." Grant went through the cupboard and refrigerator. There was enough there to last awhile. "I think I'm covered for now."

"Have you thought about how you'll get around? Without a car?" She checked to see if the sliding back doors were locked. They were, and the wooden stop that sat in the bottom track was still there.

"No. I guess I can Uber for a bit. I'll need to talk to my insurance about my car, though. The cop gave me some numbers for the case file and all that." He shook the plastic bag containing everything the hospital had given him, a huge stack of papers and several pill bottles.

"Does Lucas have a key to your house?" she asked, peeking through the front blinds.

"No, I think he used my keys to get in when he needed to, or maybe the garage door."

"So he has the code to the garage?"

"Maybe. I don't remember."

"How about your guns? Do you have those?"

"No, the police took them all that night as evidence or something, and I haven't tried to get them back yet."

Turning around, Tracy faced him. "We need to talk about your neighbor." She laid out everything she'd learned since she and Grant had last spoken, winding through Hector Camargo's connection to Miguel, and finally explaining how she had witnessed Lucas meeting with Carlos the night before.

"What did he say about it?" Grant finally asked.

"He said he was just trying to help me with my investigation."

"That makes sense. He *is* in real estate."

"No, it only seems like it makes sense. Have you seen him do any actual work?"

Grant thought for a moment. "He once brought me some printouts to look at."

"That's nothing. Anyone could print out property listings."

"What are you saying? He isn't an investor?"

"I don't know. I just know that his story is very believable and also very flimsy."

Grant looked around the room he was in. The concrete beneath his feet was bleached white from the cleaners. Lucas had told him that they'd removed a lot of the carpet in this room. It made more sense than trying to clean it. The carpet probably wouldn't have survived that process anyway. Now the room had a weird construction vibe to it, the entire room empty and cold except for the sagging bookshelves at one end. A lot had happened in here since Grant was last in this room. Lucas had handled it for him while Grant was comatose on the couch. "If he wanted to hurt me, he would've already done it. I've been sleeping on his couch the past few nights."

"I know!" Tracy shouted back, causing Grant to jump a little bit. "It doesn't make sense, but I still think he's trying to kill you. There's something off with him."

"He was acting weird at the Silk House."

"Yes, he's weird and always around. He isn't in the middle of it, but he's just close enough to be involved. Like with the break-in!"

"He wasn't here for that, though. You said yourself they were serial robbers. You were already looking for them."

"Yeah, he was here just before it happened, and he was the first one here afterwards." Grant shrugged, as Tracy continued. "And why did they come at night? All their other crimes were during the day while the homeowners were at work."

"I don't know. People on drugs make bad decisions."

"Exactly. That's why he was pumping you full of Xanax, so you would crash your car."

Tracy's voice was rising with excitement, but Grant still wasn't buying it. "That's silly. I'm the one who ran out of there and drove my car all messed up."

"From a brothel he dragged you to, on drugs he supplied," she shot back.

"Maybe." Grant shrugged.

"Why didn't you guys drive his car? He drove you out there in your car and then gave you the keys? He was setting you up!"

Grant paused. He hadn't thought too much about that night yet; the memories were fuzzy and emotionally draining. "I don't remember why we took my car," he finally answered.

"Exactly. There was no reason to do it unless he wanted you to drive off, and you wouldn't have been able to do that with his car."

Before Grant could answer, there was a knock on the front door. Even though they had been speaking loudly, they both jumped at the sound. Tracy spun around and peeked through the peephole. Sure enough, it was Lucas Green standing on the other side. *It's him,* she mouthed back to Grant, who came over and pulled the door open.

"Hey, Lucas," he greeted his neighbor, who was holding Grant's Xbox and its cables in his hands.

"Hey, buddy. How you feeling?" Lucas's warm voice filled the space.

"I'm good," he answered, holding up his broken wrist. "Other than this, I'm just sore."

"That's great. When I saw the news story, I couldn't believe it was you." Lucas stepped into the house as Grant backed away to allow him in. "And Detective Cook, I'm sure you're glad to see him back here in one piece. You were really worried this morning."

"I was," she answered curtly, her right hand falling instinctively down toward where her service weapon was holstered.

"I just thought you were living at a bar or watching the girls down at one of the topless pools this whole time." He laughed, giving Grant a playful punch in his good arm.

"Nope. Just taking a nap in the desert, I guess."

"Well, hey, if you need anything, just let me know.

Food, a ride. I brought your Xbox back so you can play games if you want."

"I appreciate that."

"Might have some trouble working the controller if you want to play *Call of Duty*, though." He pointed at the cast.

"Yeah, probably." Grant laughed, taking the Xbox in his good arm and moving the group toward the kitchen.

"Smells a lot better in here than last time I checked on it. That industrial smell's finally starting to go away."

"And they cleaned up the kitchen a good bit," Grant added.

"Yeah, I think I still got that list at home of the things they had to throw away. I'll bring it over later and we can go pick the stuff up. You're going to need a toaster, after all." Lucas motioned toward the empty spot on the counter where the toaster had lived. "Though maybe Detective Cook will take you. She seems really interested in what you're doing." He looked directly into Tracy's eyes.

"I already told Grant I can help him with whatever he needs," she answered evenly.

"That's great!" He smiled at both of them and then turned toward the door. "I guess I'll be leaving the two of you to handle things, then. Give me a shout if you need anything, either one of you." He gave Tracy another hard look.

"Thanks a lot, Lucas. I appreciate everything you've done," Grant said, following him to the door.

"No problem," he called over his shoulder as he

slipped out of the house.

Grant swung the door closed as Tracy hurried over to the curtains to watch Lucas. He reached his 4Runner and climbed in. "Make sure you keep that door locked," she ordered. She was already pulling her phone up to her ear. "And you need to get a gun." She pointed a finger at his chest, then said into the phone, "Bill, he's on the move."

Day 10, 4:00 pm

LUCAS GREEN

Unsurprisingly, stores in Las Vegas do not carry a wide range of jackets. Jackets are probably my favorite clothing article; the right jacket can pull an outfit together better than any other piece of apparel. There's such a wide range of possible options; however, that is not the case at the sporting goods stores located in the desert.

I had been hoping to knock out my shopping at a single location, my other need being two bicycles. I had spent the better part of the day running the numbers on the outcomes, and there seemed to be two available. Or at least two that were predictable; there were a million possible outcomes if you truly looked at the numbers, but those were too scattered to be able to make any plans for. So it was the two most obvious plans that I prepared for, and those each needed a bike and a jacket. The bike was easy. I'm not much of a bike rider, but you know what they say about it; all bikes lead home and elephants never forget, or something like that.

I realized as I looked at the bikes how few of them you actually see on the street here. A lot of places you visit have the wannabe Lance Armstrong types blocking traffic under the slogan of "share the road," except you can't because the idiot on the bike is doing thirty miles under the speed limit while you're trying to get to work. My preferred solution would be to treat them like Lance and rip their testicles off. Maybe that's mean, but hitmen aren't known for their accommodating personalities.

"I'll take two of those." I pointed to the base model bike hanging on the wall. Nothing fancy and darkly colored was what I was looking for.

"Is there anything else you need?" the employee asked, pointing toward the aisle of biking accessories.

"I got a couple other things to get, then I'll be up front." I headed back to the clothing section of the store. Maybe a second pass would reveal the perfect jacket. If we were doing this in Minnesota it would be a lot simpler. Of course, it's always easier to kill someone when it's cold—sliding on the ice, freezing to death, bad propane heater, the options are endless. If Grant had crashed his car in the cold, he would've frozen to death before he ever woke up. He was lucky it wasn't hot enough to completely dry him out, though his skin still had a pretty leathery look this afternoon. Like a piece of fruit coming out of a dehydrator.

Maybe a rain jacket would be best. Those are fairly lightweight.

Day 10, 4:05 pm

CARLOS GUERRA

"Where's Juan?" Carlos demanded.

"He's on his way," Javy assured him.

Ever since the phone call with Lucas, Carlos had been running hot. It had taken about thirty minutes afterwards to calm down enough to even start putting a plan together. Javy had gotten used to his temper tantrums over the years, but this one was bigger than normal. His biggest recent eruption had been when they'd realized that Paul Sherman had died naturally before Carlos could handle it himself. Carlos had spent three days planning exactly how he would capture, torment, and then dispose of the real estate agent. Once Carlos was satisfied that the plan was perfect, they'd started looking for Paul, only to realize he'd disappeared. That didn't upset Carlos; he seemed to be enthused about a hunting expedition. It was later when the body was finally found that Carlos melted down.

Miguel had come through the office to deliver the bad news and squashed any outlandish plans that involved corpse mutilation or posthumous destruction. Any move against the dead man would attract attention, so he forbade it. Carlos handled it as would be expected, with screaming, throwing things, and slamming many doors.

He cycled through those emotions again pretty strongly today but had eventually calmed down enough to put together a fast action plan. There wouldn't be any waiting to let nature take its course this time. All that was needed now was to brief the other participants, which was why he was asking every two minutes where Juan was. He wasn't going to repeat the plan.

"Where have you been?" Carlos shouted as Juan entered the house.

"I was looking for a thermostat," Juan explained, holding up the shopping bag, a box outlined through the plastic.

Carlos snatched the bag from his hands and tossed it across the room. "That shit doesn't matter right now." He launched into a full-blown denunciation of Lucas and his failed plans. It was interesting; however, William and Juan weren't completely in the loop on what Lucas was doing to begin with, so what looked like interest from them was probably more confusion. Carlos got to the point after a while; there were going to be some deaths tonight, and not accidental. "Did you get enough plastic?" he snarled at Javy.

"Yeah, it's all in the back of my truck." As home renovators, large amounts of plastic sheeting being on hand wasn't suspicious because there were legitimate uses for the product. Today, however, it wouldn't be protecting the cabinets from paint; it would be keeping blood from misting all over the new carpet and paint.

"You're gonna be with me," Carlos declared to Juan, jabbing a finger in his chest.

"I'm not good at this shit," Juan protested.

"If you're in this crew, you do the shit that's needed. No more being Miguel's pet."

Juan fell silent. His behavior was the reason he and Hector Camargo had been detained all those years ago. He wasn't great under pressure, especially when guns were involved. Since then, he'd transitioned to a more peaceful version of outlaw behavior. Drop-offs, pick-ups, the kind of work a rookie usually does, but Juan did it without complaint and handled the legitimate work perfectly. The gun he kept in the cab of his vehicle was more for general protection against the threats that life might throw at you.

"You and William are picking Lucas up and bringing him here. Don't let it get messy," he said to Javy. "Miguel will be back soon, and we don't want to be explaining why the walls needed another coat of paint."

"If they're handling Lucas, what are we doing?" Juan found his voice again.

"We're going to kill Anderson," Carlos answered, unable to conceal his smile at the thought.

"I don't think I'll be very much help," Juan protested. "I can stay here and help Javy."

"No, I don't think you should be left to deal with the professional killer," Carlos snapped back. "I'm bringing you with me to kill an idiot real-estate agent with a broken arm. Think you can handle that?"

Juan looked around the room. Javy's mind had slipped out of the room, or at least out of the present, as he daydreamed about his work tonight. William was the quiet type, but he looked eager about the experience as well. Juan was the only one in the room who found the prospect of a double murder this evening unwanted. He'd been planning on making dinner on the grill and watching a movie with his wife.

"Go get the plastic and start covering this place up," Carlos ordered him. "But not the entryway. You don't want him to expect it."

Day 10, 4:23 pm

BILL STRIDER

Bill was four cars behind Lucas. It was a little farther back than he wanted to be, but traffic wasn't cooperating. He had picked up Lucas's 4Runner as it came out of the neighborhood a little over an hour ago. Lucas had stopped for gas and then headed toward the shopping centers on Charleston. A sporting goods store was the first stop. Bill had waited in the car; it didn't look busy enough inside to stay inconspicuous. Lucas had emerged a while later with two bikes and a shopping bag full of something. Bill wouldn't have pegged this guy as a bicyclist, but maybe he wanted to get into it. Though two bikes were odd; they looked identical and, as far as he knew, you could only ride one bike at a time.

After that, Lucas led them to a bookstore, and now they were both inside Home Depot. Bill was familiar with the layout of this store, so he decided to risk following on foot. Lucas took a shopping cart and was working his way through the aisles. He clearly wasn't here with a purpose; his route through the store was pretty random, doubling back and walking down the same aisle several times as if he was searching for things. It was hard to buy this guy as anything more than just a run-of-the-mill joe, not the criminal mastermind Tracy was hyping him up to be. If this guy was serious, he would've come into the store with a plan, but instead it looked like he was just guessing. Or maybe he was trying to throw Bill off the scent. The conflicting notions played through Bill's head the entire shopping spree.

Lucas paid for his purchases at a self-service kiosk and marched out to his car, Bill trailing along behind him. If he was plotting some kind of strike against Grant, he wasn't showing any signs of it at Home Depot. He then worked his way toward downtown and ended up at a shabby-looking office building. With no idea what the building looked like inside, Bill didn't dare follow him in; it would've been extra awkward if they bumped into each other on the elevator. It didn't matter, though, since Lucas returned to his car in only a matter of minutes. He'd taken the surface roads to get down here, but this time he headed for the highway, driving north on I-15. It was in the general direction of home, but at this time of day it was bumper to bumper.

If Lucas had been an actual local, he would've known better than to jump on the highway here; *but that's what I get for tailing some idiot tourist around*, Bill thought to himself. Hunter's baseball game was going to be starting in a little over an hour and he didn't want to still be stuck in traffic. He'd explained to Becky in vague terms that they had a case that was getting hot and that's why he was going to be busy for the majority of his day off. He hadn't told her the investigation was being run out of Tracy's extra bedroom, and that there definitely wouldn't be any overtime on this one.

Lucas guided them into the right lanes that took them off of I-15 and onto SR-95. The highways converged just north of the Strip and Lucas had chosen the correct direction. SR-95 would lead them back toward home. The traffic thinned out a bit as they continued forward. Lucas's car was maintaining speed in the left lane. The farthest left lane was a HOV lane; but with only himself in the car, Lucas stayed in the lane he was legally allowed in. Bill was two lanes over and keeping up with him. Tailing while in traffic on the highway was a delicate balance of keeping up and not being obvious about it.

His phone started to ring. It was Tracy. "How's it going?" she asked.

"It's fine," Bill answered. "He did a bunch of shopping, nothing very interesting, and then went down by Spring Valley to an office building. He went in and came out just a minute later with an envelope."

"Who'd he get it from?"

"I don't know. I couldn't follow him inside."

"What do you think was in it?"

"Tracy."

"What?"

"How would I know what's in the envelope? He went inside and came out with it. That's all I can tell you."

"Where are you now?" she continued, ignoring the frustration coming from Bill's side of the conversation.

"On 95 north, just passing Decatur."

"Is he heading home?"

"That's my guess."

"Okay, well, I think you can park like three doors down and he won't be able to see you there."

"Tracy, I can't stake out his house all night. Hunter has a game."

Tracy didn't answer; just the sound of her breathing came through the receiver. Finally, she said, "I'll head there now and take over."

"Are you going to sit there all night?"

"Yes."

"No! You have your actual job tomorrow, and you can't spend all night watching this guy's house for no reason."

"Bill! Something is going on!"

"You don't know that!" Regardless of her determination to find a mystery, she hadn't found one yet. It was all conjecture, and she was getting desperate.

She refused to answer this time, more silence over the phone. Bill's multitasking was being put to the test; arguing with Tracy while driving and watching Lucas was a lot at one time. However, even if he'd had his whole attention focused on Lucas, he probably couldn't have stopped what happened. Glancing over at Lucas's car, he saw it swerve left, into the HOV lane, a minor violation. However, it was where he did it that mattered. The HOV lane at this particular spot offered the driver an option, continuing on SR-95 toward the north or accessing the westward-bound Summerlin Parkway. Lucas cruised into the west bound branch. Bill hit the brakes, but it was too late; he was already passing the regular Summerlin Parkway exit and the lane to his right was full of cars. He couldn't have gotten over even if he'd wanted to. Lucas had timed his move perfectly; in the blink of an eye, he had shifted to a different highway and made it impossible for Bill to follow him.

"I lost him," Bill muttered into the phone as he continued northward, watching Lucas's 4Runner disappear from sight on the ramp to the west.

"What?! Go after him!"

"He got on Summerlin Parkway. I have no idea where he's going. You want me to just start patrolling that whole side of the city?"

"I'll go find him!" she shouted back.

"Tracy! Listen to me. You need to stop and think for a minute. You're letting this get out of hand."

"He just slipped a police tail!"

"Or he decided to go to Red Rocks at the last minute."

"He had to know you were following him."

"He didn't. Just call Grant and tell him to be safe, lock his doors, and everything will be fine."

"I'll talk to you later." She abruptly ended the call.

Bill shook his head and forced his way into the right lane. He needed to get off at Lake Mead to get home.

Day 10, 5:27 pm

JUAN HEREDIA

Juan and his wife had enjoyed watching the show *Dexter*, although the final season had been a letdown. The plot had a little too much theoretical incest for his tastes, but the reboot had been better. He used that show as inspiration as he covered every surface in the room. He started with the walls, plastic sheeting all the way down, with masking tape holding it tight to the walls. Loosely hung plastic has a very distinctive sound in an empty room. The air currents play with it and lets your subconscious mind know even before you can see it. That's something they needed to avoid with an experienced killer like Lucas Green. Some plastic could be expected; after all, the house was under renovation, and covering things up was part of the business. However, if he got a whiff of suspicion too early, it might end up being messier than they wanted. Patching bullet holes in the walls or having the cops called would complicate things. So the walls had to be covered tightly so they didn't warn him before he turned the corner. The floor was even more interesting. The freshly installed carpet had to be covered with a type of cling-wrap plastic, which was sticky and grabbed ahold of the carpet. Juan carefully rolled it out in two-foot-wide sections and made sure every seam overlapped. It stuck tightly together where the overlap was, so nothing would seep through to the carpet.

At the walls, he cut the plastic extra-long so about a foot of it extended onto the floor. He put the cling wrap over it so that the walls and floors were connected. When it was time to clean up, you simply pulled it down from the wall, and the entire room should wrap up into a nice bundle of blood-soaked plastic.

It wasn't perfect; he couldn't cover the doorways or else risk scaring Lucas as he entered, so they might have to deal with some misting out of the room, depending on where the shots would be fired. But Juan had already made a list of cleaning products he was going to purchase before everything went down tonight and have them ready to go for Javy and William. They could scrub the walls before anything dried and have it look perfect before the body even cooled down.

Juan scoffed at that thought as he opened another roll of masking tape. Javy and William were probably only interested in pulling the trigger. Most likely they'd be at the bar celebrating before the body had cooled down, and Juan would be dispatched from one murder to the other to handle the clean-up. It wouldn't be the first time. He didn't mind the work; someone had to do it, and there was a certain thrill in making a crime like that completely disappear. However, normally he got to just wait in the background for his moment to shine on the clean-up; instead, here he was actually going to be pulling triggers somewhere else and then having to clean up Javy's mess. That didn't sit as well as he liked. He would say something to Carlos. The last thing he wanted to do after helping him kill this real estate agent was go clean up some other murder. Carlos would insist on it, though; if he said anything, Carlos would make him clean up the hitman just on principle. So it would be better to remain quiet and hope Javy took care of his own work.

The room looked perfect; all that was left was to light it properly. The overhead lights would reflect on the plastic pretty aggressively and might warn the victim. Instead, Juan placed several floodlights in strategic spots around the room. With more tape and some plastic, he was able to dampen the brightness so they just emitted a dull glow.

The room was ready. It was just missing a dead body.

Day 10, 6:00 pm

GRANT ANDERSON

After Tracy's nearly hysterical phone call, Grant had been staring out the window at Lucas's house. There was no sign of him and the house was absolutely still. He could imagine Deputy sitting in there, sleeping on his dog bed. But that was all that was happening in there. Looking over at the kitchen knife he had brought with him, he decided it wouldn't do. He'd already witnessed one home invasion, and the people with the hand-to-hand weapons had lost decisively. He thumbed through his phone until he had an Uber on the way. Destination, Sportsman's Warehouse. Grant had been there several times, mostly to just look around, though he'd bought a pair of hiking boots there and given them a test run up on Mount Charleston. He always liked looking at the guns prominently displayed in the back of the store. Even if you aren't an active gun owner, there's always a desire to look at them.

A black Malibu pulled up in front of his house and he walked out. "Grant?" the driver asked as he opened the door.

"That's me." He climbed into the car.

His driver's name was Sam, a chubby white guy who looked like he took Uber driving very seriously. Clipped to the back of the passenger seat was a laminated list. It caught Grant's eye as soon as he opened the door, and now that they were on their way, he looked it over. It was a menu of the different experiences Sam offered to his riders: deep conversations, silence, karaoke sing-alongs, or dinner suggestions. Sam had given each option a cutesy nickname and encouraged the rider to pick one and enjoy the experience. Grant defaulted to silence. Normally he was happy to converse in the back of an Uber, but on the way to buy a gun didn't seem like the proper time to be chit-chatting.

Sam didn't press the issue and drove him the four miles to the store quietly. "Have a good day," he offered as he came to a stop in front of the entrance of Sportsman's Warehouse.

"Thanks," Grant muttered back. He'd started this day stumbling out of his flipped-over car in the middle of the desert, and now he was shopping for a gun because his friend thought his neighbor was trying to kill him. Nothing that had happened to him would've happened on a "good" day, he felt like screaming at Sam. But that experience wasn't listed on Sam's menu, and it wasn't his fault anyway that things had played out the way they had. So Grant stepped out and blinked in the brightness of the sun. You could forget how bright and hot it was when you were inside, but Vegas always reminded you what she was capable of when you gave her the chance.

Inside the store, he made a beeline for the gun counter and started looking. They stocked just about every brand in existence; however, as far as Grant knew, there weren't any designed to be used one-handed. The cast on his left wrist locked his entire hand in position; only his fingers were flexible.

"Looking for anything special?" a woman's voice asked from behind the counter.

"I'm not sure," Grant answered, his eyes still working their way over every gun in the case.

"Well, I'm partial to the Springfields over here. Have you ever shot an XD?" She waved her hand toward the next glass counter that was filled with more handguns.

"No." Grant straightened up and held up his encased wrist. "I need a gun I can shoot with this on."

"Oh," the woman responded. She looked to be in her twenties and not the type you would peg to be working behind a gun counter; long red hair tied back tight, pushing six feet tall, and maybe a hundred pounds. "Let's see if you can work a slide with that on," she said, unlocking the cabinet in front of her and pulling out a Kimber. She checked that the chamber was empty and handed it over with the slide forward. "Are you familiar with handguns?"

"I've shot a few." Grant accepted the gun and got a feel for it in his good hand.

"Okay, try racking the slide with your left hand."

It was harder than it looked with the cast; he could

manage to rack it twice, but it took more effort than it should have. Your instincts are to use a bit of your palm in the process, but with the edge of the cast sticking out, it was all on the fingers.

"Let's try one of these down here." She led him farther down the countertop. "These are normally easier to manipulate." She was right—the slide did move easier under his fingers, but it still wasn't a smooth motion. "What do you think?"

"I don't know. Is that the easiest one?"

"It's gonna be the easiest of the semi-autos, but maybe we should try a revolver. Have you ever used one?"

"I've had a .38 Special."

"Okay, so you're familiar with them." She led him back to the far end of the gun section where the revolvers were lined up next to each other, starting with cowboy-style long-barreled six-shooters and ending with the snub-nose ones you see in the movies. "Try this one," she said, handing over a mid-sized silver revolver.

It felt heavier in his hands than the traditional semi-autos. With their composite pieces, they were designed to shed weight. "That's a Colt King Cobra," she explained. "I think it'll sit in your hand better for one-handed shooting, and there's no slide to work."

"How about reloading?"

"That shouldn't be too hard with a speed loader." She pointed out the cylinder release, which popped it out of the gun frame. "You would press the extract here and dump out the spent brass, then pop in the new bullets with a loader." She walked Grant through the process a few times until he got the hang of doing it without any actual bullets.

"I like this one," he decided. It felt good in his hand, and with the simple loading mechanics it seemed like the best way to do it one-handed. His fingers on the left hand were free enough to manage the speed loader.

"Perfect! Do you need a holster for it as well?" she asked, accepting the gun back and placing it in its case.

"Yeah. Holster, bullets, and the speed loader."

"Okay, I'll get you started on the paperwork and find those items for you. Can I get your driver's license?"

Day 10, 7:00 pm

JAVY SANTANA

"Why isn't this covered?" Javy snapped at Juan, pointing to the entryway floor.

"I thought he'd be suspicious of walking on the plastic there," Juan explained.

"I don't give a fuck about his feelings. I don't want to be here all night scrubbing the floor. Carlos told you we can't leave a mess!"

"Alright," Juan gave in. It was Javy's job, after all. He went to retrieve what was left of the plastic sheeting and tape. Maybe this guy would be too focused on the meeting to notice he was walking on plastic.

Javy checked the time on his phone and decided it was time to make the call. He dialed Lucas's phone and he answered on the first ring. "What?"

"The boss wants to meet tonight."

"I have plans."

"He doesn't care. You need to explain yourself, face to face." Javy had opted for the confrontational tactic. If he played too nice, it might alert Lucas that something wasn't right.

"What time?" Lucas grumbled.

"9:45, the usual spot."

"That's kinda late."

"The boss has things going on as well."

"Fine."

Javy ended the call and slipped the phone back into his pocket. Juan had done a decent job prepping the room; he could dissect Lucas like a frog in biology class and not get any blood on the carpet. Even the light was at a pleasant level. He felt for the gun at his side. He had checked it several times already today. It made him anxious to know he'd be using his gun tonight and that it was just sitting there waiting in his waistband. He felt like it should get a couple of warm-up shots before the action started. But it was too late to go out into the desert, and he hated visiting the gun ranges down by the Strip. Bunch of NRA nerds who talked down to him, even though they'd probably never aimed at a target that wasn't paper.

"Hey, do we have shovels here?" he shouted out at Juan. They were going to have to get this body out into the desert tonight.

Day 10, 8:15 pm

TRACY COOK

Tracy normally had detailed plans for her days off. Work kept her so busy that she liked to plan what she was going to do with her time off, so that each break felt like a little vacation. It helped that she enjoyed her work, so she never resented the return to the office. But today, the off day felt pretty much like a work-day —an interrogation to start with, a visit to jail to see Mom, and then picking Grant up at the hospital. She had finally made it back home after dropping Grant off, but the work hadn't stopped there. She was frantically scribbling on Post-it notes every detail she could think of that linked Lucas, the Guerras, Mencia, and Grant.

The pegboard she had been working on was overwhelmed with her thoughts now, so she had commandeered a wall in the guest bedroom and just started sticking them there. Once she ran out of things to write down, she resorted to her laptop and started digging through every available piece of information the Internet held. She'd already seen most of the online stuff that pertained to the BBR crew, and most everything about Mencia was recorded in newspaper articles. But there remained nothing on Lucas, just the basic information recorded on his driver's license. No social media, no websites listing his name; even his employer couldn't be tracked down. After two hours she was able to find the corporation that owned the home he was living in, another faceless entity registered overseas. Again, it wasn't a total red flag. However, it wasn't really a sign of honesty, either. As far as she could tell, Lucas Green barely existed; he was a legal citizen who had a spotless record and was employed by a phantom of a company.

Tracy's bladder interceded and forced her to leave the room. Stepping in front of the mirror, she saw herself for the first time since the morning. The day hadn't been kind to her. Her hair was a mess, she had a pen mark on her cheek, and her lipstick was smeared. She looked like…her mother…

Oh shit. Grabbing her phone, she set about organizing bail. Despite her position as a police detective, Tracy was wholly unfamiliar with the bail procedure from this side of the process. It was easier than she expected, and Tracy wasn't particularly upset about her mom being stuck down there longer. Shelly seemed to have placed all the blame for her predicament on Tracy anyway, so she might as well give her a real reason to be annoyed with her daughter.

Day 10, 9:30 pm

LUCAS GREEN

I tossed the shovel into the back of the car and brushed the dirt off my knees. Everything was in place at this site and nobody had been around the entire time, so it was as safe as could be. Checking the time, I saw that it was going to be close to make it to the meet in time. When people in the real world were late to things, they could just be a little generous with the gas pedal and make up the time. That unfortunately isn't an option when you're lugging around the tools of murder. Having spent this much time double-checking every single variable, getting detained because of the speed limit would be an embarrassing story.

If that stupid cop hadn't been following me around for half the day, I would've been able to finish my tasks in a timely manner. Instead, I spent a couple hours strolling around and trying not to look suspicious. Finally, it got too late and he had to be ditched. I tried to make it look as accidental as possible, but at this point, actions had to be taken and risk the suspicion. Maybe they'll affect tonight; all the players would be a little more on edge, which should make it interesting to say the least.

I dropped the car into gear and rolled out of the shadows on my way to the big meeting. The mental checklist I had running through my head was longer than I wanted it to be. I always preferred to make lists, but these steps weren't the type to be written down. I guess that's why they're paying me the big bucks.

Day 10, 9:50 pm

TRACY COOK

"Carry the Diet Coke for me," Shelly said as Tracy eased into the parking spot in front of her building. The last time Tracy had been in an apartment complex like this, she'd been wearing her body armor.

"Do you know those guys?" Tracy asked, nodding to the two men sitting just out beyond the glow of the street-lamp.

"Oh yeah, that's Mikey and Drew. Drew is my… friend." Shelly climbed out of the car with her takeout bags.

"Your friend?"

"I'm gonna need a ride to get my car tomorrow," Shelly said, ignoring Tracy's question.

"I have work tomorrow, Mom."

"What am I supposed to do? You said I need to go meet with the lawyer."

"I don't know, the bus? A taxi? An Uber?"

Shelly ignored those suggestions as well, leading the way up the exterior stairs to her second-floor apartment. "Princess!" she shouted as she opened the door and her tiny dog leaped against her legs, yipping loud enough to wake the entire block. After the initial excitement wore off, the dog spotted Tracy and shifted into barking at her and nipping at her calves. "Oh, she's a feisty one. Very good judge of character." Shelly laughed as Tracy played defense with her feet to keep the small jaws away.

"But she likes you?" Tracy shot back.

"She loves me!" Shelly cooed, setting the food down and scooping up Princess. "I'm sorry Mommy was gone for so long, yes I am." She buried her face into the fur as Princess struggled in her arms to keep barking at Tracy.

"Alright, I'm gonna go." Tracy set her mom's drink down on the kitchen counter next to the half-dozen other takeout drinks. The day was catching up to her and all she could think about was getting back to her bed. Maybe that was the key to making sense of the day.

"Yeah, fine," Shelly answered. "Just leave me here. I'll figure it all out by myself like always."

"I said I'll help you!"

"Nope, nope, it's fine, I'm used to it. Wherever I go, everyone's just out for themselves. Your dad didn't care about me back in Michigan, and you don't care about me out here. I came out here to be in your life, and you just betray me in the desert this time." Shelly dropped the dog and stalked into the kitchen, slamming cabinet doors.

"What did you say?" Tracy asked. She had come to a stop mid-stride.

"You aren't even listening to me!" Shelly shrieked.

Betray in the desert. That sentence hung with her as her mind cycled through the phrase. Lucas had said that to her…about…what did he say? Then it was clear. "Betrayal in the desert." He had said that to her when they first met.

"Have you ever seen *Dune?*" she asked, her voice cloudy with the confusion of still-forming thoughts.

"Ugh, it was so boring," Shelly answered.

"But it was a book first. Have you ever read the book?" Tracy asked, more of the conversation flooding back.

"No, I'm dyslexic. I don't read."

Tracy blinked a couple of times, processing the information. She had always known her mother was dyslexic. If Shelly Louis had a problem, everyone was bound to hear about it. However, she had gotten so accustomed to tuning her mother out she had completely forgotten about it. "You are dyslexic…"

"Yes! How many times do I have to tell you that!"

"So you don't read books."

"No. What's wrong with you?"

"How many books do you own?" Tracy knew the answer before she asked. Paul Sherman was dyslexic; they had talked about it when he was showing her a house. Grant had mentioned it as well. But that was in the background of her thoughts; all she could see were the giant bookshelves that lined his living room, sagging under the weight of the dusty books.

"Why would you have a wall full of books if you

can't read?" Tracy said out loud, but to herself. Lucas had pointed it out the other day; he was paying attention to the books right there in front of her. "I have to go!" she said, bolting to the door and tripping over Princess as she fumbled for her phone.

Day 10, 9:50 pm

GRANT ANDERSON

Flipping the chamber of the Colt King Cobra closed, Grant double-checked that the hammer was down. He'd spent the past hour watching YouTube videos about how to properly reload a revolver. He couldn't do it exactly like the pros did, since they made good use of their left hands, which weren't in casts. But he worked out a system that accommodated his limitations and had been practicing, to the point that he was pretty confident now. The holster was tucked into the back of his pants on the right side, with the two speed-load cartridges sitting in the kangaroo pocket of his hoodie. It was the only place he could think of to hold the extra bullets where he could reach them easily with his left hand. The extra-large opening fit the cast through it nicely.

Now that he felt set with the gun, it was time to dig into the house. In the garage he stuck the handle end of a socket wrench into the track of the garage door. Disconnecting the door from the automated system, he tested his blockage. He could only lift the door a few inches before the wrench blocked the path of the rollers. There was no getting through that door. The sliding back door already had a door stopper in the bottom track. That was as secure as it could get, although, of course, it would be easy to just smash through the glass. There wasn't any stopping that.

Upstairs, he checked every window. They were all locked. Again, smashing through them would be the only way to get in, and the invader would also need a ladder to get to that level. But Grant took it a step further. With the two guest bedroom doors located so close to each other, he tied a piece of rope around the doorknobs and cinched it tight. With the knobs tied together, you couldn't open the doors since they pulled against the other. You could come through the window, but then you'd have to break your way through the bedroom door. Slowing down the attacker would be a clear advantage for Grant. The master bedroom was entered through a pair of double doors, so he tied those knobs together as well. It wasn't as secure as the two guest rooms, but it would work well enough.

With the upstairs sealed off, he returned to the main floor. With a roll of tape, he worked his way around the rooms, taping the edges of the curtains to the walls so that there was no gap around them to peek through. After all of that, it left only the front door. The deadbolt was locked and the handle's knob as well. Looking around, his eyes fell on the bookshelves. One of those would work well to prevent the door being opened, but he decided it would take too much effort to move them. Grant settled on wedging one of the kitchen chairs under the knob. With that and the deadbolt, the door would stand up to a hammering.

Stepping back into the kitchen, he flipped off the last light in the house. It took about two minutes for his eyes to fully adjust to the darkness, which was as thick as possible with the curtains sealed tight to block out the moon. His flashlight was also waiting to be used in his hoodie pocket, but he didn't need it yet as he felt his way to the couch. The house was as secure as he could make it. After several days of living in a fog, it felt good to do something productive. Though he chuckled to himself for a moment, most people would view him barricading his house against an invasion as just another manifestation of manic behavior. Maybe it was, but he felt safer knowing that if a storm was coming, he was as prepared as he could be.

Day 10, 10:00 pm

CARLOS GUERRA

"Park right here," Carlos commanded. Juan obeyed. He was in the driver's seat of an old beater the organization kept stashed away for moments like this. Its registration was faked and not traceable back to anyone. It was one of the smartest decisions Carlos had made this evening, Juan thought to himself as he slipped the car into park. He wouldn't have been surprised if Carlos had insisted on driving up here in his personal car; it was one of those kinds of nights.

"Seems early to have all the lights off," Carlos commented as he surveyed the street. Most of the houses on the block had some form of light coming from them, but Grant's house was as black as a tomb, with the same amount of movement to it.

"Are you sure he's in there?" Juan asked, hoping that Grant had slipped out already.

"William said he was there twenty minutes ago,

and he doesn't have a car." Javy had dispatched William to keep an eye on the houses. Grant had left in an Uber for a short time, but he had returned with some shopping bags. Lucas hadn't been back to the house all day.

"How are we going in?" Juan asked. "He got the last two guys who went through the front door."

"Don't worry about that. This guy just spent the night in the desert. He's probably so zonked out on painkillers, the gunshot won't even wake him up." Carlos tapped his Glock against his leg. It was the actions of someone who was nervous but didn't want to look nervous. Juan, someone very open about his nervousness, took note of the behavior.

"Still, how are we getting in?"

Carlos laughed. "Did you see what Javy put in the trunk with the rifles?"

"No," Juan admitted. He'd been busy trying to figure out what vest to wear while they'd been at the stash house collecting the equipment. When no one was looking, Juan had slipped two vests on. The first one was a flexible version that was designed to stop pistols, and the second carried ballistic plates over the top. They were incredibly tight across his chest, but once he got his jacket on, nobody would notice that the bulk was bigger than it should be. Carlos was wearing one of the flexible ones under his t-shirt.

"Javy picked up an acetylene torch that's small enough to be carried around. It'll cut a hole through the garage door in five seconds."

"So we climb through the hole?" Juan asked, wondering if the extra layer of protection would impede that process. He didn't want to get stuck in a hole that had just been melted open.

"Yep. There's a packing blanket to throw on the opening so we don't burn ourselves."

Juan was sort of impressed. Short of picking the lock, it'd be the quietest way to get into the house. A high-powered torch like that would cut through the thin aluminum of the garage door like a hot knife through butter and had the extra benefit of being relatively quiet. If someone was listening for it, they would hear the hiss of the torch, but it was nothing compared to the squeal of a grinder or Sawzall.

Nothing on the street had changed while they had sat there; even in the houses that had lights on, you couldn't see the flicker of the television. "When are we going in?" Juan asked. He'd made it through this day by focusing on each task at hand, instead of dwelling on what the future held. Now they were staring at the house, and there wasn't much else to focus on.

Carlos checked his watch. "I want to make sure Javy has Lucas with him first. Don't want him sneaking back here while we're inside."

"Do you think he's expecting us to do something?" Juan asked, checking the mirrors. Everything around them was still unmoving and dark. But if there was an assassin out there waiting for them, he probably was good enough at his job to not get spotted in a rearview mirror.

"That dumbfuck doesn't know what's going on," Carlos snorted.

Juan nodded but kept checking the mirrors.

Day 10, 10:04 pm

TRACY COOK

"Fuck!" Tracy slammed her phone onto the passenger seat. She had been dialing Grant's phone the entire drive over and he still hadn't answered. *What could he be doing?* she thought to herself. He was supposed to be alone at home with a broken arm. Most people would practically have their phone glued to their good hand at this point of the night. Even if he was just watching TV, the phone should still be right there. She whipped a left turn at a red light to get into Grant's neighborhood. Her car didn't have any markings of a police vehicle, so she should be obeying the traffic laws, but there wasn't anyone coming and this was an emergency. Tracy's route from her mother's brought her to the rear entrance of Grant's neighborhood, which she hadn't driven through previously; so she worked her way through the streets carefully, guided towards his house on instinct instead of good directions or

Google Maps.

She found the right road, so she spun the wheel and clicked off her headlights at the same time. Another moving violation, but with the streetlights all in working order, the road was plenty bright enough to drive down, and there didn't seem to be anything moving on the street to begin with. Coasting down the street, she leaned on the wheel and slowed the car to a stop in front of the house next to Lucas's. She was on the other side of the street and one door down from Grant's, but she had a good view of the front. Everything looked normal, except for it being completely dark. Perhaps he'd passed out, she thought; after all, he'd been in the hospital just this morning. He might've just called it an early night and dosed himself, which would explain his unanswered phone. Though that didn't bode well for knocking on his door.

Tracy settled into her seat and thought through her options. Unfortunately, the most prominent idea involved sitting in this car all night, watching his front door, which sucked because there were back doors that could be entered without her seeing it from here, as well as the fact that she'd be sitting awake in her car all night. Bill wouldn't be amused with that story in the morning. No amount of caffeine would be able to hide that fact, either. The next option was waking Grant up and taking him to her house. He could sleep there and be safe through the night. She should've suggested that earlier in the day when she called him.

She wondered if UberEats would deliver to her car. She hadn't brought anything to help her stay awake, and she knew she wouldn't be able to stay up all night without some kind of help. A couple of coffees or Red Bulls would be needed.

She didn't notice the man at first; he was in the middle of the road before her brain registered the movement. She jumped and focused on him for a moment. He was bathed in the orange glow of the street-lamp, but there wasn't much to see; he was basically just a shadow from this distance. Her left hand found the door latch, easing it open as her right fumbled for the flashlight she had on the passenger seat. The man reached the opposite sidewalk and became one with the darkness of Grant's house. She hadn't had to wait all night, after all; what she'd come for was happening right now, she thought, as she shoved the door all the way open and jumped out, the flashlight going to her left hand as her right settled onto the handle of her weapon.

Day 10, 10:04 pm

LUCAS GREEN

It'd been close, but I made it to the Home Depot parking lot before Javy had shown up. Instead of parking in the middle of the lot like I'd done previously, I put the car against the far wall that separated the retail space from the residential property behind it. It was the darkest place in the lot and would be the easiest place to get back to when I returned.

Javy's truck pulled in and circled toward where we normally met. I flashed my lights at him and he turned toward me. "Why are you over here?" he demanded out the window once he pulled into the spot next to me.

"I like the dark."

The passenger seat was occupied. One of the workers I recognized from the job site was sitting up there. "It's a little late to be dropping him off here to look for work," I said, motioning toward the man.

"Just get in the fucking back."

I complied and enjoyed the view from the back seat. Everything seemed completely normal from this vantage point. Javy and his friend didn't give anything away, and Javy drove the familiar route toward the flip. Several minutes later he eased the truck into the driveway and we were there. I noticed Carlos's car sitting on the street, suggesting Carlos was waiting for me inside, a good touch. The dim glow from the windows of the house, though, had an ominous look to it; it was clear it wasn't coming from the overhead lights as it should be. It wasn't much of a giveaway, but details like these mattered when dealing with life and death.

"You cold?" Javy sneered at my jacket as we climbed out.

"It always seems like it should be chillier at night than it ends up being." The desert chill was a real thing. Nights in Vegas could get very cold during the right time of year.

"After you, Santa," he said, motioning me forward and indicating I should follow behind his friend into the house.

"Sure thing, Rudolph Fucknose." I willingly stepped forward as he wanted. That put me in the middle of the pack as we went to the front door; a fair strategy, but also the most obvious. A shot in the back from Javy, that's what they were setting up, because they thought I deserved it. Maybe I do, but like the song says, we don't always get what we deserve.

Day 10, 10:05 pm

TRACY COOK

"Police! Identify yourself!" Tracy yelled into the night, her flashlight's beam searching for the man who had disappeared into the shadows. She left the car door open behind her as she advanced toward Grant's house, but she still couldn't see the man she'd watched cross the street.

"Shoot her!" the voice echoed out of the darkness ahead of her as her eyes caught a glimpse of motion to her right. Spinning her aim in that direction, she saw the source of movement; another man, this one looking bulky and lugging something heavy in his right hand. He was halfway between the car behind him, its trunk open, and Grant's house. He'd come to a sudden stop in the street when the yelling commenced. The flashlight beam found him, and he shielded his eyes. Tracy couldn't tell what he was carrying—it looked like some kind of oxygen tank—but whatever it was, it wasn't an immediate threat.

Swinging her focus back to the house, the light finally found the first man. He was leaning around one of the pillars on Grant's front porch, the unmistakable profile of a rifle aimed directly at her. Diving to her left, she only saw the flash from the muzzle out of the corner of her eye. Hitting the pavement, she rolled two more times until she was pressing against a parked car. The crack of the first gunshot had been enough to shock her eardrums. The tightly packed houses had channeled the sound, causing each ensuing gunshot to become more like muffled *whumps* as her ringing ears tried to shut out the noise. The shock hadn't spread any farther, though; she clearly saw the sparks as the bullets skipped across the pavement around her and heard the thumps of them burying themselves into the body of the car between her and the shooter.

"Get over here!" the voice screamed through a pause in the gunfire. The second man had finally regained his wits and was on the move again; however, he'd decided that retracing his steps to the vehicle behind him was the most prudent choice, and this time he was in a hurry.

"Fuck you!" the voice screamed again. The second man had thrown himself into the driver's seat and the car woke up promptly, its headlights pointing straight at Grant's house.

Popping around the bullet-riddled car body, Tracy took aim at the last place she'd seen the man. Her flashlight had gone rolling when she dove, but she still had her service weapon gripped tightly. For a brief second she saw the first man crouched behind the pillar, readjusting his aim toward the freshly started car, and the man who had just a few moments ago been his conspirator. Squeezing the trigger, Tracy saw the scene change. The man with the gun jumped as he felt her bullets impacting near him, which caused him to refocus his attention on her. The car's tires squealed loudly as the driver reversed away from the battlefield, the headlights shifting away from the house and returning the porch to darkness. The gun in Tracy's hands fell silent as the slide locked open. The magazine had been emptied in a matter of seconds.

"Fuck!" Tracy swore, ejecting the mag and fumbling for the spare one she had in her pocket. Normally when she was working, she kept two extras on her belt; but she wasn't really working, so her belt was sitting in the back of the car. But she'd had the presence of mind to slip a fully loaded mag into her pants before she climbed out of the car, and now that was all she had left.

For a moment the only sound came from the fleeing car as it roared out of the neighborhood, the engine screaming in pain as the driver pushed it to the limit to escape. The new magazine locked into the gun. Thumbing the release, she felt the slide fall forward, chambering the next round. Tracy was back in the fight, which was the moment her hidden attacker began his assault again. The first round he fired shattered the headlight inches from Tracy's body. Dropping behind the car again, the bullets continued to come.

In the movies, they often show the protagonist go through some kind of shock during the firefight; the sound goes dull and the movements become blurry. But even though her ears were shutting down in protest of the racket, Tracy was still very clear on where she was, even as she experienced the slowing down of reality. Not from the shock or terror, but from the processing of the situation. The adrenaline that had taken command of her body paused for a moment, her mind went clear, and the situation presented itself as if it was a book in her lap.

Her handgun was outmatched. Sooner rather than later, one of those high-powered rifle rounds would skip or plow its way through the obstructions into her flesh. She'd already had her best shot at the assailant when he turned his attention to his cowardly friend, and she'd missed that shot; in fact, she'd missed multiple shots. She knew she could've probably hit the target on the firing lane, but this wasn't the sterile environment of a gun range; and even there, a pistol shot at this distance was hard to make. She was overpowered and outranged. That meant retreat.

Behind her, there were no more cars lined up on the street. She could run that way, but it'd be in the open and moving straight away from the shooter's position, an easier shot to make. Across the street was her own car, the driver's door still open. She could slide behind it. Her path would take her diagonally away from Grant's porch, a marginally harder shot to make, but not that much. It appeared her foe was carrying an AR-15, and there was a reason the US military had adopted that firing chassis as its primary infantry weapon; it was accurate and easy to shoot. If another big war came, you could hand those rifles out to anyone over four feet tall, and they'd be able to put accurate fire down range.

If she made it to her car, she might be able to

resupply her ammo from the mags in the back seat; the car was in the open by itself, so she could curl up behind the wheel well, which would give her the best protection. If the attacker came for her, he'd have to cross the open street, which would give her the best chance to return fire. More importantly, though, her opening the distance between them might encourage him to disengage and make a run for it before the cavalry arrived. There was probably about a hundred panicked 911 calls going out right now, as the neighborhood collectively fumbled for their phones to report the gunfight that had broken out.

Her mind ran through the options and a decision was made in moments; retreat to a safer spot for a last stand or rescue, whichever came first. Closing her eyes, she envisioned the image she'd seen only a moment before—the pillar, a man, a gun bathed in light. Peeking up above the car, Tracy held that image in her mind's eye as she returned fire at the spot she'd last seen the man. He fired a couple of times but erratically, as the surprise shook his aim again. Half the mag is what she planned on firing, but in the heat of the moment it was impossible to tell. Her suppressing fire outbound, she leapt to her feet, running as hard as she could for the car behind her.

First step. She had a chance; if he'd stayed on target, she would've caught a bullet as soon as she stood up.

Second step. She exhaled with the lunge.

Third step. Halfway.

Fourth step. The bullets had returned. They shot sparks around the hood of her car as the gunman tracked the target.

Fifth step. A moment before she started the dive, her right leg gave out. She found herself flying forward, toward the back of the car. Hitting the ground, her body came to a stop in the open. Her sliding plan had fallen apart. Kicking her right leg, she tried to propel herself behind the car, but nothing happened. Her leg was responding as if it was asleep, no feeling and no strength.

Shifting her focus to her other three limbs, they gave her everything they had for the final jump behind the car. Rolling over, she scooted toward the safety of the tire, the bullets still flicking through her vision. The numbness of the leg hadn't connected with reality yet, but now she could see it. A burst of bullets had caught her there; one above the knee that was already bleeding profusely, another that had ripped through her calf, and a final one that had buried itself right into her ankle, shattering the bone and leaving her foot hanging sideways, only attached by the strength of her skin as she dragged it along behind her.

The pain was starting to break through Tracy's concentration, but her body kept working as if on autopilot. Reaching up for the door handle, she squeezed it and the door popped open. The glass from the window showered down on her as it swung open. Her belt was sitting where she'd left it, behind the driver's seat. Aiming the gun through the car, toward Grant's porch, she was firing again, three shots before the slide locked back. It was empty. Her thumb went to the magazine ejection button automatically and the empty one slid out. The last three shots gave her the only chance she'd have to reload. From her knees she was reaching forward across the back seat when the next round of firing started. The first bullet went straight through her outstretched hand. The next bullet caught her chest, the angle of the trajectory causing it to skim under the skin along her breastplate until it lodged its full force into her right shoulder. The impact didn't knock her down, but it did knock the wind out of her chest, staggering her enough to stop the momentum. She dropped back out of the car, onto the sidewalk behind her.

"Arrgghhh," she groaned, gasping for air. It felt like she'd taken a baseball bat across her chest, and that was the least of the pain. The holes in her body were being felt with full force now; the adrenaline of the moment had broken and all that was left was pain and fear. From her back she rolled to her left side. It improved the pain slightly. Apparently laying on the side that was bullet-riddled wasn't a good idea. Her right arm swung with her. She was still holding the gun tightly in her right hand, but she had no control over it; it was just sitting there. It didn't matter, though; even if she could aim it, there were no bullets left. Squirming around on the ground, Tracy was searching for anything that could help her, but there was nothing left. She couldn't walk, her right arm was limp, and her left hand was shattered.

In the midst of the pain, she recognized that the shooting had stopped. Her ears pulsed. Maybe something had happened; maybe the police had arrived. But her eyes told her that the street was the same color it'd always been, no flashing lights bouncing off the walls to protect her. In the sudden silence, the sounds of footsteps on the pavement echoed as loud as the gunshots. Someone was crossing the street. A guardian angel? Then a clattering sound overwhelmed the steps. It was the hollow aluminum sound of an emptied AR-15 magazine hitting the ground.

He was coming, and he had reloaded.

Day 10, 10:05 pm

LUCAS GREEN

The door was unlocked. William led us through it. My senses tingled crossing the threshold. It wasn't my ears that discovered the plastic, but my nose. The scent of packaged plastic was faint, but it was by far the most noticeable smell in a house that should've smelled of carpet and paint. Instead, it smelled like a freshly wrapped body. Not a thing most people would associate with new plastic; but once you've done it, the memory lingers. William turned toward the living room, which led to the kitchen. It was routine, the path we had walked each time I had come here, but I wasn't going to make it to the kitchen this time. Although keeping a crime scene clean is an important part of surviving, the most integral part is catching the victim unaware.

My hands were in my jacket pockets. If they had frisked me, they would've found my guns; but if they had frisked me, they also would've revealed that this time was different. They should've been frisking me every time we met, but that's why pride is a deadly sin. The gun in my right hand was for Javy. Spinning to the left, I brought it to bear on his chest. The shock registered on his face even as his gun was half-drawn from its holster; but it was still pointed at the ground as I fired, one shot through the chest. His face flashed from shock to anger to slackness in the half a second it took for it all to happen. That's a lot of emotions for a blink of an eye.

Javy's body was still dropping when I spun back to my right. William only looked confused as the gun in my left hand fired. He went limp and collapsed backwards. I let my breath out. It was that quick; inhale, kill two men, exhale. Both the bodies were laid out perfectly, their feet pointing at each other. Tapping the button on my watch, I started the timer. Those shots would be heard and noticed in this neighborhood, and every second counted. Slipping the nitrile gloves out of my pants pockets and over my hands, I was ready to work.

The gun in the right pocket killed Javy, so he got the left gun. His eyes were still fluttering as I kneeled next to him. The seconds mattered to him as much as to me, as they're the last ones he had left in this life. I ejected the mag from my gun and put it into my pants pocket, along with the bullet that chambered after the kill shot was fired. Taking his gun, I opened his mag and checked the bullets. Seventeen bullets fit in the Glock 17 magazine, plus one in the chamber made eighteen. His mag was full. Slipping it into my gun, I released the slide. It was now chambered with his bullets, most likely loaded by his hands and more importantly his fingertips. Both guns had the serial numbers filed off, so tracing them was impossible, but a telltale sign of a staged scene is a gun loaded with bullets with someone else's fingerprints. Producing a cloth from my other pocket, I wiped the gun down again. I had cleaned it perfectly this afternoon, so there were only a few new prints to wipe clean. I took his dead hands in my own and pressed them against my gun, rubbing his index finger around the trigger. It doesn't have to be perfect, just good enough to not trigger an investigation. Stepping up, I stood where he stood, another act that just had to be good enough, not perfect. I imagined I was standing here when I got shot in the chest, letting go of the gun and letting it tumble to the floor, just beyond his hand. One last element, the empty shell casing from my pocket. I flicked it against the wall. It went bouncing along the plastic and landed next to the floorboard.

I checked my watch. Sixty-five seconds had passed and there was one more body to set up. William never tried to draw his gun, so I had to yank it out myself, but no one would notice. He got my gun instead, the one that killed Javy, but loaded with his bullets and the spent casing flicked in the other direction, across the open room. The scene was set. Two men entered this room and then they shot each other in the chest. Why? Drugs? Gambling? Sexual tension? Didn't matter; after Carlos set the world on fire, it would look like they were taking care of loose ends or whatever drove criminals to behave criminally. Either way, they were both holding the guns that killed the other person— ballistics would confirm that—and the state would be saved the expense of a trial.

The back door was unlocked, and the yard was unlit. The most dangerous part was going to be the fence-hopping. I went over the cinder block wall in the back and dropped into the neighbor's yard. No lights came from the windows, so either they were watching me in the dark or didn't respond to the gunshots. The gate opened easily, putting me on the street. In a neighborhood like this, it was hard to disappear when everything was packed so tightly, but the street-lights were off this evening. A short at the breaker box; that had taken a while to engineer, but it might have been the most important part of the plan. It was dark enough that someone would have to be looking very hard to spot me. Checking both ways, I saw that there was no one outside and no moving cars on the street. Only one more fence to hop.

Day 10, 10:07 pm

GRANT ANDERSON

Grant had been sitting in his room watching *Seinfeld* on his laptop when the shooting had started. The first couple shots were confusing as they echoed down the street, giving them a unique sound. The second round of shots were even stranger; the shots rang out, followed by thumping, which Grant finally recognized as the sounds of the bullets impacting the front wall of his house. The shattering glass from the living room windows followed in the next wave of bullets.

Tossing the laptop aside and lunging off the bed, he posted up against the doorframe of his bedroom. The chair he'd placed there earlier provided a steady platform on which to mount his gun. He wasn't the best shot in the world even when he had two working hands, so he needed all the help he could get. The gun's handle sat flat on the armrest of the chair, the barrel pointing directly at the open space that led to the living room where the previous two intruders had met their end. The shooting continued sporadically. The moments of lull gave him a chance to think. He needed to call the police. There was no telling how many people were outside, but judging from the number of gunshots, it was a lot. He might have dug in as deep as he could into his home, but he wasn't going to hold off many attackers, once they sorted out what they were shooting at out there.

His phone wasn't in his pocket, and his casted hand searched his body. He had set it down on the kitchen counter, the memory springing back as the next salvo of bullets echoed throughout the house. Kicking the chair out of the way, he ran for the kitchen. Even if the guns were still firing out there, they weren't trying to get into the house yet. The phone was laying on the counter where he'd left it. A faint light outside was seeping through the living room curtains, which were now blowing in the wind. The gunfire had shattered the glass and broken the curtains free from their duct-tape restraints, open to the night sky now. Kneeling down and using the counter as a new gun platform, he worked the phone with his left hand. The entire lock screen was covered in notifications from Tracy. A dozen missed calls and unanswered text messages gleamed back at him.

He wondered for a moment why she'd been trying to get ahold of him so desperately, before the gunfire opened up again. From the new vantage point, he could tell the firing was coming from his front porch. The shots stopped suddenly with the sound of a woman screaming. It was the first noise Grant had registered as human. The bullets had found a soft target. Glancing back at his phone, he saw that the most recent text from Tracy had arrived a few minutes before, simply stating "IT'S THE BOOKS!" He now realized it was Tracy who'd just been shot.

Dropping the phone, he sprinted to the front door. Without pausing to catch his breath, he flipped the locks, flinging the door open. The pistol in his hand led his body. The space just outside the door was empty, save for dozens of empty shell casings. One more step forward and he saw the man. He was in the middle of the street, holding the rifle up in the air and laughing as he slammed a new magazine into the gun's frame. The orange light of the streetlamps gave a strange hue to everything in front of him, but Grant could see a glimmer of liquid on the street ahead of the man, a blood trail leading behind a car on the opposite side of the street. Squeezing the gun tightly, Grant tried to aim it dead center at the man's back, but he was too far away. He would only warn him of his presence if he fired from here.

The man was crossing in front of the car as Grant started sprinting toward him. If the man had been paying attention, he would've heard the footsteps behind him, but he was completely focused on what was behind the car. His rifle shouldered, he stepped behind the car as Grant closed the distance. "Fucking bitch!" the man roared as he rounded the corner. "Shoulda stayed the fuck out of my shit!"

Grant reached the car directly behind the man and saw what he was looking at. Tracy was slumped against one of the car's tires, blood soaking through her clothes and streaming down the side of her face. Clutched in her shaking right hand was her gun, the slide locked back. Her jaw was set as she glared at the man towering over her. Her eyes softened as she saw Grant appear behind the man. Grant saw the change in her face when she looked at him, as did the attacker. He responded swiftly, his instincts taking over. The man started to drop and spin at the same time to get his weapon pointed at Grant. It didn't matter, though. In one swift motion, Grant raised the pistol and fired at point-blank range. He couldn't miss, even with one hand. The man's skull collapsed as his body crumpled to the ground.

Day 10, 10:13 pm

LUCAS GREEN

My jacket, the plastic pieces of the guns, and the gloves were now sitting underground in a five-gallon bucket I'd buried earlier in the day. It took two jugs of acid to submerge all the items, before I popped the lid back into place. If anyone ever found them, they'd just see a lump of acid-smelling mush. In the future, this hiding spot would most likely be uncovered by a bulldozer at some point when the dirt lot across from the neighborhood was finally sold. At that point, whatever was left in the bucket would get crushed and spread throughout the shifted earth, never to be found again. All that was left with me were the gun barrels, bullets, magazines, and the drill bit I had used to de-rifle the barrels. Without the intact grooves of the rifling, there was no way to identify what was left of the gun.

Taking a bit of an erratic route back to the Home

Depot allowed me to dispose of the rest of the items in my pockets separately; a gun barrel in a sewer on one street, the drill thrown into a dumpster on the next street, one mag into a trashcan and the other into an aqueduct running alongside the street. They'd only be discovered by a comprehensive search, and only if it was undertaken immediately, which it wouldn't be. By the time some bureaucratic captain approved a ground search of that magnitude, half the pieces would be out to Lake Mead.

Now the only focus was on pedaling. Distances look a lot shorter when a gasoline-powered engine is propelling you along them; when it's your own muscles, you feel every yard traveled. Even with all of this, the job wasn't finished, so focus was needed. Too many slip-ups happen after the fact. Once the hardest part is completed, it's easy to relax and coast toward the finish line, but that's where amateurs get caught. Until I was safely off the plane tomorrow and blending back into the crowd around me, the danger remained.

Day 10, 10:13 pm

GRANT ANDERSON

With his gun still aimed at the man, Grant considered shooting a second time or even a third as the body crumpled in front of the home, the assault rifle clattering to the sidewalk. But it would've been pointless. Grant was getting used to seeing gunshot victims, so he knew this one was already dead. Lowering his gun, he looked back to Tracy. She had dropped her own gun that she'd been clutching so tightly, the pain of her situation taking full hold of her.

"Where are you hit?" he asked, his voice cracking across his dry throat.

"Everywhere," she mumbled back.

Dropping to his knees, Grant pulled her shirt open to see her shoulder. Her entire chest looked mangled. He could only imagine what had happened internally. "Ahrgg!" she screamed as he pressed his hand against the wound that was still streaming blood.

"We have to stop the bleeding."

"First aid in the trunk," she sputtered as she spit out a mouth full of blood. She'd hit her face harder than she'd realized when she had fallen down.

Springing up, Grant grabbed for the trunk release, but the lid wouldn't open. The panic was starting to set back in. "It won't open!" he screamed, slamming it with all his might.

"Button," Tracy responded from her spot on the ground.

"Fuck!" Grant swore. Shifting to the driver's seat in the car, he searched for the trunk button, the car shaking slightly once he found it and pressed it. An orange bag with a red cross on it was sitting there next to a gym bag. "Okay, what do we need?" Grant asked, back at Tracy's side and tearing the bag open.

"Tourniquet." She motioned to her leg.

"Right." Grant was pulling equipment from the bag. Nitrile gloves—no time for those. Scissors—not yet. Bandages—he would need those, but Tracy was right, cutting the blood flow to her shattered ankle was the top priority.

"That one," Tracy instructed, as his hands found the elastic orange bandage in its sealed packaging. Snipping the plastic open with the scissors, he had it wrapped around her leg in a few moments. The stretchiness of the bandage let him pull it tightly around her leg, even with her pants in the way.

"How does that feel?" he asked, but Tracy didn't answer this time. Her head was starting to drop to her good shoulder as the blood loss mounted. "Tracy!" he yelled, slapping her cheeks.

"Huh."

"Stay with me!" His voice rose as he finally heard the sound of sirens approaching. "They're almost here!" Slapping a pressure bandage onto her bleeding shoulder caused her eyes to bulge, the fresh pain fighting through the fog of the trauma. There wasn't anything left to do once the bandage was secure. Her hand was bloodied with a mangled hole through it, but the bleeding there was minor compared to the other wounds. Digging out some more gauze from the first aid bag and pressing it around her hand was all he could do. "Stay with me, Tracy!" Grant kept repeating, shaking her hand back and forth. The constant movement seemed to keep her slightly tethered to reality as her head bobbed back and forth.

His encouragement was drowned out by the wailing of the sirens as the first patrol car screeched into the street. The officers jumped out of the car with their guns drawn. "Over here! We need help!" Grant screamed over the noise, waving wildly for them. They both approached, one with his gun holstered and the other with it still out. "Help her! She's a cop!" he pleaded.

The second officer slipped his gun back into its holster, grabbing the radio on his chest instead. "Officer down, repeat, officer down. Need immediate EMS on site." His eyes focused on the body strewn across the sidewalk "One DOA as well."

"How bad is she hit?" the first officer asked Grant, kneeling down on her other side.

"Her chest and leg." The tourniquet had staunched the blood, but her foot was still laying awkwardly, the skin swollen and turning a sickly yellow color. "And her hand." He gestured with her hand still clenched firmly in his. "She was talking a minute ago, but she's fading now."

"Okay. Keep the pressure on her hand." He reached around to her shoulder and clamped his hands across the fresh bandage as the blood started dripping from it again. "Tell them to hurry!" he shouted over his shoulder to his partner.

Day 10, 10:44 pm

JUAN HEREDIA

Juan hadn't slowed down since he'd peeled away from Grant's home. He may have run a few lights, but largely they'd been favoring him so far during his flight. He was halfway into the desert when he called his wife. He should've called her immediately, but the panic had clouded his judgment. If Carlos had survived, finding Juan would be number one on his priority list. But luck was still with him. William and Javy would've left their cellphones somewhere else, so to not let their movements be traceable while they committed their crimes. If they were out of contact, Carlos wouldn't know for a while to send someone to Juan's house.

His wife answered on the first ring. "Hi, honey. Where are you?"

"Remember that place we talked about?"

"What?"

"The place we talked about. For having a nice picnic?" he said slowly.

"Yes," she answered, hesitation in her voice.

"Pack a bag and meet me there, as fast as you can."

"Okay." She hung up quickly.

He tossed the phone out the window. It was still ten miles before the turnoff and another thirty minutes down the dirt road to get to the spot. It was secluded enough that no one would notice the burning car. Someone would eventually find it, but considering how much junk was scattered out in the desert, it'd probably just get chalked up to joyriding kids or pyromaniacs.

Once they were together and out of town, Juan would be able to stop and think about what to do. If Carlos hadn't made it or had gotten arrested, then his trouble would be with the police, but Miguel would help him in that case. After it all calmed down, he'd get ahold of Miguel and see what he should do. But for now, he had to destroy the car. He eased his foot down on the accelerator a bit more as he pressed on into the darkness.

Day 10, 11:50 pm

LUCAS GREEN

My street had been a blaze of activity when I pulled back onto it nearly an hour ago. Every house was lit up as the inhabitants scurried around. The flashing lights from the emergency vehicles bounced across the surfaces, adding to the feeling that the night itself was pulsing with energy. One by one the vehicles rolled off; first the coroner's van with its black-draped body, followed by the police cars, until there was only one patrol car left, guarding the yellow tape of the police line.

"You'll have to park over there," the officer explained as I approached. I could cross into the restricted zone on foot, but they wanted the street to remain open. Fair enough, I figured. I put the 4Runner into an open space between two houses and walked the remainder of the way. I wasn't going to be there very long anyway.

"Lucas!" Grant's voice came from the darkened space of the garage. The door was fully open. Peering through the shadows, I saw he had a folding chair set up, like he was waiting for Fourth of July fireworks to start.

"Oh, hey. Are you okay?" I asked, walking over to him.

"Yeah. Although, could you maybe give me a ride to the hospital?" He looked as pale as the last time he'd been involved in a shooting, but his senses remained intact. "I want to be there for Tracy."

"Uh, sure. But I need to get some things from my house."

"Okay, I'll wait here."

I shrugged and headed across the street. I was still ahead of schedule, so an unplanned trip to the hospital wouldn't be an issue. My bags were already packed and waiting in the front closet. Deputy was waiting for me when I opened the door. He slipped right past me and went out into the yard, letting loose a torrent of urine on the rocky ground. "Sorry, bud," I said with a sigh. I was surprised he'd kept control of his bladder even with all of the shooting going on; even a lot of humans couldn't manage that skill. Throwing my bags over my shoulder, I sent Deputy back inside. He didn't bother looking at me as he sidled by, apparently holding me personally responsible for his uncomfortable evening.

Grant climbed into the passenger side of the 4Runner and launched into a detailed explanation of everything that had happened that night. "I don't know when she'll get out of surgery, but I want to be there when she does."

"She'll appreciate that."

"Thanks for taking me. My car is totaled and now my house is all shot up. Does insurance cover something like that? I've never heard about a gunfire claim before." The shock of the situation seemed to have affected Grant's ability to have an inner monologue; everything was coming out.

"I'd at least try calling them."

"Do you think it's even worth it?"

"What do you mean?"

"I mean I hadn't even gotten the carpet replaced since the last gunfight at my house. How long before something like this happens again?"

"Ha. You've already fended off two different attacks. You're practically John Wick at this point."

"John Wick never totaled his car and got picked up from the hospital with his butt hanging out." Grant fidgeted slightly in his seat, like he was afraid his butt might still be hanging out.

"Grant, buddy, I don't think you'll have to worry about any more crazy stuff happening for a while."

"You think so?"

"Yeah. Things happen in threes. So I think you're set for a very peaceful life for the foreseeable future."

"I hope," Grant replied, looking out the window as we came to a stop at the light.

We continued in silence for a bit longer before I had my own questions to ask. "Do you think you could do me a favor?"

"What is it?"

"I actually have to leave town for a week or so for work. Do you think you could watch Deputy for me while I'm gone?"

"Oh, sure." He sounded a bit surprised and excited.

"His stuff is all in the living room. It might be easiest if you just bring him over to your house."

"Yeah, no problem. He can keep me company."

"One more thing. Could you give these to Tracy when she wakes up?" I handed him a manila envelope from the pocket on the driver's door. "I had a friend do some digging, and he tracked down who's been receiving the money from the fraudulent charges at the casino."

"Oh, wow, that's awesome. I wonder if anyone's told Tracy's mom yet what happened."

"Probably not yet." I steered us into the hospital parking lot and toward the visitor's entrance. "Here's the key to the house," I offered once we came to a stop.

"Okay. You'll be back in a week, you said?"

"Give or take."

"Sounds good. See you then."

"Take care. Tell Tracy I'll be thinking of her."

"Will do." He jumped out of the car. I checked my watch. Just enough time to get to the airport for the early flight.

Day 11, 9:45 am

TRACY COOK

Some people have lucid dreams during their surgeries, or at least that's what Hollywood would have us believe. The opportunity to transport the main character to a dreamworld where they can confront truths about themselves is irresistible to most writers. Tracy didn't experience any of that, or at least she didn't remember any of it. She could recall being loaded into the ambulance, and the next thing she knew, she was lying in a hospital bed with Bill sitting next to her. "You okay?" he asked when noticing her awake, leaning forward in his chair.

"Yeah," Tracy mumbled. "How long have I been here?"

"It's just the next morning. Do you want me to call the doctor?"

"No." She took stock of her situation. Her rational mind told her she should be in pain—she remembered the searing pain of the night before—but instead, everything just felt cloudy, even though the threat of the prior pain lingered in the back of her mind. Her legs were covered by the blanket, though it was clear from the shape that there was an excessive amount of bandages underneath. Her right arm was fully covered as well. Only her left hand was visible. She flexed it and watched her fingers move like she commanded. One out of four wasn't bad.

"We found the bodies of Javy Santana and William Rosario this morning at the house Battle Born was renovating. Looks like they shot each other."

"Why?" Tracy asked. Her thoughts were crowding up in her mind, slipping through one by one.

"No idea so far. Some kind of power struggle, I guess."

"Juan?"

"No sign of him. We had uniform check his house, but no one's home."

Tracy tried to shift in the bed. All of a sudden her neck was killing her with stiffness. "Wait, wait!" Bill shouted, jumping up and helping her get repositioned. He fluffed the pillows and slid another behind her head. "The nurses say we have to be really careful. You've got so many holes in you, you're liable to start bleeding anytime you move."

"How's Grant?" Tracy asked once she'd recovered from the exertion of the tiny movement.

"You can ask him yourself; he's in the lobby. Been here all night waiting for you."

"Lucas?"

"Well," Bill said, settling deeper into his chair, "I

didn't see him. But Grant says he got back to his house around midnight, then dropped Grant off here before taking off again."

"Where is he now?"

"No idea. But he gave Grant the key to his house and asked him to take care of his dog for him."

"That seems...weird." It was hard to get an accurate feeling on her thoughts in her current state.

"Yeah, let's add it to the gigantic list of weird things here to look into. Including the fact that he apparently solved your mom's case."

"What?" Tracy blurted out.

"He handed Grant some papers with the accounts the money was being routed into. Account numbers, names, everything."

"What name was on the accounts?"

Bill pulled his notepad out, flipping it open. "The accounts are linked to Sarah Brantley."

"Oh, my mom mentioned her."

"Yeah, she is on the management team at the casino and her husband..." Bill paused, trying out the drama, "is a sales rep at EventRig. His office is located directly across the hall from Mark's the building manager."

Tracy nodded, the puzzle pieces fit together nicely. If Sarah really hated Shelly, it made sense she would be setting her up to take the fall.

"How's my mom?"

"Um, I called her last night, told her about everything that happened."

"And?"

"She said you had promised to drive her to pick up

her car and then demanded to know what she was supposed to do." He gave a little laugh. "So, I gave her a ride."

Tracy nodded as much as she was able to. It was honestly better without her mother here. She'd made her peace with that fact long ago. "I think I need to go back to sleep," she said.

"Can I send Grant in for a minute? Otherwise, he'll sit there all day."

"Yeah." She could keep herself awake for a couple more minutes for the guy who saved her life.

Day 11, 10:55 am

GRANT ANDERSON

Tracy had only been able to mutter a couple of words and squeeze Grant's hand for a moment before she faded back out. The nurses and Bill assured him it was normal. She needed as much rest as possible, they said; there'd be plenty of time for chitchat later as she healed up. With her extensive injuries, it wasn't like she was going to be jumping out of bed anytime soon.

Bill gave him a lift back to his house, depositing him at the edge of the police tape that still fluttered in the breeze. Bill said there wasn't much more investigating to be done—several doorbell cameras had captured most of the gun battle from multiple angles—but a police officer being shot meant that the book had to be followed to the letter, so the tape would stay up for a while.

He hadn't brought his keys with him when he had left the night before; he'd just closed the garage door behind him with the keypad when they left. He felt for the key Lucas had given him and detoured toward his door. Deputy was sitting on his haunches. He cocked his head to the side slightly at the appearance of his neighbor. "Come on," Grant called him over, scooping up a handful of dog supplies Lucas had left in the living room. Deputy fell into step, following him across the street without complaint.

The garage door creaked open at Grant's place and Deputy wrinkled his nose at the mixture of scents. Grant made a vow to himself to get the house emptied out immediately. He simply couldn't take the mess anymore, especially not with a dog now in the house. Who knew what he'd find buried under the rubble.

Deputy followed him warily through the trail into the house, giving the bedroom a solid sniff before nosing through the living room into the kitchen. He seemed dismayed by the scene as well, like he wasn't meant to live in conditions such as these. His claws clicked as he stepped onto the bare concrete in the front living room. The faint chemical smell didn't seem to bother him; rather, he seemed to appreciate the openness of the room.

"Are you hungry?" Grant called from the kitchen. The bag of dog food was still sitting over at Lucas's, but he had some lunch meat the dog would probably enjoy, a housewarming gift for his temporary home.

Deputy barked. Grant ignored the first yap, but the second got his attention. He'd never heard the dog raise his voice before now. "What is it?" he asked, joining him in the living room. Deputy was sniffing along the length of the bookshelves against the wall, pacing back and forth in front of them. He reached out

with a paw and clawed one of them. "You want to…
read?" Grant asked him incredulously, and then
jumped back as two mice went scurrying out from
behind the bookshelf and deeper into the house.

Deputy barked again. He hadn't seen them
escaping; instead, he pawed at the book, pulling it free.
The book toppled off the shelf to the ground and
opened, revealing a hollowed-out interior and a shrink-
wrapped block of cash inside it. Grant stared at it for a
moment, then grabbed the next closest book from the
shelf and flipped it open. It contained the same thing.
And so did the next one. And the next one after that.

Day 11, 11:00 am

LUCAS GREEN

The airport in Denver was the third one I'd been in today. It was a nice airport, as long as you were just passing through. It was so far outside the city that it made it very inconvenient if Denver was your final destination. I spotted my double sitting in the bench seats at the B14 gate, a flight to Seattle. Catching his eye, I proceeded into the restroom as we had agreed. He followed in moments later. The last two stalls in the row were unoccupied, which was in our favor.

Locking the door behind me, I put the toilet seat down and started the process of undressing. It was only the top layer that needed to go; my pants, shirt, jacket, and shoes went into the duffel bag I'd been carrying. Scooting the bag under the divider to him, he slid back the backpack he'd put his clothes in. A minute later, I was wearing khakis, a blue button-down, and leather loafers. He slid his laptop bag under the divider, which was empty so I could shift my belongings out of mine into it. The entire process only took five minutes and when we exited the stalls, we looked like perfect replicas of who the other person had been only a few minutes before.

The double held out his ticket, a paper copy, destination Seattle under the name Matt Harris. Taking it and tucking it into my pocket, I offered him mine, a ticket to Kansas City leaving in an hour. "Have a nice day, Mr. Harris," he offered pleasantly, taking the opportunity to wash his hands, which was a good idea considering how much touching had just been done in a public bathroom.

"You, too, Mr. Green." I stepped to the sink next to him. He rinsed his hands quickly and disappeared out the exit. That was the last I would see of Lucas Green; both the person and the name were gone from my life. The entire job was behind me now, or it almost was. There was just one more item that needed addressing, and that was why I was at Denver International Airport.

Exiting the bathroom, I headed for the bar in the center of the terminal. I had about twenty minutes before I had to board my flight, so a stop at the bar looked natural. The moving sidewalk carried me back to the terminal hub, lined with restaurants and convenience stores. I wondered if Grant would tell Tracy about the money in the books; if she survived the surgery, that is. There was a lot of blood on the ground, but that might've been mostly from Carlos. Getting one's head blown open was bound to make a mess. No, Grant would tell her; he liked her, and now that he could be credited with saving her life, he could expect some gratitude. He'd tell her about the money, and hopefully she'd see past her cop filter and let it be. There was no evidence that the money was stolen and, considering how Paul lived his life, it was believable that he kept his income hidden as cash for legitimate if not crazy reasons. At least, that was a strong enough argument to swallow, if you were in the mood to swallow an argument, like maybe Tracy would be.

Either way, things should get easier for him. I wasn't joking when I told him the attempts on his life were bound to stop. People could only try to kill him so many times before they gave up.

Walking past the hostess stand, I found a seat at the bar, next to a very well-dressed businessman; Mexican by the looks of him, though he seemed to be trying to hide that fact. "Can I buy you a drink?" the man asked as I settled into the seat.

"Sure, but it'll have to be quick. My flight won't wait."

"So it's done?" he asked, his voice stiff.

"You know it is. That's why you're flying right now yourself. The death of one's brother is rush-home type of news."

"Shot by a cop?"

"No, he shot the cop. Paul's nephew shot him in the head before he could finish the cop off."

"What did he think was going to happen?" The man shook his head. "Even if it went perfectly, how was he going to get away with something like that?"

"He didn't think about things like that. That's why you hired me, and he proved you correct."

Miguel Guerra slid a piece of paper across the

bartop, a sequence of numbers listed on it. "It's all in these accounts, spread across, just how you asked for it to be."

Miguel had hired me months before to deal with his younger brother, once he realized that Carlos's dreams of usurping him in the Cortez cartel would never be dissuaded. Only his death was going to halt his quest for power.

Slipping the paper into my pocket I continued, "The detective he shot had gotten pretty deep into the investigation of your Battle Born Renovation scheme, thought you should know."

Miguel lifted his fingers from the table to signal it didn't matter. "I'm shutting the entire business down. My lawyers are already drafting the paperwork. This time next week there won't be trace of it to look into anymore."

"Plus, everyone involved is already dead, except for yourself."

He nodded, taking a sip of his drink. Most of my clients were overjoyed when I delivered the news that the target had been eliminated successfully. Miguel, though, was showing signs of grief. He had taken no pleasure in dispatching me against his brother and friends. "And the money?" he finally asked.

"Right where you said it would be, tucked away in all of Paul's books."

He snorted. "I feel like he is the one who started this mess, and he got out of it without an ounce of pain."

"He died alone in the parking garage; that's not a happy ending," I answered. "The nephew found the money, but I think he will keep it to himself."

"I guess he deserves a reward for everything you put him through. I'm glad you didn't get him killed in all of this."

"It was close a few times, but I was able to put my fingers on the scales just enough," I replied, thinking back to the long-distance TV remote and the block I had slipped behind the gas pedal at the brothel so his car couldn't go over sixty miles per hour.

Miguel nodded again but didn't say anything. He was consumed by what was waiting for him when he got back to Las Vegas.

"On second thought," I said, standing up from my chair. "I should get to my gate. Raincheck on the drink, friend." I threw my bag around my shoulders.

"See you around."

"I hope not."

"Good point." He looked directly at me for the first time.

I nodded before walking back toward the hostess stand. I'd been on more airplanes than I could count in my life. The next one would take me away from Grant, Tracy, the Guerra brothers, and the job I'd devoted my entire life to for the past six months. No one knows where the one after this would take me, including myself, but I hope next time, it's to a tropical island.

THE END

Wonder why Lucas bought two bikes? Check out this exclusive bonus chapter to continue *The Vegas Flop* experience

Hey! You made it. It's so good to see you here at the end of the book, I know you didn't expect to see me, however, I've been here the entire time. Don't worry, I looked away when you were reading this in the bathroom.
I hope you enjoyed reading this story as much as I enjoyed writing it. Now that you've made it this far, it's time for me to ask one last favor. The success of this book relies completely on reviews from readers like you. If you could spare a minute to leave your thoughts about this story on Amazon or Goodreads it would be greatly appreciated.
Thanks, Kyle

Kyle K Wolfson grew up in Woodstock GA, the oldest of nine children. In 2008 he moved to Las Vegas and started working in the entertainment industry. He spent over a decade working as a roadie, traveling around the country and world as an automation programmer for various bands. He wrote several novels during his free time and even sometimes during concerts.
Recently he has returned to Woodstock along with his wife and daughter to be closer to his family.

Follow Kyle on social media for book updates and his thoughts on the Atlanta Braves:

instagram.com/kylekwolfsonwritings
facebook.com/kylekwolfsonwritings

Or reach out to him via email:

kyle@kylekwolfson.com